WISHES
IN THE
MOONLIGHT

MELODY TYDEN

CONTENTS

Previously in the Rocky Mountain Wolves...

Supernatural hunter Calista met Alpha Vaughan while investigating his Crimsontooth Pack for a series of murders taking place near their Montana pack territory. He knew instantly that they were mates but had recently signed a treaty with the Ravenstone Pack in Alberta to take their Alpha's daughter, Amanda, as his mate. Unable to fight the connection between them, Vaughan and Calista accepted their bond and Amanda returned to her own pack, taking Vaughan's sister Savannah and the pack Beta Felix with her.

At the Ravenstone Pack, Savannah was introduced to several eligible men, including genetic scientist Kyle, but soon discovered that her fated mate, Jasper, was a former pack member currently living as a rogue and suffering blackout episodes caused by an additional personality force inside him. Savannah almost fell victim to Kyle's experiments before discovering that he was responsible for both Jasper's exile and the Ravenstone Luna's illness. Amanda claimed authority over the pack after her father betrayed the pack's best interests in favour of saving his mate, and she asked Savannah to be her Beta.

Upon returning to Montana, Felix was sent to help another pack deal with an invisible thief. He ended up following the being through a portal into the fae realm where he met his mate, Evalina. Although Felix helped her escape, the fae prince wasn't willing to let her go without a fight since she was key to his plans to accumulate greater power. When they defeated the prince and returned home, Vaughan noted to Felix that each of their recent matings involved some kind of unusual circumstances and wondered if there might be a common thread.

Now, we return to the Ravenstone pack where Amanda is settling into her position as Alpha but has mating problems of her own...

Prologue

~Seven years ago~

~Amanda~

The light of the full moon shone down on the small gathering on the beach, shadows playing around the edges of all the guests as if the darkness were a living thing. Inside my head, my wolf howled.

Finally, a rich, sultry voice practically purred in satisfaction as we both gazed out over the assembled crowd through my eyes. *I've been waiting for this.*

'This' was my 18th birthday, the day every werewolf met their wolf for the first time and made their first shift.

I'm Amanda, I introduced myself as my mother had instructed me to do. *What's your name?*

Cinder.

I considered the name, turning it over to see whether it suited my other half. It reminded me of Cinderella, but I'd never particularly related to the story of the servant girl, not when in my pack, I'd always been the princess.

What about its actual meaning, though? Cinders were burnt pieces of coal. The flames appeared to have died out, but with enough of a spark, they could come back to life again. It sounded resilient, with a hidden strength, just right for the kind of werewolf and leader I wanted to be.

We're going to be a great team, Cinder. Now, do you see anyone special?

The day a wolf first appeared also marked the first chance for a werewolf to recognize their mate, if that person happened to be present. My parents had told me not to worry about a fated mate, that an advantageous match would be arranged for me, but deep in my heart where I kept the thoughts I didn't dare to voice aloud, I wanted to feel the sparks I'd heard so much about.

When it came to my mate, I wanted the fairy tale.

Slowly, I let my gaze wander over the assembled crowd of ranked wolves from our pack and visiting dignitaries from neighbouring packs. All the closest packs sent their eligible young men to the celebration in case they ended up being mated to the daughter and only child of the Ravenstone Alpha. That way, they could begin negotiations with my father immediately. No need to wait.

With no brother in line before me, everyone assumed that my mate, fated or chosen, would become the Alpha's heir. If I were mated to an Alpha from another, bigger pack and moved to be with him, an alternate chain of succession would be activated but that would be a last resort. Each single man in the crowd watched me eagerly, hoping that he would be my fated mate and have the chance to claim this pack as his own.

Nothing, Cinder confirmed when I'd examined the whole group. *Our mate isn't here.*

A strange mix of disappointment and relief filled my stomach. Yes, I wanted a fated mate, but I didn't want one who would care about my position more than me. That didn't sound romantic at all.

I could wait a little longer.

Taking a step forward, I bowed to my parents who sat on the only chairs on the beach, placed atop a wooden platform like thrones on a dais. "My wolf has revealed herself to me but she has not seen our mate. I'm ready to shift."

Murmurs of disappointment swept through the crowd but my father looked pleased as he nodded. "Go ahead."

Taking a deep breath to brace against the coming chill, I removed the warm robe I'd worn over a plain black bodysuit. My clothes would be destroyed when I shifted, and although tradition would have had me naked for this moment, that idea didn't appeal to me at all.

"I didn't wear anything at my celebration," my father grumbled when I suggested the bodysuit.

My mother backed me up. "Times have changed, and it's different for a woman. Leave her be, Warren."

As usual when it came to private matters, my father conceded the point to his mate, and I was grateful for the small layer of fabric over my torso as the night air nipped at my newly-exposed skin. It might have only been September, but nights were still cold in the Canadian Rockies.

My mother promised my body would know what to do when it came to my first shift and, as in so many other things, she was exactly right. Electricity rippled beneath my skin as Cinder took control of our body and began the process that would transform us from a human woman to a female wolf. Bones slid smoothly into a new place, rearranging to form the new skeleton we'd need for our animal form. Fur sprouted across my skin, a dark, charcoal grey that seemed fitting for my wolf's name, and my nails sharpened into claws.

My body twisted and dropped until I stood on all fours, fully canine.

Immediately, everything seemed amplified: the hoots of owls in the trees, the shine of the rippled moonlight on the water, the fresh fir scent of the forest. I saw the world through a wolf's eyes for the first time and its beauty stunned me even more than before.

Letting out a joyful howl that the rest of the attendees echoed, Cinder took off along the beach for her first run.

With her in control, I became a passenger in my own mind, but surprisingly, it didn't scare me. It almost felt freeing to let someone else take charge and simply *experience* it.

Instinctively, Cinder knew our land's borders, feeling the pack's authority through the bond that tied us to the Alpha and to the earth beneath our feet. We ran along the lakeshore until we reached the boundary of our territory, and she pivoted into the trees, racing with sure, steady strides beneath the canopy of evergreen branches.

As we neared an outcropping of rocks that marked another corner of our land, we caught sight of a lone wolf standing atop the tallest rock. Moonlight gilded its light-grey fur and when it turned its head at the sound of our approaching footsteps and our eyes connected across the distance, a strange energy snaked its way through my body.

Did you feel that? I asked my wolf, but Cinder didn't answer. Her pace slackened, lightening to a trot that brought us to the base of the stone outlook. The grey wolf bounded down as we approached, reaching the bottom at the same time we did.

Sea salt drifted through the air, a scent that had no natural place in our mountain home.

Cinder? What's happening?

Again, she remained silent, but when the wolf in front of us bowed its head in instinctive recognition of our Alpha blood, she stepped forward and rubbed her chin against the top of its head.

Sparks cascaded along our fur-covered skin, lighting up our body like a firework.

Mate, Cinder declared just as I put the pieces together for myself.

Shift, I ordered almost without thinking and she obeyed, relinquishing control over our body as my limbs returned to their previous length, the fur disappearing back into my skin and my long, wavy brown hair growing back out. It covered my chest as I knelt on the forest floor and the darkness hid the rest.

"Shift," I repeated out loud, that time addressing the wolf in front of me. He bowed his head and a moment later, the wolf morphed into a well-formed man. Short, light-brown hair glinted in the moonlight just as his fur had, and muscles rippled in his shoulders as he bowed even lower, keeping his face hidden.

"Lota Amanda."

Disbelief laced his words as he addressed me by the title my father insisted the pack use. It marked me as different from the other wolves in the pack, and I always disliked it for that reason.

"Just Amanda," I corrected him, dipping my head to try to see his face better. His gaze remained fixed on the ground. "Who are you? Let me see you."

Not willing to disobey a direct order, the man lifted his face until his eyes met mine. They were a pale brown, unusual and rather enticing. "My name is Troy. I'm one of the border guards, part of the pack's defense units."

"And my mate," I pointed out, since he didn't state the obvious.

His jaw ticked, restraint evident in his eyes. "And your mate," he agreed softly. "If you accept me."

Ah. That explained his reticence and the tension in his bowed body.

He anticipated a rejection, was already bracing for it.

Our pack didn't put a lot of stock in fated mates, especially among the ranked wolves. Rejections were common, or bonds were simply ignored while chosen matings were arranged instead.

Clearly, Troy expected that scenario to play out for us.

"Do you want me to accept you?"

Something primal flared in those pale brown eyes. "Nothing would make me happier. The Goddess chose you for me, blessing me above every other wolf in this pack, and if you gave yourself to me, if you let me give myself to you, I would make sure you never regretted it, not for a single day."

His impassioned response squeezed something in my chest, making it difficult to breathe. It also sent a flare of desire through me, something I'd never truly experienced before. Not like I felt it looking into the possessive, hungry stare of my would-be mate.

This was what had been missing from the introductions to all those other wolves earlier that night. It would be missing from any arranged mating too. This indescribable, unexplainable bond that already twined the two of us together in ways it would take a lifetime to fully discover. This *need* to be together that already tugged at us both.

I didn't know a single thing about him other than his name but I believed every word he just said. He'd been chosen for me.

"Come to the pack house in the morning. I'll introduce you to my father and ask for his blessing."

Surprise and tentative hope brightened his expression. "Seriously?"

"Seriously. We're fated. That might not mean much to some people but it means something to me."

He reached out his hand, as if he couldn't help himself, and brushed a piece of hair away from my face. Warmth and pleasure sparked where his fingers skimmed my skin. "It means something to me too."

Another wolf howled in the distance and Troy glanced up at the rock where he'd previously been stationed, seeming to remember himself.

"I have to get back to my post."

Every part of me wanted him to stay, but as the daughter of the Alpha, I understood duty better than most. "I'll see you tomorrow."

He bowed his head and shifted back to his wolf form and Cinder hummed her approval. Close up, I could see how strong and agile he was in that form too, though personally, I found the man more attractive.

He scrambled back up the rocks until he sat atop them again, eyes scanning the horizon for any sign of trouble. Wolves like him guarded the border all night while the rest of the pack slept securely in their beds, safe in the knowledge that we were watched over.

Would he make me feel that safe in every way?

In the night sky above him, a star broke loose and streaked across the sky. A shooting star seemed like the perfect omen for this night, and I whispered a wish beneath the moonlight.

Please let me and Troy get our happy ending.

The star blazed even brighter for just a second before winking out.

My heart racing with the weight of what just happened, I shifted again and ran back to the pack house, testing my new mind-link abilities to reach my mother.

I'm exhausted after the shift. Can I go to bed without coming back to the party?

Sure, sweetheart. I'll make an excuse for you. We're so proud of you, me and your dad.

Her approval warmed me as I shifted back outside the house and threw on some of the communal spare clothes we kept by the back door before heading inside to my room. When I fell asleep that night, thoughts of Troy filled almost every dream-soaked moment.

The shift really must have taken a lot out of me because I didn't wake up until almost ten the next morning. My heart racing, I skipped half my morning routine and raced down the stairs as soon as I'd made myself presentable.

"Has anyone come to see me?" I asked the young man working the front door.

"One of the border guards stopped by, Lota," he confirmed, his head bowed politely. "He's with your father now."

Shit. I wanted to have a chance to lay some groundwork with my dad before he met Troy, but apparently, that was no longer an option.

It only took another minute for me to reach the Alpha's office, but before I could even raise my hand to knock, the door flew open and I found myself face-to-face with my mate. His sea-salt scent washed over me, and in the daylight, cleaned up and dressed in what must have been his best clothes, he looked even better than he had the night before.

Except for the fact that his face had turned an ashen shade of grey.

"Excuse me, Lota," he mumbled, bowing his head before striding past me and down the hall, turning towards the front door without a backward glance.

What the hell?

"Dad? What happened?"

Behind the large oak desk that exuded power and control, my father wore a stony expression, one that I knew all too well. Anger simmered beneath the surface and if I didn't tread carefully, I would cause an eruption.

"That... *boy*... informed me that he is your fated mate. He tried to tell me that you would be willing to accept him if I agreed. I assured him he was mistaken."

"You... what?"

Dread flooded my veins, thinning my blood until my skin must have been the same pale pallor Troy's had been.

"I assured him my daughter, my only heir, would know her place and her value to this pack better than to ever entertain the idea of mating an unranked wolf. That she would never be so selfish."

Each word pierced my heart, his ice-cold stare freezing the wounds before they could bleed out.

"Eventually, he saw reason. He won't bother you again."

My throat closed up until it almost felt like I would choke, but somehow, I forced out a few words. "But we're fated."

"An inconvenience," he stated so firmly that I knew it was an order. "He'll stay out of your way and we'll arrange a proper match for you. All will be as it should be."

"And Troy…" His name tasted bitter in my mouth. "He agreed to that?"

"He did. He surrendered his claim to you."

Just like that? After his passionate words the night before, he gave up after one conversation with my father. He wasn't even going to try?

He *betrayed* me.

The realization slammed into my chest with a force so strong I had to take a step back. Pain and hurt swirled in my stomach, threatening to drown me until another emotion came along, bigger and louder, and pushed everything else out.

Anger.

How *dare* he? How dare he decide I wasn't worth the trouble and run away without even bothering to tell me so to my face? Fuck him, and fuck the goddess too while we were at it.

Troy was dead to me, and though I had no idea who I might end up mated to, it sure as hell wouldn't be him.

CHAPTER ONE

~Present day~

~Troy~

The familiar ache started in my chest as soon as I lay down on the narrow bed in the guard's barracks. Over the past seven years, the pull of the mate bond had shifted from an all-consuming sting, like being stabbed with a thousand small knives all at once, to a blanket of loss and sadness that covered me each time my mind quieted. If I could keep busy, I could keep the ache at bay, so I filled every waking moment with as much purpose and business as possible. Only at night did I give into the pain, indulging in it almost like an addiction.

In a twisted sort of way, I treasured each moment of the torture. When it stopped, it would mean my bond to Amanda had been completely severed and she belonged to someone else instead. That kind of emptiness would be worse than any pain.

Some nights, the nights she took other men to her bed, the pain worsened to the point that I had to bite down on my pillow to keep from crying out and alerting the other men in my unit to my distress. Did she think of me in those moments? I almost hoped she did, that it gave her some kind of cruel pleasure to imagine the suffering she inflicted on me, because the alternative would be far worse: that I didn't cross her mind at all.

Tossing onto my side, I tried to find a position that made the ache a little less so I could go to sleep, but before I managed it, a voice sounded in my head.

Captain, the Alpha has asked to see you. Are you available?

Up until a couple of weeks ago, 'the Alpha' would have referred to that smug bastard Alpha Warren who never failed to look down on me like a pile of shit that he'd accidentally stepped in. If he were the one asking, I might have come up with an excuse to put off the late-night meeting request, since it *was* a request and not an order.

However, since Amanda deposed her father, she'd become the Alpha, and the idea of her asking for me, even for work-related reasons, intensified the aching need inside me so much that sleep would have been impossible even if I wanted to refuse.

And I didn't want to. More than anything in the world, I wanted to see her.

On my way, I responded to my subordinate, trying not to be annoyed over the fact that Amanda sent the message through official channels rather than reaching out to me directly. As Alpha, she had the ability to mind-link with any of us, but I'd never heard her voice in my head. Just the idea sent a shiver of pleasure through me that in turn made the longing for her even worse.

Dressed back in my simple black uniform, I knocked at the pack house's back door. The guard on duty opened the door wide, already expecting me. "Do you know where you're going?"

The route to the Alpha's office had been firmly ingrained into my memory since the day I made my ill-fated visit to Alpha Warren. "I'm fine on my own, thanks."

Silence swelled in the empty corridors, the lights dim and most of the staff already gone to bed for the night. At the end of the hall, the door to the Alpha's office stood open, the lights shining bright compared to the darkness of the night outside.

I stopped to knock rather than walking straight in. "Alpha?"

Amanda's head raised, her nose twitching as my scent carried over to her. A subtle movement, but I didn't miss it since my nose mirrored the action. Even across the room, I could smell her wild rose scent as clear as day.

What did I smell like to her? I'd never had the chance to ask.

"Come in. Close the door behind you."

I did as instructed, doing my best to ignore the way my heart began to pound at the prospect of being alone with her. I'd tried to talk to her a couple of times since she became Alpha but there had always been other people around. She refused to see me alone. What it meant that she'd changed her mind and invited me there, I had no idea.

With her father's desk between us, I came to a stop a few feet in front of it and clasped my hands behind my back, feet spread shoulder-width apart. A warrior's pose, ready for action. "You asked to see me?"

Her beautiful brown wavy hair cascading over her shoulders, Amanda leaned back in her chair, her legs crossed and her hands gripping the armrests tightly. Nothing in her pose suggested she'd called me there for a personal discussion, so her words, when they came, took me completely by surprise.

"This can't go on any longer. Reject me and let's be done with it, once and for all."

Every muscle in my body stiffened and my jaw clenched while my wolf howled in my head.

Fuck that, Hunter snarled.

Trust me, I agree. Let me handle this.

Weighing my words carefully, I cleared my throat, finding my mouth had gone dry. "I'm afraid I can't do that."

Her nostrils flared, anger simmering in her deep brown eyes. "Why not?"

She had to be kidding me. The last time we spoke, down in the holding cells when everything with the former Alpha and the mad scientist went down, I told her I wanted to finally accept our bond. Without her father in the way, we had no reason not to. Didn't she hear a word I said that day?

Keeping my voice as even as possible, I stuck to the basics. "I won't throw away the Goddess' blessing. We were chosen for each other. There were obstacles, yes, but there don't have to be anymore. Why would I have waited all this time, held out for so long, only to reject this gift now?"

She said nothing, her lips pressed into a thin line and nothing but resentment in her expression.

Needing to provoke something more out of her than bitterness, I played my trump card, hoping she wouldn't call my bluff. "If you want to break the bond, you'll have to reject me."

We both knew the consequences of that. Rejected wolves often found second-chance fated mates. The wolves who did the rejecting rarely did. They could take chosen mates, sure, but that magical, indefinable fated connection? It would pass them by forever.

Amanda had been prepared to forsake it, ready to mate with Alpha Vaughan of the Crimsontooth Pack, that bastard who never understood what an incredible woman he'd been presented with. However, now that she was free to choose her own path forward, I had a feeling she wanted a fated bond for herself.

It means something to me, she said to me on that moonlit night so many years ago, the only time she ever looked at me with anything other than pain and resentment in her beautiful eyes. Every moment of that brief encounter would be stamped on my heart as long as I had air in my lungs.

Alpha Warren ordered me not to reject her for fear she'd find another fated mate, one who wouldn't be so easy to control. Selfishly, I agreed, hoping that somehow, against all odds, we might find a way to be together in the end.

It had seemed impossible at the time, but now? We were so close. All she had to do was say yes and we could get the happy ending we'd both been denied for so long.

Amanda didn't seem to see it that way.

Still, she didn't reject me outright.

"I could order you to do it," she reminded me instead. "As your Alpha, I could force you."

I bowed my head in acknowledgement of her logic even as I denied her conclusion. "I would renounce my pack link before I let that happen."

"And become a rogue?" Amanda scoffed. "*Now* you would risk it?"

My muscles somehow tensed even tighter. During the last conversation we had, in front of several witnesses down in the prison, I couldn't stop myself from sharing part of the conversation I had with her father the day I went to ask for his blessing. He told me in no uncertain terms that if Amanda accepted me, he would banish us both from the pack.

If it were just me, I wouldn't have cared. But to ask the Alpha's daughter, the pack Lota, to give up her family, her home, her inheritance, her legacy, just to be with me? How could I be that selfish?

I tried to explain that to her, clumsily, the last time we spoke, but clearly, she hadn't been impressed.

"I was always ready to risk anything *for* you. I just wouldn't put *you* at risk."

She snorted an exhale, still unimpressed, before lowering her head with a sigh. "This isn't over, Troy, but I'm tired. We'll talk about it later."

The sound of my name on her lips drove the ache of the bond to almost unbearable heights, coupled with the need to care for her. She *did* look tired. I could help. I could pamper her, spoil her, take on whatever responsibility she needed me to so she wouldn't have to do it alone.

I would give her anything, *every*thing she needed, if she would only let me.

But she turned in her chair, giving me her back in a clear sign of dismissal. Her Alpha authority compelled me to walk away, the ache in my chest deepening with every step I took in the opposite direction.

I wouldn't be getting any sleep that night.

CHAPTER TWO

"Good night, Alpha."

The guard at the top of the stairs nodded his head in greeting as I walked past on the way to my bedroom. It had been a long day - *another* long day - and arriving in my room for some much-needed sleep should have been a relief. However, as I entered and flipped the light on, the vast space felt utterly cold and unwelcoming.

This had been my parents' bedroom as long as I could remember, the place I ran to when I couldn't sleep as a child and the place I visited my mother almost daily during her months-long illness. When I claimed the Alpha position as my own, moving into this room had been the last thing on my mind. In fact, I tried to resist it when the house manager asked about redecorating.

"Can't I stay in my current room?" I asked.

His lips pursed in a way I had already come to learn meant that he disagreed with me but respected my position too much to say so directly. "The master suite, the Alpha's room, has the best security in the house. Everything is set up to keep you safe."

He left unsaid that asking them to change all the arrangements would be a waste of everyone's time, but I got the message. My parents' things were moved into storage until we knew their long-term plans and the staff brought my belongings to the Alpha's room, along with a brand-new bed-and-dresser set. The king-sized bed took up nearly twice the space as my old double and still looked small in the sprawling top-floor suite. Besides the bedroom with its sitting area complete with a fireplace and a door to a private balcony beyond, the room had an ensuite bathroom bigger than many of the staff bedrooms, and a walk-in closet that even my substantial wardrobe seemed to get lost in.

With a partner, the space might have seemed a little more reasonable, but for me alone, it felt excessive.

Not to mention lonely.

With a sigh, I headed to the bathroom and stripped off my clothes for the day, replacing them with the pajama set that had already been laid out for me. Even with the clothes in the hamper, Troy's scent lingered, so I scrubbed my face and applied my nighttime cream, its warm vanilla aroma drowning out any other smells. Brushing my hair and my teeth, I managed to keep my mind off him until I padded back out to the bedroom and climbed into the enormous bed, reaching over to the panel on the wall that turned off all the lights.

The room plunged into darkness and the ache in my chest swelled.

For years, I'd been living with this pain, this unfulfilled *need* inside me. Most of the time, I could ignore it, but since returning from the Crimsontooth pack, since seeing Troy more in the past few weeks than I had in years, the pull of the bond seemed to be growing stronger again. I called him to my office that night out of sheer desperation for it to stop. I had enough on my plate without throwing my fated mate into the mix.

I'm glad he didn't agree, Cinder mumbled quietly inside my head. *It would have hurt more if he rejected us.*

Rejection will only hurt temporarily, I corrected. *After the initial shock, the pain will stop.*

I don't mean physical pain. Emotionally, it would hurt you if he gave in.

We'd had some variation of this discussion too many times to count over the past seven years. Cinder swore she could feel Troy's wolf's devotion whenever we were near him. He wanted us more than anything, she declared.

The same couldn't be said of his human side, though. He wanted us *now*, once the hardship and struggle had vanished, but he'd never been willing to fight for it before.

He told you what your father said, Cinder reminded me, as if I hadn't just listened to Troy's excuses for myself. *We would have been kicked out of the pack.*

And? I'm not some fragile princess who needs to live in the lap of luxury. I would have gone with him if it came to that.

He didn't know that.

Only because he never bothered to ask! My frustration boiled over as I tossed onto my other side, still trying to ease the ache in my soul. *That's what bothers me more than anything. He made the decision for both of us without talking to me, without asking me what I wanted. And now he's doing the same thing, deciding on his own that we should accept the bond instead of really listening to me.*

All he'd done since I became Alpha was tell me how we could finally be together. Not once did he ask me how I felt about the past seven years or if I even wanted a mate at all.

That should have been the end of it but Cinder refused to let it go. *You never gave him a chance, Amanda. He tried to talk to you over the years. You never let him get close.*

We were never going to agree on this. *I really need to go to sleep. Can we pick this fight back up in the morning?*

Fine, but don't think I'll forget.

Wouldn't dream of it. Good night, Cin.

My wolf fell silent and soon, sleep thankfully claimed me.

The reprieve didn't last long. A sharp knock on my door woke me up just after three in the morning.

"Alpha?" The muffled sound of the guard's voice filtered through my bedroom door. "Are you alright?"

"I'm fine," I called back groggily, hauling myself up to check the time. "What's going on?"

"A skirmish at the border. It's under control but my protocol is to check on you and make sure it wasn't a distraction and you're secure."

At the sound of the word 'border', an image of Troy's wolf, standing atop the rock on the night we met, flashed through my mind. Was he on duty? Had he been involved in the 'skirmish'? Was he okay?

Pushing those thoughts aside, I swung my feet over the side of the bed, wiping the last of the sleep from my eyes.

"Have the senior officer responsible for the team in my office in ten minutes to make a report."

"Yes, sir," the response came through the door. "I mean, ma'am."

It would take some time for *that* particular habit to die off among my staff.

With the clock ticking, I tied my hair back into a loose ponytail and threw on some workout clothes, a fitted top and yoga pants, before heading back down to my office. Things were just as I'd left them only a few hours earlier, and I woke up my computer screen just in time to see the camera feed from the back door showing a tall, broad man walking in.

Most of the men in the pack fit that description, but somehow, even though I could only see the back of his head, I recognized Troy immediately. Cinder stirred in my head and the ache in my chest deepened.

Apparently, fate took my comment about picking things up again in the morning a little too literally.

Chapter Three

~Troy~

With sleep out of the question, I volunteered to take over the night shift from my counterpart, Devon. He gratefully headed home to his bed and family while I shifted and let Hunter take control as we headed to the territory's southern border. Clouds blowing in over the mountains obscured the light of the moon, making it darker than usual. Through our pack mind-link, I checked in with the wolves leading the teams on each of the other borders and they all reported quiet and calm.

Most nights on patrol were uneventful, even boring at times. That didn't bother me. I would take boredom over the alternative of an attack any day.

At the southern border, I found a new recruit, Shaun, pacing along the small creek that marked the edge of our land.

Something wrong? I asked through our link as Hunter came up behind him. Shaun's shoulders looked tense, his ears twitching as they strained to hear something.

I think there's something in the trees on the other side. The wind's blowing in the other direction but every now and then, I can smell something strange.

With a deep sniff, Hunter inhaled. He didn't smell anything but as Shaun said, the wind came from the northwest, carrying any scents south of the creek away from us. *Have you alerted the others?*

I reported it to Lily, my team leader, he confirmed. *She's on her way.*

Sure enough, something rustled in the trees to our left, and a moment later, the smaller wolf appeared.

Captain. Her spine straightened at the sight of me. *I didn't realize you were coming this way too.*

Why didn't you call in Shaun's report? My tone, though non-confrontational, still demanded an answer. We had protocol for these kinds of situations, especially after all the trouble we had with rogues recently.

I wanted to confirm it for myself first before bothering anyone, she explained, her wolf bowing its head in apology. *I'm sorry.*

Well, we're all here now, so let's check it out.

The three of us split up, moving as quietly as possible along the waterway, eyes and ears trained on the dark forest outside our territory. After five minutes, I was ready to call an all-clear when the wind shifted and a new scent drifted over to me.

Definitely a wolf. Not one of ours and not a rogue either.

Before I could act, a howl sounded from the opposite direction, the way Lily had gone, and I set off at a sprint back towards her. A moment later, I got the alert that someone had crossed into our territory, a buzzing vibration that rumbled through me and all wolves on the border team.

As the senior officer on duty, the others would all wait to hear from me, but first, I needed to see what we were dealing with.

Shaun reached Lily's position a few steps before I did, and we found her backed into a defensive position, three unknown wolves closing in on her, their legs still wet from crossing the creek.

Shaun, you have the one on the left with the grey face. Lily, you take the one in the centre. I've got the big brown one. Move in now!

They obeyed without question, Lily switching from defense to attack as Shaun and I sprang into action as her back-up. My target was a wolf a little smaller than Hunter, brown fur interrupted by a bald patch near its hindquarters. I aimed for that spot, charging straight into him as he reacted too slowly to my approach. With a thud, we both hit the forest floor, grappling for the upper hand until I managed to sink my teeth into his shoulder in warning, a deep growl accompanying the action.

Get the fuck off our land, my actions said in no uncertain terms.

Lily had her opponent in a similar position, but Shaun's target had seen him coming and had the young wolf pinned on the ground. Snarling at the brown wolf one more time, I dashed over to assist my teammate, knocking the other wolf off-balance and giving Shaun a chance to scramble back to his feet.

I howled in warning and, thankfully, the three turned tail and ran back across the creek, into the forest.

What the fuck was the point of that?

You both okay? I checked in with my team members and when they confirmed they were, I sent out a message to the whole team. *The intruders are gone. Keep your position in case it was a distraction. Someone check on the Alpha.*

My chest tightened at the idea of anyone going after Amanda, but she should be asleep in her bed, safe and sound. Unless I heard otherwise, I would take comfort in that fact.

As I debated my next move, a voice called out from the distant forest, a deep, male human voice that must have belonged to one of the werewolves we just chased off.

"You won't be able to keep us out for long with that weak woman as your Alpha. Consider this a warning."

Rage boiled in my blood and every instinct of the mating bond urged me to chase after the son of a bitch and force him into submission for insulting my mate. Before I could do anything, though, another voice echoed in my head.

This is Ewan at the pack house. The Alpha is secure and wants to see you in ten minutes in her office.

Unable to refuse a direct summons, I turned to Lily and Shaun.

*I have to go report to the Alpha. If there's any sign of further trouble, report it **immediately.***

Yes, Captain. They both bowed their heads in acknowledgement as I set off at full speed back towards the pack house. At the back door, I helped myself to one of the spare sets of clothes left out for such occasions and made my way to the Alpha's office for the second time that night.

The door stood open, and again, I knocked out of politeness.

"Come in."

Amanda sat at her desk, just like before, but instead of the business-casual clothes she'd been wearing earlier, the stretchy fabric of her workout clothes hugged every curve of her body. My heart began to thump so loudly she must have been able to hear it as I stepped closer. I went to swallow, realized my mouth was hanging open and quickly closed it as I took my usual military stance.

"What happened out there tonight?" she asked briskly, her mind clearly focused only on business.

I kept my report as factual as if I were reporting it to her father or any other Alpha. "Three wolves from another pack tried to intimidate one of our guards. We were able to chase them off. No injuries."

Amanda absorbed all of that with a nod. "What did they want?"

There, I couldn't keep myself quite as detached. My lips twisting into a grimace, I repeated the words the wolf had yelled into the night.

She sighed but said nothing, the silence stretching between us until I felt compelled to speak again.

"If it was a test to see if we were ready, we proved we are. The team is well-trained and ready to defend our territory against any threat. They're loyal to you."

Her brown eyes snapped up to meet mine. "Are they? Some people in the pack aren't happy about having a female Alpha. There's been grumbling, and apparently, someone has been leaking information too. How did these wolves even know about me? No formal announcement of the change in leadership has gone out."

I hadn't been aware of any grumbling. In our pack, internal and external security were separate. My team defended our borders while the other team, our pack's equivalent of the police, dealt with problems within our ranks.

"You think people are plotting against you inside the pack?"

"I think it's a possibility," she confirmed grimly. "I need more information but I'm not sure who I can trust. Savannah and Jasper, for sure, but beyond that it's..."

"And me," I interrupted, unable to help myself. "You can trust me completely."

The wariness in her eyes stabbed at my chest. Obviously, the past seven years had taken their toll on her, as they had on me, but deep down, she must have known that I had always had her best interests at heart?

Relaxing my posture, I took a seat across the desk from her, speaking to her not as the captain reporting to his Alpha but as the mate she refused to acknowledge.

"You might not believe it, not yet, but I've never done anything to intentionally hurt you. I didn't reveal our bond when it might have made things difficult for you. I didn't interfere when you agreed to take Alpha Vaughan as your mate. Every time you left pack land and took an escort, I made sure I was on that team to keep you safe. I would have laid down my life for you then and I still will. Anything you ask of me, I'll do."

She opened her mouth to object and I held up my hand in acknowledgement before she said the words.

"Anything except rejecting you. There isn't a person on this earth who is more loyal to you than I am, Amanda. That's the truth."

For a long moment, she held my gaze, the world around us fading into the background until all I knew was the light in her pretty brown eyes and the sweet wild rose scent of her.

Finally, her eyes dropped to her lap.

"Alpha," she said softly. "Please call me Alpha."

The words stung, as she must have known they would. They were intended to keep distance between us where I wanted to erase it, but since she *was* my Alpha, I wouldn't argue. "Of course, Alpha."

Exhaling a slow breath, she looked over her shoulder at the large windows overlooking the lake, the mountains, and the night sky. "I'm going to try to get some sleep, but in the morning, I'll convene a small working group to come up with a plan on how to deal with... all of this."

My lips parted, ready to beg her to include me, but it turned out to be unnecessary. She said the words before I had to.

"There's a spot for you on that team if you want it."

"It would be my honour, Alpha."

With her dismissal clear, I rose to my feet and bowed my head before taking my leave. At the door, I paused a moment, glancing back just in case she had anything she wanted to add, but her eyes remained fixed on the world outside.

I'd give anything to know the thoughts in her head, to know all her hopes and fears and dreams, but I understood that the trust I'd asked her to put in me would have to be earned.

At least she would give me a chance to prove my loyalty to her. For now, that would have to be enough.

CHAPTER FOUR

~Amanda~

By nine o'clock that morning, anyone who walked into the Alpha's office would never have guessed I'd been up half the night. Unable to get back to sleep after meeting with Troy, I went to the pack house gym instead, working off my frustration through physical exertion. After a long shower and a facial mask, I got dressed for the day in my carefully chosen clothes, elegant but not *too* formal, and did my makeup in a way that conveyed femininity without being too flirty.

As the Alpha's daughter, I'd been walking the tightrope between competent and desirable for as long as I could remember. Appearances counted for a lot, especially in a traditional pack like ours. The pressure could be intense but knowing how to play the game gave me a sense of power. I prepared for the day like a warrior preparing for battle, and Savannah whistled in appreciation when she and Jasper sat down to join me at the oval table I used for informal meetings.

"Do you ever take a day off, Amanda? I mean: sweats, no make-up, eating ice cream out of the tub in front of the TV?"

She helped herself to one of the muffins I'd requested to be on the table this morning while Jasper poured a cup of coffee for his mate before taking one for himself. When he offered me one too, I shook my head. Caffeine wouldn't help my nerves at that point.

"I can't remember the last time I had a day like that," I told Savannah truthfully, glancing down at her more casual clothes with a pang of something that felt suspiciously like envy. Her curly hair bounced around her shoulders in a haphazard way that complemented her energy and her lack of conformity. She looked completely comfortable in her skin, unconcerned with how anyone else viewed her, and it made her shine. Did that come from having found her mate, I wondered, or had she always been that way?

Savannah had an Alpha for a father too, but our situations were different. Her brother had always been the heir, bearing the weight of that responsibility and giving Savannah more freedom to live her life on her own terms.

At least it seemed that way to me, looking in from the outside. She probably saw it differently since she made the choice to stay in my pack when I offered her the position as my Beta rather than returning home.

"Are we expecting someone else?" Jasper asked, his attention snagging on the fourth cup and plate that the staff had set out when I requested refreshments for the meeting.

"Yes. Troy from the external security team will be joining us."

It would have been impossible to miss the glance shared between the two people across from me, or the way that their eyes momentarily glazed over, indicating that they were speaking to each other through their mind-link. It also didn't take a genius to guess what they must have been discussing. Savannah and Jasper were both present when Troy made his declaration to me, after I became Alpha, that he wanted to acknowledge our mate bond at long last.

So far, neither my new Beta nor her mate had mentioned it again or questioned me about it, but they wouldn't have been half-human if they hadn't wondered about our situation.

As if me saying his name broke the taboo on the subject, Savannah blurted out a question I'd been anticipating. "Is he still your mate?"

Lying to my Beta would be pointless, especially when we were still building trust between us, so I gave her the truth. "He is. I asked him to reject me and he refused, so for the time being, we're at an impasse."

Jasper's full lips pursed into a frown. "Why do you want him to reject you?"

"Because he didn't put her first," Savannah answered for me before shoving a large chunk of the blueberry muffin into her mouth and chasing it down with a gulp of coffee. "He kept her dangling for seven years. I'd tell him to take a fucking hike too."

Jasper winced at the expletive, or maybe the fact that his mate used it in front of me, but I didn't mind her cursing. Savannah's lack of filter was one of my favourite things about her.

"He must have had his reasons," Jasper pointed out, his tone cautious but firm. "It can't have been easy for him either, so there had to be a reason he kept hanging on."

"Not a good enough one," Savannah responded with equal certainty. "Felix just nearly started a war with an entirely different realm to win his mate. And look at Vaughan and Calista! Duty's all well and good, but when it's your mate, you gotta throw caution to the wind and go for it. Sorry, Amanda."

She grimaced as if only just remembering my place as the 'other woman' in Vaughan and Calista's story, but I shook my head to dismiss her apology as unnecessary. She had it exactly right. By rejecting me, Vaughan risked the treaty with my father and the safety of his pack so he could be with the woman he was fated to. Why did I deserve any less than that?

"All I'm saying is that there might be more to the story than we know," Jasper suggested. "Jumping to conclusions doesn't help anyone."

"He said something recently that I didn't know," I found myself admitting. "He said he requested to be on my escort team whenever I left the pack's territory."

Jasper frowned over his cup of coffee. "You didn't know he was there?"

"No, that part I knew. With his scent and the way he scowled at me every time we were in the same room, he would have been hard to miss. But I thought he was as unhappy to be in that situation as I was. I thought my father arranged it as some kind of test. I didn't know Troy requested it."

Why would he, other than the reason he gave me: because he didn't trust anyone else to protect me as fervently as he would? But that raised more questions than it answered. His actions and his words didn't match up and I didn't know which to believe.

"Well, until he convinces me otherwise, I still think Troy can go fuck himself," Savannah declared before popping the last of her muffin into her mouth.

Before either Jasper or I could respond to that, someone else cleared their throat from the doorway.

"Sorry I'm late."

Chapter Five

~**Troy**~

I only intended to rest my eyes for a few seconds after the long, sleepless night, but when Devon gave me a playful shove, I realized the barracks had come to life around me and I must have fallen asleep.

"Just saw on the duty board that you're expected for a meeting in the Alpha's office in fifteen minutes," he informed me as I sat up, giving my head a shake as I tried to clear the sleep from my foggy mind. "Did you know about that?"

Shit. The call must have come in while I was dead to the world. "Not exactly, but it must be to discuss what happened last night. I'll head over now."

I hauled myself to my feet, intending to head to the pack house immediately, but Devon pushed me back down with a smirk. "Clothes first, Troy."

Hunter snickered in my head as I glanced down to see I'd been sleeping in nothing but my underwear.

I would have realized it when I got outside, I grumbled back to him.

Would you? Amanda gets you so turned around, I wouldn't put it past you to walk into her office naked.

Since he might have a point, I didn't say anything in response.

Devon helpfully pulled open my locker and tossed me a pair of combat pants and a black t-shirt, my standard uniform for a work day, and I pulled them on while also shoving one of our standard ration breakfast bars into my mouth. "What time is it, anyway?"

"Quarter to nine. Well, ten to, now. You're going to have to hustle."

I did, brushing my teeth and running a comb through my hair before jogging over to the pack house. The guard at the door tried to ask me about the overnight alert, but I brushed off the question in my hurry. "There'll be a briefing later today. I'm sorry, the Alpha's expecting me."

Even with my rushing, it was still past nine o'clock by the time I got to Amanda's door, which stood slightly open. My hand raised to knock, I froze when I heard voices coming from inside.

"You didn't know he was there?"

The speaker was male but I didn't recognize the voice immediately. The person who replied to him, however, couldn't be anyone but my mate.

"No, that part I knew. With his scent and the way he scowled at me every time we were in the same room, he would have been hard to miss. But I thought he was as unhappy to be in that situation as I was. I thought my father arranged it as some kind of test. I didn't know he requested it."

With each word, my heart rate kicked up a little more. Was she talking about me? It almost felt like too much to hope that I would be on her mind, that she would take the time to speak to someone else about me. It suggested her feelings for me weren't quite as cut-and-dried as she pretended they were.

Any doubt about whether I was the topic of conversation died as soon as another voice joined the conversation, one I also recognized.

"Well, until he convinces me otherwise, I still think Troy can go fuck himself."

That broad, blunt tone couldn't belong to anyone but our pack's new Beta, a woman I hadn't interacted with directly but had been around enough to be able to pick her out of a crowd. Apparently, she wasn't my biggest fan, though I couldn't think of a thing I'd done to her personally to earn her contempt.

Knowing my presence could be noticed at any time, I decided to step in before anything else was said, pushing the door fully open.

"Sorry I'm late."

Three heads swivelled towards me: Amanda, Savannah, and Savannah's mate, Jasper, one of the men unfairly exiled from the pack in the rogue situation we dealt with a couple of weeks earlier. Jasper gave the only friendly acknowledgement of my arrival, nodding his head in greeting, while Savannah, rather than looking embarrassed at the possibility that I might have overheard her last statement, simply looked me up and down, sizing me up in a way that made me very aware of my haphazard preparation for this meeting.

Amanda got straight down to business with no mention of the conversation I'd just interrupted. "Close the door behind you, Troy, and take a seat. There's coffee and some food here if you haven't eaten."

"Thank you, Alpha." I kept my tone polite and neutral as I followed her instructions, grabbing a cup of coffee before taking a seat at the oval table across from Amanda and next to Jasper.

Sitting perfectly straight in her chair, Amanda appeared the picture of propriety and control. "I've asked you here to talk about an incident that happened on the border last night and the wider implications of it. Troy, can you fill Savannah and Jasper in on the first part?"

"Of course." As thoroughly as possible, I relayed the skirmish at the border and what the wolf said once we drove them back.

"Is this kind of thing common?" Jasper asked once I'd finished. "I mean, aside from the rogue stuff, do we often have other wolves coming into the territory?"

"I wouldn't say common, but it happens. There are packs nearby who aren't allies or enemies, and wolves will occasionally cross over just to cause trouble with no bigger purpose. Sometimes, they're drunk; other times, it's young kids with new wolves looking for a thrill. In this case, there were only three of them and they gave up pretty easily. I wouldn't be all that worried about it if it weren't for the wolf's threat afterwards. That's what makes this especially unusual."

"How do they even know about you?" Savannah asked Amanda, mirroring the question Amanda herself had voiced during our earlier meeting.

"Someone must have told them, but who and why are the questions we need answered."

Her hand drifted absent-mindedly to a pendant she wore around her neck, her fingers closing around it almost as if seeking some comfort there.

"Where did you get that necklace?"

The words were out of my mouth before I could think better of them, and everyone's attention immediately went to the pendant in question. Amanda lowered her hand, her lips pressing together. "Let's stick to the topic at hand, shall we?"

The rebuke was clear, but Savannah leaned a little closer, examining the necklace curiously. "It's pretty. Is it new? How do *you* know it's new?"

She directed the last question at me, and I answered honestly. "I'm familiar with all of the Alpha's jewellery and I haven't seen that one before."

It didn't resemble any of the sleek, professional pieces she usually favoured. A burnished gold colour with an oval gemstone pendant, it looked like an antique; pretty, as Savannah said, but not Amanda's style at all.

Still not looking pleased about the change of subject, Amanda responded tightly. "Several of my mother's accessories, those that belong to the pack, were added to my own collection when I moved to my new room. This is one of them. Not that it's any of your business."

Again, the final statement was meant for me, and I bowed my head in acknowledgement. It *wasn't* my business, but something about her wearing that necklace didn't sit right with me. I couldn't explain it but gut feelings rarely had any basis in logic.

When I raised my eyes again, Amanda's hand had returned to the pendant, which also struck me as odd. She didn't play with her jewellery. She was always too much in control for that.

"I just wish I knew who in the pack I could trust, who I need to win over, and who would sell me out."

"Well, we'll do our best to figure that out," Jasper promised. "If we can find out what pack the wolves came from last night, we can start…"

A knock at the door interrupted him before he could finish his sentence, and Amanda frowned. Her staff would have instructions not to interrupt her unless it really couldn't wait, so something else must have happened.

"Yes?" she called out.

The door opened to reveal the guard I'd spoken to briefly at the back door that morning. "I'm sorry to disturb you, Alpha, but there's someone here to see you. He says it's important."

"Someone?" she repeated sharply. "Who?"

"That's the thing," the man explained apologetically. "We have no idea. He just turned up at the front door and will only speak to you."

It was my turn to repeat his words, unsure I understood what he was saying. "Turned up at the front door? Someone from outside the pack? Without us knowing about it?"

"Yes, Captain," he confirmed with a grave nod of his head. "He didn't set off any alarms and he has no scent at all."

The four of us at the table exchanged confused glances but Amanda quickly regained her composure. "If he can move around the territory at will but came here to talk, it's worth hearing what he has to say. Let him in."

The guard bowed and turned back to the hall while Amanda stood from the table to take her seat at her desk instead. Without a word between us, Jasper and I positioned ourselves on either side of her desk, just in front of it, putting ourselves between our Alpha and any potential danger. Savannah stayed at the table, reaching for another muffin from the tray as the guard returned, accompanied by the strangest-looking man I'd ever seen.

CHAPTER SIX

~Amanda~

Although I would never admit it, having Troy in the room while the guard let the stranger in made me feel safer and stronger than I would have on my own. Every tensed muscle in his strong body that hovered just on the edge of my peripheral vision confirmed that he would do anything necessary to keep me safe, not only because he had to as a member of the pack, but because he wouldn't let anyone harm his mate.

For once, the bond actually worked in my favour.

When the stranger appeared, Troy somehow tensed even further, and I could see why. The person who strolled through the door looked like he had wandered out of some kind of costume party, dressed in dark, leather clothing that appeared to come from another time. White hair framed a dark brown face that looked no older than my own, and gold rings dotted almost every finger of his hands.

Exotic-looking, certainly. Handsome? Yes, but I gave that consideration little weight as I sized him up.

As the guard had warned me, no smell accompanied our guest, giving me no hint as to what he might be or what brought him to our territory, but he wore a friendly smile as he walked right up to my desk, ignoring everyone else in the room.

"Amanda. It's a pleasure to meet you."

A low growl rumbled from my right. "That's *Alpha* Amanda," Troy gritted out.

The stranger inclined his head in Troy's direction before turning his attention back to me. "My apologies. Alpha Amanda."

His eyes seemed to almost glow, a shade of brown so light they appeared nearly golden. This man didn't look like any werewolf I'd ever met, nor any human either, but the longer I looked at him, the more attractive he seemed.

"I'd say it's a pleasure to meet you too, but I have no idea who you are, what you want, or how you ended up in my territory without me being notified, so I'll have to reserve that judgement for now."

His smile revealed two rows of perfectly straight teeth, so white they seemed to glow against his burnished skin. "Where are my manners? My name is Kalo and I've come to provide the help you need. As for how I got here, that will have to be my secret for the time being. A man needs to maintain a little bit of mystery during a negotiation, don't you think?"

Without waiting for an invitation, he took a seat in the chair across from me, leaning back and crossing one ankle over the opposite knee, revealing a shoe that matched his clothes in style and apparent age. I'd never seen one like it.

"What exactly are we negotiating?" I asked, leaning back to mirror his body language and steepling my hands in front of me. Whoever Kalo might be, I had no intention of letting him know how much his presence unnerved me. Had my father ever been visited by someone so unusual, completely out of the blue? He never mentioned it, but I supposed there were many things about being Alpha that he never shared.

"We're negotiating the services I can provide to you," he said, as if it were obvious. "The help you need. My particular skills will be very useful, I promise you."

"Which skills? And what help do I need?"

He spoke as if we were already acquainted, as if he'd walked into a conversation already in progress, while I struggled to keep up.

"Well, you've already seen one of my skills." He gave another wide, white smile as he gestured around the office. "I can move around among your kind without attracting attention. It's a useful talent in a spy."

That made sense, but nothing else he said did. Each statement only raised several new questions. "What do I need a spy for? How do you know anything about me and my pack? And what are you if not one of 'my kind'?"

Kalo surveyed the room again, his gaze landing that time on Jasper and Troy, still standing sentry at either side of my desk. "The guard dogs really aren't necessary. Your man at the door searched me. I'm unarmed."

Troy growled again, his wolf close to breaking free and sounding very much like the guard dog he'd just been labelled as. "No one meets with the Alpha alone without being fully vetted. Standard protocol."

That was absolutely true for external visitors, but it surprised me to hear Troy say it. I didn't realize he paid so much attention to visitor procedures. Maybe he studied them for the visits he accompanied me on?

"Answer my questions," I cut back in. "What are you?"

"That one, I'm going to have to decline to answer." He shrugged his leather-clad shoulders, as if the choice were out of his hands. "It's a matter of personal security for *me*. Standard protocol."

Troy stiffened at the mimicking of his statement, but I kept my eyes trained on Kalo, my expression neutral, waiting for him to continue.

"As for your other questions, I know that you've very recently taken over the pack and that there are some in your ranks who would prefer you hadn't. I know there's been talk among your neighbours about whether you're strong enough to defend your territories. And I know that if your internal rivals teamed up with your external ones, it could go very badly for you. *That's* what you need a spy for: to help you determine the source of the threat internally before things get out of hand."

Every muscle in my face tensed as I tried not to react in any way, but inside, my head spun.

How does he know all of this? I asked Cinder, my most-trusted confidante.

I don't know, but you literally just said you wanted to figure all this out and he appeared. It's like you called him into existence.

That sounded crazy but I had no better explanation. *I said I needed to know who to trust, though, and I can't trust him. I literally don't know anything about him. He just said he'd make a perfect spy and for all I know, someone has sent him to spy **on** me, not for me.*

"What does your wolf think about me?" Kalo asked, shooting me another of his casual, confident smiles. He really did look good when he smiled.

My expression didn't shift. "What makes you think I'm talking with my wolf?"

"Your eyes haven't done that weird glazing thing they do when werewolves talk to each other, so I'm guessing you're not speaking to anyone else in the room, but your pupils are moving as if you're processing something being said to you. Your wolf is the obvious choice. Observation is another of my skills, you see."

He bent forward in a self-congratulatory bow, and though I did my best not to show it, I *was* impressed. "And you really won't tell me what you are?"

"I'm afraid not."

"Where do you come from?" I tried instead.

"That's also confidential."

I had a feeling that would be the case, so I moved on. "You haven't mentioned your price for providing these 'services'."

"I have not," he confirmed good-naturedly. "And I can only tell you that it won't cost you anything financially. I will only require a favour of you when you're satisfied my work is complete, but the nature of that favour, I'm not at liberty to disclose right now."

"Ludicrous," Troy snorted. "You can't seriously expect..."

"Troy." His name from my lips stopped his words immediately, and though I could tell it went against every instinct he had, he said no more.

To Kalo, I made an offer.

"Give me a few minutes to discuss your offer with my team before we proceed any further with the negotiations. My staff will make sure you're comfortable while you wait."

"Certainly. Thank you, Alpha Amanda."

His tongue lingered on my name in a way that made Troy's fists clench, and Kalo rose gracefully from his seat, gave me a nod of acknowledgement, and turned on his heel. I immediately mind-linked the guard outside the door so that by the time Kalo reached it, it opened for him.

When the door closed again behind him, I let out a long breath as the three other people in the room all turned to me, looking for any direction on what to do next.

Chapter Seven

~Troy~

Not since my very first shift as a teenager had I felt so close to losing control of my wolf. Hunter clawed against the barrier in our mind every time Kalo spoke, desperate to take over and neutralize the threat the stranger posed to our mate.

The fact that he *was* a threat, I didn't doubt for a second. Everything about the man screamed danger, and the fact that Amanda could sit there so calmly, carrying on a conversation with him as if nothing out of the ordinary were happening, defied my understanding.

When he at last left the room so that the rest of us could speak freely, I could barely stop myself from blurting out what seemed obvious to me: we should throw him in our basement cell and interrogate him until he gave us some straight answers about who sent him to us and why.

However, I managed to restrain myself until my Alpha asked for my opinion. I owed her that sign of respect.

"Do any of you have any idea what he is? What species?" was her first question, and on that point, I could only shake my head mutely. I'd never encountered anyone like him before, from his almost-glowing eyes to his old-fashioned clothing and distinct lack of any scent.

Jasper also shook his head, but Savannah immediately pulled out her phone. "I don't know off the top of my head but if anyone has a clue, it'll be Felix or Calista. Let's ask them."

She tapped at her phone screen, sending a message to the members of her former pack who she thought would have some insight. Amanda let her finish before continuing.

"What does your gut say, Savannah?"

Hunter growled in my head, frustrated that she didn't ask for our opinion first, and I clenched my jaw tight to keep from speaking out of turn.

"I don't trust him for a second," the Beta stated as she got to her feet and came over to stand in front of Amanda's desk between me and Jasper, facing the Alpha straight-on. "However, I don't think we should piss him off either. Whoever he is, he knows a lot about the situation here and has some unusual abilities. He could do a lot of damage against us if he chose to. I say we keep him close until we figure out exactly what's going on."

That time, I couldn't entirely hold the growl in, and Amanda narrowed her eyes at me before turning to the other man in the room. "Jasper?"

"I'm with Savannah," he said, unsurprisingly. The man clearly adored his new mate. "He's holding back a lot of information but if his intentions were simply to cause harm, I don't see why he would have approached us this way. Something else is at play, and we need to figure out his motivation before making any firm move one way or the other."

Amanda nodded thoughtfully before her eyes finally flicked over to me. "Troy?"

Swallowing down my protective anger, I stated my opinion as calmly as possible.

"He's trespassing on our territory mere hours after a threat was issued against us by another pack. It's too risky to give him the benefit of the doubt. We should put him in the prison where we can keep an eye on him while we get some answers."

"We have no idea what powers he has," Savannah immediately argued. Despite barely coming up to my shoulders, she had no problem standing her ground. "We don't even know if we *can* hold him. He doesn't register on our sensors. How did he get to the pack house? Maybe he can teleport or turn invisible. There's too much we don't know, and if we respond too aggressively, we might lose our chance to negotiate with him at all."

"Good," I shot back. "We shouldn't be negotiating with anyone who won't give us a straight answer. As for holding him, we just need to figure out what he is and we'll know how to do it. Every species has a vulnerability, and you can bet that's why he doesn't want to tell us what he is."

"We have the right to hold him temporarily under our pack laws," Jasper conceded, clearly attempting to take the middle ground between my position and Savannah's. "However, not being a werewolf, he might not understand all the intricacies of our border security. Simply refusing to answer questions isn't a crime. Technically, we could do it, but if we want to act in good faith, he hasn't done anything to warrant incarceration."

"So you want to wait until he commits a crime?" I snarled. "Until he puts this pack, our *Alpha*, in danger?"

"Enough." Amanda's firm voice silenced the room immediately and we all turned to her to await her decision. Sitting there in her chair while the rest of us stood, she appeared poised and completely in control. "I agree with Savannah. There's too much we don't know to make an enemy of him. Finding out his species is our top priority, and once we know that, we can reevaluate. In the meantime, I'll speak with him again to try to find out more about why he's here. Alone."

My growl rattled the mugs still sitting on the table where we'd abandoned our earlier meeting.

Amanda shot me a warning look. "I mean that our conversation will be private, but naturally, there will be security in the room. Since I already know you'll insist on being there, you can choose one other guard to join you. I'll meet him in the library where we can maintain a little privacy but still be watched. Savannah and Jasper, you work on figuring out his species. We'll reconvene here for lunch."

I still didn't like it, but being able to keep her in my line of sight quieted my wolf and my protective instincts enough that I could nod.

In my head, I reached out to Devon through mind-link. I wouldn't trust this to anyone else. *How quickly can you be at the pack house?*

His reply came instantaneously. *Less than ten minutes. You need me? As fast as you can get here. Meet me in the library.*

Out loud, I confirmed the arrangements to Amanda. "Devon can be here in ten minutes."

"Good. I'll use that time to review my father's files and see if there's anything I might have missed about unusual visitors in the past. Maybe Kalo is even someone my father knows. I'll run a search through his records."

Just hearing her speak the stranger's name aloud stung at my chest like a red-hot poker. This man was bad news, I could feel it in my bones, but until I had the proof everyone else seemed to want, I'd have to satisfy myself with keeping Amanda safe.

If Kalo wanted to harm my mate, he'd have to do it over my dead body.

Chapter Eight

~Amanda~

When the door closed behind the others, I let out a deep sigh simmering with anxiety and frustration.

The anxiety stemmed from the unexpected turn this day had taken and the unusual visitor waiting to speak with me again.

The frustration? Well, that mostly came from Troy.

He seemed to take everything I did or said as a personal affront to him. When I cut him off for speaking out of turn in front of Kalo, he bristled, even though he'd been the one in the wrong. His impatience when I asked Savannah and Jasper for their thoughts before him practically vibrated off him even though I simply followed protocol. Our pack cleaved to its traditions, and one of the ones I'd learned from my father had been always addressing his advisers in order of rank. My Beta came first, obviously, and Jasper, as her mate, outranked a captain of the guards.

Yes, if we'd accepted each other as mates, Troy would outrank them both, but at the current moment, when nothing at all had been agreed between us, he held the lowest position in the room. That wasn't me being vindictive towards him; it was simply a fact.

Him not understanding that or just not accepting it added another layer of stress to my day that I really didn't need.

Pushing my growly, overprotective mate from my thoughts, I pulled up my father's personal archive on my computer. With all the other business of taking over the pack, I hadn't had a chance to really delve into any of his files yet, but I knew where to find them and how they were organized.

First, I accessed his visitor log where he maintained a full list of all formal visitors to our territory during his tenure as Alpha. Names, dates, pack affiliations and more were all carefully documented. I did a search for the name Kalo, in every spelling variation I could think of, but each search returned the same message: 'no results found'.

So, Kalo had never met with my father, at least not under that name.

Broadening my search, I clicked into the folder of his personal notes, made up of hundreds of documents over the years of his rule. Each week, he summarized the important activities that had taken place in the pack, and a search for 'white-haired man' and 'strange visitor' returned several results, none of which were relevant.

My eyes flitted to the phone on my desk, wondering if it would be more efficient to simply call my father and ask him. He and my mother were still in the United States, staying with the scientist who had helped treat my mother from the illness which nearly claimed her life. Calling my father would be the most direct route, but he might be busy and the idea of adding to the worries they already had didn't appeal to me, especially since nothing was necessarily wrong.

Not yet, anyway.

Besides, I needed to prove to the pack that I could handle things on my own without running to my father every time I had a question.

I needed to prove it to myself too.

With a sigh, I locked my computer and stood up, straightening out my clothes. From my drawer, I pulled a small compact mirror to check my makeup and hair, ensuring nothing had come out of place before I squared my shoulders and headed to the library to meet Kalo.

The library had always been my favourite place in the pack house. As a child, I spent hours sitting in one of the window bays, curled up on the cushioned bench with a book until someone called me for dinner or to work on my lessons or to go to bed. My father approved of reading as a hobby since it meant staying inside and away from any potential dangers, so he instructed my tutors to indulge me in it.

The library sat on the ground floor of the pack house, directly beneath the ballroom upstairs and almost the same size. Rectangular and wide, the walls were lined with in-set bookshelves, complemented by free-standing ones forming a back-to-back column in the centre of the room. A comfortable seating area by the fireplace had been my mother's preferred place to read on the occasions she took advantage of the space, but I preferred the privacy of the window bay, pulling the curtain closed around it when I really wanted to escape.

That morning, Kalo stood in the centre of the room, perusing the titles on the middle shelves with his hands behind his back. The posture added to the old-fashioned air that surrounded him despite his youth. At the rear of the room, a man clad in black stood, his hands clasped in front of him and feet spread as he watched Kalo's every move. That had to be Devon, the man Troy mentioned bringing in, and his surveillance of our visitor was hardly subtle.

Troy himself managed a little better. He stood close to the wall by the windows, just a few steps from my favourite window seat, and his eyes, rather than watching Kalo, were fixed on me.

I gave him a nod of acknowledgement when I entered to confirm I knew he was in place before I strode over to our visitor.

"Anything catch your eye?"

Kalo turned to me, his golden gaze even more striking close up than it had been across the desk in my office. "Now that you're here, I can honestly say yes."

Fabric rustled from behind me, where Troy stood. Obviously, he overheard that and didn't appreciate the compliment. Werewolf hearing could be *too* good sometimes.

I didn't take Kalo's comment to heart, however. Flattery formed part of diplomacy, so I doubted he meant it sincerely. "I'm sorry to have kept you waiting. Let's take a seat by the fire so we can continue our conversation."

I gestured to the sofa and chairs arranged around the crackling fire, and a ghost of a smile flickered across Kalo's face. "As you wish."

I took a seat first, choosing one of the comfortable armchairs that sat perpendicular to the fireplace and Kalo took the one across from me. From his vantage point, Troy couldn't see me but he would have a full view of Kalo, exactly as I wanted.

"I think we got off on the wrong foot this morning," I started, giving him a smile as I sat back and crossed my legs, trying to look at ease. Since demanding answers hadn't worked before, perhaps a little gentle coaxing would be more effective. "Your sudden appearance took us all by surprise, and when cornered, wolves tend to get a little aggressive."

"My introduction was clumsy," he agreed, relaxing into his chair a little more with my words and softened tone. "I'm a little rusty at offering my services and I apologize if I've been too forward."

Now we were getting somewhere. "Is this something you do often, then? Go around offering to help people out of the blue?"

"That is pretty much my business model, yes." His golden eyes twinkled with amusement. "Very few of my clients are quite so charming, though."

I ignored that to focus on the first part of what he said. "And your business deals are usually successful?"

"I suppose that depends on your definition of success." For a moment, a dark cloud of something close to pain passed over his expression, erasing the merriment that had been there a moment earlier. When I blinked, it had gone. "My clients are satisfied in the short term. I'm usually less so."

"Aren't you the one who sets the terms?"

He inclined his head in agreement, his eyes never leaving mine. "Yes, but people rarely keep their word when the time comes to settle our debt. I've been disappointed many times, but I live in hope that each time will be different."

A hidden meaning lingered beneath the surface of his statement, so close I could almost feel it, but what that meaning might be, I had no idea.

Before I could say anything else, he turned his head, glancing around the room. "This space holds a special significance for you, doesn't it?"

The blood in my veins cooled, remembering how I had just been thinking about that before I came into the library, and how he had appeared moments after I said that I needed some help. Could he read my mind? Some species had that ability, and if I was dealing with one of them, he might be more dangerous than even Troy believed.

"What makes you say that?"

He lifted a shoulder in a shrug, the light from the fire playing along his bronzed skin with the movement. "You're more relaxed in here than in your office. A lot of our behaviours are rooted in our childhood memories, even when we don't realize it. I'm guessing that as a child, you felt safe in here and on edge in your father's office. Is that right?"

I didn't answer, mostly because I was still stuck on wondering whether he had dug that out of some part of my memory without me realizing it. Finding out his species seemed more urgent than ever.

Kalo chuckled at my silence. "I'm sorry. I told you: observation is one of my skills. People tell you all sorts of things about themselves if you know where to look, but sometimes, they find it off-putting when you point it out."

My eyes narrowed on him as I considered his explanation. "Do they ever accuse you of reading their minds?"

His head tilted back as he laughed, a deep, melodic sound pushing past his white teeth. "You can't imagine how often. Unfortunately, that's a skill I don't possess, as useful as it would be."

That's too bad. If you could hear this, I'd take you to my bed tonight.

I put the thought out into the space between us, the same way I did when mind-linking with one of my pack, and watched Kalo carefully for any sign that he'd heard me. A twitch of his jaw, a flare of his nostrils or a widening of his eyes would be proof enough for me.

However, nothing changed, other than his smile slowly fading as he watched me.

"If you're trying to talk to me telepathically now, I'm afraid it truly won't work. I'm good at reading people but I'm not a mind-reader. I promise."

"A promise means little without an honourable person behind it, and I don't know enough about you to know whether you fit that bill," I replied, and he bowed his head again.

"That's fair, but I hope you'll give me a chance to prove myself to you. I think we could be good for each other, Alpha Amanda. There's no reason we can't be friends."

Friends were never something I had many of and not at the top of my list of concerns now. "You said you won't tell me what you are or where you come from, but if we're going to work together, I do need to know one thing: how do you know anything about me or my pack?"

His smile reappeared, lighting up his face once again. "That, I can tell you."

Chapter Nine

~**Troy**~

One of my eyelids had begun to itch but I fought down the urge to scratch at it, afraid to move and miss a single word being spoken at the end of the room. Although I stood roughly twenty metres away from them, I could hear every word thanks to the device worn in my ear, a piece of tech the border guards used to amplify their werewolf hearing. Amanda didn't seem to know about them but that didn't surprise me. Alphas looked at the big picture, not the details of how each team in the pack performed their job.

She thought she and Kalo were speaking in private, but I had no intention of missing any crumb of information the stranger might drop.

So far, he hadn't said much that I considered useful, but when he agreed to explain how he knew about our pack, I found myself holding my breath.

"Last night, I was in a bar in Canmore when three men came in, looking like they'd been in some kind of fight. One had a blood stain covering half his grey t-shirt but he didn't seem to care. I offered to buy them a drink if they told me what they'd been up to."

Canmore was a human town about fifty kilometres away from us as the crow flew. Several mountains stood in the way.

"Why did you care?"

Amanda's voice sounded clipped and controlled, and although I couldn't see her from my current position, my imagination quickly filled in the blanks, picturing the way she did her best to appear casual when she didn't want anyone to know how uncertain she actually felt.

Kalo shrugged, an easy gesture that conveyed casual confidence. "I like a good story. Besides, I was bored and had nothing better to do."

That sounded like bullshit to me but I kept my mouth shut as he continued.

"One drink turned into a few and their tongues loosened. I found out they belong to a werewolf pack located on a large ranch south of Calgary and they were testing out the border security of another pack, one which had just been taken over by a new Alpha. It didn't take long to realize they meant this one."

My eyes darted to Devon at the other end of the hall who also wore one of the enhancing earpieces. *You hearing this?* I asked him in my head.

The guys from the border last night, he confirmed. *It has to be.*

"Another drink or two and they told me they're making preparations to move against you since they've heard not all of the pack members are happy about a woman being their new Alpha. They believe enough of your own pack can be swayed to switch sides or at least not to put up a fight if it means removing *you*."

The emphasis he put on the last word made it sound far too close to a threat for my comfort.

Hunter growled inside my head. *Why haven't we locked this asshole up yet?*

I didn't know, so I gave him the only answer I could. *It's not our call to make.*

Amanda, for her part, took the revelation calmly. "Did they say where they learned any of this information?"

"They didn't, but considering the distance over which news seems to have travelled, I would hazard a guess that it's not by word of mouth."

Online, then. If people within our pack were planning a mutiny, cutting off their internet access would be an easy first step. We were too far into the wilderness to get a reliable signal without the pack's central service. That went for phone calls too. With a flip of a switch, Amanda could disrupt all communication with the outside world.

It didn't solve the problem of the external people who were already conspiring against us, though. That would be where my team came in.

Apparently, it was also where Kalo's thoughts were headed.

"I have some useful tricks to secure your borders more forcefully in the short term if necessary, along with helping you to determine where the internal threat might be coming from. You can see why I thought you might appreciate my services at this particular moment."

"It's very convenient," Amanda agreed, but despite the calm words, I could hear the undertone of suspicion in them. *Too* convenient, she meant, and on that point, we were in complete agreement. "I suppose you'll need access to our defense systems to make your preparations."

Kalo's smile felt entirely too intimate. "You really don't trust me. I can see I'll have to prove myself, but that's okay. I enjoy a challenge."

If he kept flirting with my mate, he'd have to face the challenge of my wolf ripping his throat out. Somehow, I suspected he wouldn't enjoy *that* very much.

"You won't have to let me in on any secrets. As long as I can speak to the appropriate members of your team, I can work with them to implement changes at no risk to you."

"This all sounds a little too good to be true," Amanda told him frankly. "Especially since I don't know what I'm expected to give you in return. You say that people you've worked with previously haven't kept up their end of the bargain, so what happens then? What if I can't give you what you're asking for?"

Kalo inclined his head in a show of submission that rang false. "I promise you will be able to meet my requirements, as long as you're willing. As for those who chose not to... well, they discovered that the work done for them wasn't as permanent as they wanted to believe."

What the fuck did that mean?

"I wouldn't wait too long to make your decision," Kalo warned, leaning forward and resting his elbows on his knees. Though I couldn't see Amanda, I could tell his gaze was locked on her. "The wolves I spoke to last night intend to move soon. A delay of even a day could be dangerous."

"Of course you'd say that," I muttered out loud, unable to stop myself, and a second later, Amanda's voice echoed in my head.

Did you hear all of that?

Shit. I hadn't meant to give myself away, but facing a direct question from my Alpha and my mate, I couldn't lie. *Yes.*

What do you think?

Surprise flickered in my chest that she wanted my opinion, followed quickly by pride. I'd expected a scolding but this felt like an olive branch.

He's trying to create a sense of urgency to make you give in. It's a classic sales technique. Give nothing away until you speak to the Beta and see if she's learned anything. I can offer to give him a tour of the territory to give you more time.

Spending time with Kalo appealed to me about as much as taking a bath with piranhas but I'd rather have him where I could keep an eye on him and as far away from Amanda as possible.

Thank you, was all she said in reply before responding to Kalo out loud.

"I have an important matter that needs my attention now, but one of our border guard captains will show you around. I understand you won't begin any work until we come to an agreement, *if* we come to an agreement, but at least in the meantime you can get a better understanding of our territory so no time is wasted. If we can't work out a deal, at the very least you'll get a pleasant walk."

Kalo smiled again as he sat back in his chair once more. "As you wish."

Amanda's face appeared from around the high back of her armchair. "Troy, could you please join us?"

Ensuring I wore as neutral an expression as possible, I strode over to the sitting area and bowed my head to her. "Alpha."

"I'm leaving our visitor in your hands for the next few hours. Please ensure he's given something to eat and drink and give him an overview of our land."

"Of course." I bowed to her once more before turning my attention to Kalo, my back stiffening as our eyes met. "Come with me."

Please, Amanda's voice said in my head.

"Please," I added through gritted teeth.

As the stranger stood and followed me from the room, I realized that for the first time, Amanda and I had spoken by mind-link and I hadn't even been able to truly enjoy it. As important as our mate bond was to me, her safety took priority.

The sooner we figured out the truth about Kalo, the better.

Chapter Ten

~Amanda~

My conversation with Kalo left me both reassured and more agitated than before. He didn't seem to pose an immediate threat, more interested in negotiating than intimidating, and he'd shared some useful information about the conversation he overheard.

On the other hand, we still had no idea what he was, what he might be capable of, and what he wanted in exchange for his assistance.

Hopeful that Savannah and Jasper had made some progress with the first of those questions during my absence, I returned to my office eager to hear their report.

"Where's Troy?" was my Beta's first question when she and her mate returned at the designated time. Lunch had already been brought to the table where we'd had our breakfast meeting a few hours earlier and they found me sitting there alone, picking at my salad.

"He's keeping Kalo busy for me," I explained, grateful once again that he'd made the offer to do so, taking some of the pressure off me. "I expect them to return in about an hour, so I'm hoping you have some news."

Savannah and Jasper exchanged grim glances. "Not yet, unfortunately," he replied for them both. "Calista was in a meeting when we called and Felix was... uh... occupied with his new mate."

'Occupied' clearly meant 'in bed with', and I did my best to ignore the pang of jealousy that tightened my chest. That was the dream for all werewolves, honestly: spending as many hours as humanly possible enjoying the pleasure of your fated mate as soon as you found them. It hadn't worked out that way for me, and though I'd taken my pleasure elsewhere over the years, the knowledge always lingered in the back of my head that it would never be as good as it would have been with the one meant for me.

Not to mention it had been a long time since I'd had *any* pleasure. My father began negotiations with the Crimsontooth pack nearly a year ago and I'd stayed celibate in anticipation of the mating arrangement between myself and Vaughan, figuring I wouldn't like it if my chosen mate fucked around in the meantime, so I'd return the courtesy. In the end, it turned out to be unnecessary since Vaughan found his own fated mate and never so much as kissed me.

My body craved a man's touch, which only made being around Troy lately even harder than usual.

"We left a detailed message explaining the situation," Savannah added, helping herself to one of the large deli-style sandwiches on the table and passing the other to Jasper. "At least one of them should be calling us back soon. How did your conversation with Kalo go?"

As thoroughly as possible, I filled them in on what we'd discussed. "He seems to understand our situation pretty well, knows a lot about werewolves in general, and has some unusual abilities. I'm also pretty certain he was being truthful about not being able to read my mind. However, the fact that he refuses to say what kind of payment he wants makes it almost impossible for me to agree, no matter what he can do for us. What if he asked me to hand over control of the pack? To sacrifice someone's life? There are too many awful possibilities."

Savannah nodded thoughtfully. "Maybe we could try to set some terms around it? If he can't tell us what the payment is, at least he could confirm what it isn't. No murder, no power trips, no sexual favours..."

She ticked the items off on her fingers as she spoke, and at even the mention of sex, my body clenched again. This was getting ridiculous. Was I so hard up that the thought of trading sexual favours to protect my pack didn't seem as awful to me as it should? Technically, an arranged mating with Vaughan amounted to the same thing, didn't it?

Kalo wasn't unattractive, if I were being honest. Unusual-looking, certainly, but he was young and strong, with a confidence and grace that could be appealing under the right circumstances.

Circumstances like a year-long dry spell, for instance.

"Alpha?"

Jasper's head cocked to the side quizzically as my eyes darted to him, and I realized I must have missed part of the conversation. "Sorry. What did you say?"

"Only that it would be easy to miss something off Savannah's proposed list, or for his price to slip past those barriers on a technicality. I don't think it's worth it."

Thankfully, Savannah's phone rang, giving me a chance to collect myself further before needing to make a response. "It's Calista," she announced before answering the call and placing it on speaker in the middle of the table. "Thanks for calling me back. I'm here with Jasper and Alpha Amanda."

"Oh. Hi, everyone." Awkwardness infused her tone at the sound of my name, and I understood it completely. Based on the way we met, Vaughan's Luna and I would probably never be friends, but we were both capable of putting our past behind us, as she did then. "I have Felix here with me. We reviewed your message and compared notes."

"What can you tell us?" I asked, eager to get to the bottom of the mystery of Kalo's species. It might not tell us everything, but it would certainly be a good start.

"This is an interesting one." Felix's friendly tone filled the room, and I could picture his enthusiastic smile as easily as if he were there with us. "Not setting off the pack's alarm narrows down the possibilities considerably. Even the fae, while invisible, set it off. Usually, the only things that won't are animals with no human counterpart or beings lacking a corporeal state, like a spirit."

"Are you saying this guy's a ghost?" Jasper asked.

"Not necessarily," Calista cut in. "He said *like* a spirit, but spirits aren't the only beings who exist outside of a solid state."

All of this was outside my realm of experience. Besides the vengeful spirit that had attacked Vaughan's pack by possessing the sasquatches, I'd never dealt with a non-solid being before. "What are the other options?"

"Demons are a big one," Felix offered. "Or angels, on the flip side. Various gods or god-like beings. Based on his offer to help you in exchange for payment, demon was my first guess."

My hand found my mother's necklace, the weight of it between my fingers strangely comforting. "You think his price is my soul?"

That made sense, actually. It didn't cost anything and I was free to give it, if I so chose. I could see why people would balk at it when the price was revealed. All the pieces fit.

"That's Felix's suggestion, but I'm not entirely convinced he's a demon," Calista countered. "Usually, you have to summon a demon, they don't just appear. I assume you haven't performed a summoning ritual recently?"

"Not unless wishing I knew who to trust counts as summoning," I tried to joke, but based on the silence that immediately swallowed the room, it obviously didn't land very well.

"Did you use those exact words? Out loud?" Calista asked, her voice sounding sharper all of a sudden, the words clipped.

I looked to Savannah and Jasper for confirmation and they both nodded. "Something along those lines, yes. During our meeting this morning, just before Kalo appeared. I thought maybe he'd read my mind somehow, but I tested him later and it didn't seem like he could."

Papers shuffled in the background through the phone, Felix and Calista murmuring to each other too quietly for me to make out any of the words.

"Did you recently pick up any new possessions?" Calista asked next, and I had to purse my lips to keep from scoffing.

"I just took over as Alpha of the pack. Most of what I own now is new to me."

"Right." She blew out a breath, the speaker crackling with the force of it. "Is there anything in particular that caught your attention? Something that you feel an unusual urge to touch?"

My fingers froze over the pendant in my hand and Savannah and Jasper's gazes immediately dropped to the necklace too. I dropped my hand as though the metal scalded it. "How... how is that related?"

"What is it?" Felix demanded, his tone more urgent than before. "Were you touching it when you made your wish this morning?"

I couldn't remember for certain, but it was possible.

"It's a necklace, and I think she was," Savannah answered for me. "What does it have to do with Kalo?"

"It might have everything to do with him," Felix breathed out, sounding both excited and concerned at the same time. "I think you *did* summon him, Amanda, but he's not a demon at all. If we're right, you might have your very own genie."

"A genie?" I repeated in disbelief. "Those are real?"

"Real and very dangerous," Calista stated, sounding just as concerned as Felix but not nearly as enthused. "He might be able to help you, like he said, but wishes don't come free. You're going to have to proceed very, very carefully or a mutiny within the pack might be the least of your worries."

Chapter Eleven

~**Troy**~

My hands clenched into fists at my side as I led Kalo through the house to the pack house mess hall. Unlike the formal dining room where the Alpha's family and important ranked members of the pack ate, the mess hall catered to the staff that kept the house running and wolves like me whose business might bring them to the house. Utilitarian tables filled the clean but slightly cramped space, and several groups of workers were already partaking of their midday rations. Curious glances flew our way, but a well-directed scowl from me had them all quickly turning their heads away again.

I grabbed two of the pre-packed hot meals from the warming tray and brought them to the quietest corner of the room, placing them down unceremoniously in front of two chairs.

"Water or coffee?"

Kalo's gaze drifted from the packaged meals to the other tables in the room, taking everything in. "Coffee. The hotter, the better."

With a grunt of acknowledgement, I returned to the serving area and poured two cups from the pot already sitting there. By the time I returned to the table, the stranger had opened his meal and was examining its contents, poking at the various items with his fork.

"You aren't given a choice of what to eat?" he asked as I took the seat across from him, using my body to block his escape route. He couldn't leave the room without going through me.

"The former Alpha implemented a new nutrition program. Meals are carefully planned."

I didn't bother to explain the genetic modifications that had been part of that program. Since the downfall of Kyle, the geneticist responsible for both that and the Luna's near-death, it didn't seem like something to brag about. Besides, I didn't trust the man in front of me one bit and had no intention of giving up more information than required about our pack in general.

"You didn't like the previous Alpha," he stated, the words an observation rather than an accusation.

Kalo had already proven with Amanda that he could read people well, so I didn't bother to argue with that assessment. "I had my reasons," I replied instead.

"And you're very protective of Alpha Amanda," Kalo added. "Unusually so."

"And?"

Again, I didn't deny it. Had he already guessed we were mates? How good were his powers of deduction?

"I simply find it interesting. That's all." He offered me a smile obviously meant to be charming but my expression remained stony. "Werewolf pack dynamics are incredibly interesting to an outsider like me."

"Do you deal with a lot of werewolves?" Maybe I could get a bit more information about his background than Amanda had managed in their limited time together since he wanted to chat.

"I deal with a lot of everything." He took a delicate bite of his food before giving it an approving nod. "Well, at least it tastes good since you don't get a choice."

He really seemed stuck on the limited menu, and I felt an urge to defend our pack's practices simply because they now reflected on Amanda. "I don't mind having the meals selected for me. Saves decision-making energy for more important things."

"The freedom to make your own decisions should never be taken for granted."

Something pained flickered across his golden irises, but I focused on the hypocrisy of his words. "And yet you want to force my Alpha into a deal with you where she doesn't have the necessary information to make an informed choice. How is that free or fair?"

Rather than answering, Kalo placed another forkful of food into his mouth, so I followed suit, shovelling in as much as I could to try to make this meal go faster.

"How long has this pack been on this land?" Kalo asked after a few moments of silent eating had passed. My plate was nearly empty but he paused in his eating to take a long sip of his coffee, holding the mug between his hands as if drawing heat from it.

"Almost a hundred years. Wolves were breaking off and founding new packs as settlers moved further west. Some located closer to the human towns. The Alpha's family chose this location instead, remote and unoccupied. It's served us well and there are plenty of packs who would like to get their hands on it."

Based on what he told Amanda in the library, I assumed he asked for that reason, and Kalo's nod seemed to confirm it. "I imagine it has some attractive natural resources too. Are people still looking for gold in the mountains?"

"Gold?" A frown pursed my lips as I searched my memory for any mention of gold on our land. A vague memory of a field trip back in school sprung up from somewhere deep in the back of my brain. "There are old stories about people coming this far east during the gold rush in the mid 1800s, but as far as I know, they never found anything. It was a dead end, and all of that happened long before our pack got here."

"I suppose it was a while ago." His eyes drifted to a spot over my shoulder, unfocused, as if he were deep in thought. I waited a few moments before clearing my throat.

"Are you almost finished?"

He blinked, his eyes refocusing as if waking up from a dream. "Not quite."

My foot tapped impatiently on the floor while he finished his meal, completely unhurried, and at last, we stepped together out into the fall afternoon. A light drizzle had started and grudgingly, I offered to get him a raincoat, knowing my Alpha expected me to be hospitable.

"The weather doesn't bother me," he said, turning his face upwards to let the drops hit his cheeks. "Without the rain, we can't appreciate the sun."

This guy is fucking weird, Hunter grumbled in my head, and I couldn't disagree. Hopefully, Amanda was making some progress on figuring out his species and true motive because the more time I spent with him, the more confused I became.

Together, we set off towards the north, towards a mountain ledge that would give us a full view of our territory and its natural defenses. What he was able to glean from that would tell me a lot about his knowledge of the challenges we faced, and whether he might have anything worthwhile to offer if Amanda decided to trust him.

The whole thing still felt like a terrible idea to me.

Chapter Twelve

~Amanda~

I stared at the phone in the centre of the table as if the rectangular device could somehow sense my confusion and consternation. Not knowing Calista very well and not being able to see her facial expressions and body language as we spoke didn't help matters. Was she serious that Kalo was dangerous? *How* dangerous? In what way?

I still had a lot of questions.

Thankfully, Felix started talking again before I had to put any of them into words.

"Most people only know genies from stories or fairy tales, where you get three wishes and the only problem is deciding what those wishes are going to be. In reality, it's not nearly as simple."

Pages flipped in the background, a sign that they were researching on the fly to get us as much information as possible.

"Genies *do* have the power to make wishes come true. They possess real and strong magic. Whatever you ask will happen, but it's hardly ever straightforward. The consequences of the wish can be worse than the problem you're trying to get rid of in the first place."

Savannah gasped from across the table. "Like that story we read in school with the monkey paw?"

"Exactly like that," Felix agreed while Jasper and I exchanged confused looks.

"We must not have had the same school curriculum," I said. "What's the story?"

Savannah leaned forward, her eyes wide. "The details are fuzzy but there was this cursed monkey paw, and when the owner wished for money, his son died, leaving behind an insurance payment. So yeah, the wish came true, but in a horrible way."

"Fuck," Jasper muttered as my gut twisted remembering some of Kalo's earlier answers to my questions.

"When I asked him what would happen if I couldn't meet his price, he said the work done for me wouldn't be as permanent as I hoped. Do you think that's the same thing Savannah is talking about?"

"It definitely sounds like it's along the same lines," Calista agreed. "He might grant your wish for a time, fulfilling the requirements, and undo it when it suits him. It's better not to get involved with a genie in the first place, but since you already are, we'll have to think this through carefully."

"Wait, why am I already involved? I haven't agreed to anything yet."

"You summoned him," Felix explained. "He's bound to you now unless someone else calls on him. You'd have to give the necklace away and the new owner would need to summon him to transfer the connection. Until then, he'll keep turning up every time you need something, trying to entice you into a deal."

"Fuck," Jasper repeated, and I had to agree. None of this sounded good.

"What if I just wish for him to go away?" It wouldn't solve my pack security issue, but at least I'd only have that to deal with. What seemed like a major problem just that morning now felt significantly easier than dealing with an underhanded magical being.

"It doesn't work that way," Calista said apologetically, her sigh echoing through the line. "I remember hearing about a case where someone tried but the genie returned anyway. Until the third wish is made or ownership is transferred, he belongs to you."

"So she can wish for him to go away three times," Savannah suggested, giving me a nod of encouragement. "Right?"

However, even I could see the flaw in that plan. "In order to grant my wish at all, he'll require his payment, whatever that might be."

"Do you guys have any information about what kind of payment he wants?" Jasper asked the two people on the phone. "What do genies care about?"

"I've never heard of a genie requesting payment," Felix admitted. "Calista?"

"No, me neither. Although, I've never personally talked to anyone who survived an encounter with a genie."

Foreboding prickled down my spine. "What do you mean 'survived'?"

"Like I said, there are usually consequences to wishes, and often, the final consequence is the wisher's life. But don't worry," she hastened to add. "We'll make sure that doesn't happen to you."

Her reassurance didn't make me feel a lot better, and as the full extent of the danger began to sink in, I realized I might not be the only one at risk.

Troy?

I reached out to my mate via mind-link, sending the signal as far as I could since I didn't know how far he might have gone.

Yes, Alpha? His reply was faint, but within range.

Where are you?

At the mountain lookout with Kalo. Are you alright?

Asking about my well-being seemed ironic considering he was the one in more immediate danger. *Bring Kalo back to the pack house as soon as you can but without arousing his suspicion. Whatever you do, don't agree to anything he might suggest.*

Of course not. He sounded almost insulted that I would think he might. *Did you get some answers?*

Some. We're still figuring it all out, but he might be dangerous. I don't want you to be alone with him.

The pause on the other end of our link suggested my words took him by surprise, though I couldn't be sure exactly why.

We'll head back as soon as possible. I'll be careful.

Thank you.

Closing the link, I turned my attention back to the others at the table. They had carried on talking without me, but I interrupted to get my most pressing question asked.

"If I were to restrain him, would he be able to escape from our prison cell?"

"In about half a second," Felix answered dryly. "He seems solid but his body forms and dissolves at will. A regular cell will do nothing to him."

"And there's no way to counteract that?" Jasper asked. "Nothing that weakens his power, like silver weakens us?"

"That's a good question." Calista sounded thoughtful as more paper rustled in the background. "Let me do some research and I'll get back to you, but I'd say to use incarceration as a last resort. Stay on his good side as much as possible until we can formulate a game plan."

"Is there any reason not to tell him what I know?"

Savannah and Jasper exchanged a look with each other, and I could imagine Felix and Calista doing the same on the other end of the phone, considering the question thoroughly.

"I don't see why not," Calista finally answered. "It might make him more forthcoming about this payment he wants if he's aware that you understand the situation. As much as we know about genies, they're still individuals and he may have his own agenda completely separate from anything that's been recorded before."

"So, I should get to know him," I summarized.

"I discovered werewolves weren't so bad when I talked to a few. Maybe Kalo will turn out to be a friend."

Maybe he would, but I had to prepare for the other alternative as well. "When you're looking up ways to weaken him, can you also find out how to kill a genie, if it comes to that?"

"We'll see what we can do," Felix promised. "Good luck. We'll be in touch."

With that, the line went dead, leaving me wiser than before they called but not much clearer on what to do next.

CHAPTER THIRTEEN

~**Troy**~

Hunter yipped happily in my head as Amanda closed the link between us.

She's concerned about us. That's why she reached out.

I felt it too, though I didn't want to get my hopes up too much. It might have simply been the same level of concern she'd feel for any member of the pack. As Alpha, she cared for us all. However, something in her tone, in the way her voice vibrated in my head, made it feel like a little bit more. Not an acceptance, not by a long shot, but maybe a thawing in the icy wall she'd built between us.

A step had been made in the right direction, and it made me more determined than ever to assist her in this situation with Kalo and prove my worth to her, as a member of her council and, more importantly, as her mate.

We had reached the lookout ledge just before Amanda linked me, and Kalo seemed content to gaze out over the scene in front of us without the need for conversation. However, since I now had instructions to return him to the pack house, I would need to move this along.

"This mountain forms a natural border to our land on this side," I explained, gesturing to the ground below us that marked the northern reach of our territory. "Crossing it would take a lot of effort. The lake serves the same purpose on the west. Therefore, we focus our defensive measures primarily in the east and south."

Kalo nodded, his gaze following each movement of my hand as I drew the border lines onto the landscape in front of us. "Do you have any kind of early warning system? Something to alert you before the border is breached?"

"No. We tried setting up a laser system several years ago but large animals kept setting it off. It caused more trouble than it was worth."

I'd had several sleepless nights because of it, patrolling outside our territory only to find a moose wandering around harmlessly.

"Any allies you could call for assistance in the event of a large-scale attack?"

"We recently allied ourselves with the Crimsontooth pack in Montana. They're a large, well-equipped pack with a well-trained fighting force."

As much as I'd been against the treaty when it involved Amanda being mated to their Alpha, I could understand why Alpha Warren initiated the agreement. Any pack tempted to attack us would face repercussions from the biggest pack in the whole Rocky Mountain region. It made a powerful deterrent.

Or it should have, anyway. The pack conspiring against us now didn't seem to feel too threatened by it. Were they counting on Crimsontooth not coming to Amanda's defense? I'd heard stories about mutinies in other packs where allies refused to intervene if the insurrection came from within the pack itself, so maybe they counted on that being the case this time too.

Unease roiled in my stomach as the words Alpha Warren spoke to me all those years ago echoed once again in my head.

She may be my blood but she's still a female. Disposable. If you think her lineage will protect her, you're wrong.

The certainty in his voice had shaken me so much that when I ran into Amanda in the hall afterwards and she asked what was wrong, I couldn't answer. I didn't want to have to tell her the awful things her father said, not when she obviously loved and admired him so much.

Some of that shine had worn off for her after the situation with her mother and Kyle, but still, I hadn't shared the full details of that conversation with her and I doubted her father ever had. Exactly what he told her, I couldn't be sure, but it had been enough to make her turn her back on me. Seeing the disappointment, hurt and resentment in her eyes never got easier, no matter how much time passed.

"Troy?"

It took a second to realize Kalo was talking to me. He must have asked me a question while I got lost in my thoughts. "Sorry. What did you say?"

"I asked how quickly these allies could respond to a call for help, if you needed it?"

"It would take at least 12 hours," I admitted. "Probably a little more by the time they mobilized."

None of that could be considered a secret; anyone looking at a map could see that Alpha Vaughan and his warriors were a day's drive away from us. Perhaps we should call on them now, as a precaution, until things felt a little more solidified.

Kalo echoed my thoughts almost precisely. "Could they spare a portion of their forces in the short term?"

"I'll discuss it with the Alpha. She should have concluded her business by now, so we can head back if you'd like."

He took one last, lingering look at the vista spread out before us. "Yes, I've seen what I need to for now."

Beneath the evergreen trees on the forest floor, the drizzle of rain halted, the drops gathering in the branches above us and falling in large splats rather than tiny droplets. Every so often, one would land directly on my head or shoulder. Kalo chuckled with delight when one hit his nose.

"You're lucky to have a position that allows you to spend so much time outdoors. It's peaceful here."

The first part, I definitely agreed with. I joined the border guard for two reasons; first, to protect my pack, and second, to spend as much time outside as possible. After discovering Amanda was my mate, my primary purpose became to protect her first and the pack second.

Not that she knew that.

"It's only peaceful when no one is trying to attack us," I pointed out. "I don't relax when I'm on duty."

"Would it make your life easier to have a better security system around the perimeter of your territory? Is that what you'd wish for?"

Something in the way he phrased the question prickled the hairs on the back of my neck. "What I'd wish for?" I repeated slowly.

"Yes. If you could have anything you wanted."

Kalo reached up to a branch above us, pulling it towards the ground before releasing it and letting it spring upwards again. Water droplets flew around us, making him laugh with an almost childlike pleasure. Innocent, in a way.

Meanwhile, I turned his question over in my head. I knew without hesitation what I wanted more than anything in the world, but voicing the thought out loud, to a stranger, went against every protective instinct I had.

"I don't believe in wishes," I answered instead. "Hard work and determination will get you much farther."

Kalo's smile twisted into something more complicated. "Don't underestimate the power of wishing. If the timing's right, there's no stronger power."

Weird, Hunter repeated in my head, still baffled by Kalo in general.

Instead of agreeing with him, though, I asked a different question. "What would *you* wish for?"

The expression on his face shifted once more into one of forlorn hopelessness, a look I recognized from staring into the mirror over years of heartbreak. "I would wish to undo something I once did. Unfortunately, that's not possible, not with a wish and not through hard work or determination either."

I knew exactly how that felt, and for the first time, the stranger in front of me didn't seem entirely foreign to me. "Maybe it can't be undone, but that doesn't mean there isn't another way to make it right, one way or another."

His golden eyes met mine and I could have sworn the sadness lifted, just a little.

"I'm counting on it," he replied right as another large drop of water hit my neck and slithered down my back, sending a shiver down my spine along with it.

Chapter Fourteen

~**Amanda**~

The guard at the door alerted me that Troy had returned less than a minute before the man in question showed up at my door.

"Are you free to talk, Alpha?"

Fresh from his walk outside, he brought the scent of pine trees along with his sea-salt mate scent, and the combination filled the space between us, warm and inviting. His cheeks carried a hint of red from either the fresh air or the exertion, and with each deep breath he took, his broad chest expanded, stretching against the black of his uniform.

Mentally shaking away those observations, I motioned for him to come into my office and he did, closing the door behind him. "Where's Kalo?"

"He was curious to see the kitchens and Jasper promised to keep him occupied there as long as possible. What have you learned?"

His eyes swept over me as he approached my desk, looking for any signs of injury or distress, a protectiveness that seemed to be so instinctual in him, I couldn't even be sure he knew that he did it. When I gestured again, this time for him to sit, he lowered his large frame into the chair in front of my desk, his whole body still on high alert.

"Kalo is a genie." Easiest to get that fact out into the open right off the bat. "That's what Savannah's contacts at her old pack think, anyway. They believe I summoned him here using this necklace."

I picked up the piece of jewellery from where I'd left it on my desk after taking it off. Wearing it seemed like an invitation for more trouble even if the damage had already been done.

"A *genie?*" Deep creases lined Troy's brow as he took in that piece of information. "Seriously?"

"Apparently so. The people we spoke to have a great deal of experience with other species between them, so I trust their expertise. As our allies, they have no reason to lie to me. Since Kalo doesn't set off our sensors and he appeared just after I made a wish this morning, it all fits."

At the word 'wish', something dawned in Troy's pale brown eyes. "He was just talking about wishes on our walk. I thought it was an odd way to phrase things, but if he's a genie..."

"He's using the language he's comfortable with," I filled in for him. "What did he say to you? You didn't wish for anything, did you?"

Troy shook his head, his eyes never leaving me. "The only thing I truly want, I need to prove myself worthy of on my own."

Longing panged deep in my abdomen, courtesy of the pull of our bond that never stayed silent for long. He must have felt it too since his lips twisted into a grimace and he shifted in his seat.

Silence pressed down on us for a long moment until he spoke again, his voice gruffer than before. "How do we get rid of him?"

I relayed the rest of what Calista and Felix said, about how I couldn't simply wish myself free of my guest and how any wishes I made might have unintended side effects. Troy listened carefully, his jaw clenching harder with every word that made it clear just how precarious my situation might be.

"You said this necklace came from your mother's collection. Do you remember her wearing it?"

I'd asked myself the same question earlier. "When I came across it in her things, something drew me to it immediately, but I didn't recognize it."

"Is it possible she knew how dangerous it was but forgot to tell you?"

"It's possible. Her illness came on so suddenly, and my father giving up his position happened even more unexpectedly. But she's mentioned other heirlooms to me over the years, so it seems strange that she'd forget to mention this one."

The more I talked it through, the more something about it didn't sit right with me, and before I could second guess myself, I pressed a button on my desk phone to call my mother's cell. The ringing sound filled the office for the space of three rings until she picked up.

"Hello?"

Her voice, once so vibrant, shook with the effort of speaking. Her life had been saved but she remained very weak while we waited for a permanent cure for her condition. "Hi, Mom. It's me. How are you?"

"Better," she claimed, but we both knew 'better' wasn't the same as 'good'. "How are things at home?"

As much as I wanted to confide in her, there was too much to tell and she didn't have the energy for it anyway. "Things are okay but I have a quick question for you. What can you tell me about the antique necklace in your collection? The gold one with the oval pendant?"

A pause followed, long enough to make me wonder if the connection had dropped, before she finally answered. "I don't have a necklace like that."

My eyes met Troy's over the desk, the concern in his gaze mirroring the unease in my chest. "Are you sure? Let me send you a picture."

Grabbing my own cell phone, I snapped a quick photo and sent it to her. We heard the ding through the line, confirming it had arrived, and a moment later, she spoke again.

"I've never seen that before in my life."

Rustling sounds replaced her voice, followed by the sound of my father's deep baritone. "Amanda? Your mother's tired, she needs to rest. What is this about?"

I didn't miss the way Troy stiffened at the sound of my father's voice, but I kept my eyes on the phone speaker. "Don't worry about it. She told me what I needed to know. Take care, both of you."

I hung up before he could say anything else, only looking up at Troy when the line had disconnected.

"If it didn't belong to my mother..."

"Where did it come from?" he wondered, completing my sentence just as I'd finished his earlier. "I don't like this. We need to lock down access to the house, and to you, and I think we should disconnect the wi-fi and cell service. If anyone within the pack is communicating with other packs, we need to cut them off."

His suggestion made sense, and it didn't necessarily need to raise an alarm within the pack. Being as remote as we were, connection could be spotty. I could claim we were having technical issues and no one would find it suspicious. It would give us a day or two's grace, at least.

"Can I leave you to coordinate that with Jasper? He'll have the necessary access and Savannah can authorize it."

Troy's lips pursed into a frown. "What are you going to do?"

"I need to speak to Kalo."

Protests jumped to the tip of his tongue, but I cut him off with a firm shake of my head.

"If I'm going to find a safe way out of this, I need to know more about him. That means talking to him."

"I'll go with you," he tried to insist, but I shook my head again, more gently this time.

"As long as he wants something from me, I don't think I'm in any danger, and he might open up more one-on-one. Diplomacy is my job, Troy. I can handle it."

Pride and protectiveness warred across his face, but in the end, he bowed his head in acceptance. "I know you can. And I'll take care of everything else. Like a team."

A team. That sounded nice, I had to admit. Even if I still had very strong reservations about the man across from me as a mate, I couldn't doubt that he had my back in this scenario.

"We'll regroup here for dinner, along with Savannah and Jasper."

"Yes, Alpha." With one more bow of his head, he took his leave, and I prepared to once again face our mysterious visitor, armed with a little more information than before and even more questions.

Chapter Fifteen

~Troy~

I found Jasper at the internal security team's office, the building located next to my own team's headquarters just a short distance from the pack house. Despite being so close to my workplace, I'd never been inside the two-storey, wood-framed building. While my team's office consisted of a large, open space, its walls lined with maps of the territory and team schedules, the internal security team felt almost corporate in comparison. Each person had their own office, sharing the space with the interrogation rooms I'd thankfully never had a reason to be called into.

Jasper's office had a window facing the pack house with a glimpse of the lake beyond, a pleasant view that emphasized his team's role in protecting the internal functioning of the pack. "This is nice," I complimented him as I took a seat at his sleek, black desk.

"It's a recent upgrade," he informed me wryly. "Getting on the Alpha's good side comes with some perks."

I could only imagine.

"What are her orders?" he went on to ask. When I called him a few minutes earlier, I said only that Amanda asked us to work together on something, leaving the details for a face-to-face conversation.

"We need to shut down all the pack's access to the outside world. Phone lines, internet, everything. Make it seem like a technical malfunction. She said Beta Savannah can authorize it if necessary."

Jasper's nod confirmed he'd seen that coming. "I was going to suggest it if she didn't. My team has a few satellite phones that we can't disable as easily but we can track who accesses them. I'll leave them active for emergencies, and if anyone tries to use them for anything else, we'll know about it."

He began to type into his computer while I waited, not feeling particularly helpful but not wanting to leave either since we still had a lot to talk about. Eventually, Jasper's eyes drifted to me over the top of his computer screen and he gave me a sympathetic near-smile, closer to a grimace.

"I'm sorry about the conversation you walked in on earlier."

With everything that had happened since, it took me a moment to realize what he meant, but soon, Savannah's words came back to me. *I still think Troy can go fuck himself.*

The 'still' suggested it wasn't the first time I'd been the subject of conversation, and though I wouldn't have brought it up myself, since Jasper broached the subject, I decided to tentatively feel him out. "I guess the Alpha told you about the situation between us?"

"We were in the prison the day you told her that you were free to be together," he reminded me, phrasing his response equally as carefully as I had my question. "She offered us a brief explanation this morning. That's as far as it went."

He obviously didn't want me to think they'd been sitting around gossiping about me, but honestly, that bothered me less than the idea of Amanda keeping all her feelings about me, good or bad, bottled up with no one to share them with.

Keeping everything inside sucked.

I would know.

As if he could read my thoughts, or maybe just something in my expression, Jasper leaned a little closer to me over the desk. "I didn't really have a normal experience of finding my mate either. I'm not sure how much you know, but I'd been kicked out of the pack and experimented on without my knowledge. Part of my personality literally broke off to form a whole new persona. I thought I was losing my mind.

And in the middle of that, my mate appears. It could have gone wrong in so many ways."

"It didn't, though," I pointed out. "You're together."

He nodded solemnly. "We fought hard for each other."

I could read between the lines easily enough, especially considering what Savannah said that morning. "And I didn't. That's what you think."

He held up his hands to deflect my words. "I don't have nearly enough information to make any kind of judgement."

"But it *is* what you think," I pressed. "Your mate does too, obviously. And I don't blame either of you. I don't blame Amanda either. I understand why she's angry with me, but I believe we can find a way to move past it now that she's safe."

Jasper's eyebrows raised so sharply I could almost picture him in his wolf form, his ears twitching as he picked up the sound of something important. "What do you mean 'safe'?"

I glanced around at the walls of his office, the space suddenly seeming more confined than before. "Do you mind if we take this meeting outside? Are you finished on there?"

I gestured at his computer and his gaze returned to it, typing a few more things on his keyboard before he stood up. "That should do it."

Sure enough, as soon as he opened the door for us to exit, annoyed chatter greeted us. "Is your internet down too?" a man standing at his own office door asked Jasper.

"Yeah, the whole system just went down," Jasper said, doing a good job of sounding like it had been completely unexpected for him too. "I'm going to head over to the pack house and talk to the IT team there. Hopefully it'll be back up soon. We'll just have to work offline in the meantime."

More grumbling followed but Jasper ignored it, heading back out into the cool afternoon air, and I breathed deeply as the fresh air hit my face. That was better. Being inside all day had never been for me, and even after my walk with Kalo earlier, there had still been a lot more sitting in offices than I usually endured.

We strolled together in companionable silence until we were outside of the pack's admin district, far from any ears that might pick up on our conversation. Only the rustling of tree branches and the snap of twigs underfoot accompanied us.

"Why wouldn't it have been safe for you and the Alpha to accept each other before now?" Jasper asked after taking one more look around to ensure we were entirely alone.

I'd never shared the details of my conversation with Alpha Warren with anyone, and I really didn't know Jasper well at all, but something inside me urged me to speak the words out loud. I was ready to do whatever it took to win Amanda's trust, and if that meant putting my past decisions on full display, open for scrutiny, I would have to take the risk.

"I was on patrol the night Amanda turned 18. I knew the party was happening, like everyone in the pack did, but of course I wasn't invited. I had no reason to expect to be, but all day, I felt like I should be there. Like something pulled me towards that place."

Jasper nodded in understanding. "There's no good reason I should have been at the edge of Ravenstone territory when Savannah arrived. Fate put me in that spot. I think gut feelings are often fate guiding us."

"Could be." Philosophical theorizing about fate had never been my concern, but I knew how I felt, and that night, I wanted to be there when she shifted for the first time. It didn't make any sense at the time, but in retrospect, the reason became clear. "I ignored the instinct and went to work as I should. Not even an hour into my shift, the most beautiful wolf I'd ever seen appeared, and the bond hit me like a fucking lead weight. It pulled me completely under. When she shifted and I saw who she was, I thought it had to be a trick. I didn't dare to hope. I was sure she'd reject me."

"But she didn't."

His words were quiet, non-judgmental, and I nodded in agreement. "She didn't. She told me to come to the pack house in the morning and we'd speak to her father together to get his blessing."

A frown creased Jasper's face. "So what happened?"

I knew what he really meant: how did we get from that moment to where we were seven years later? "I went to the pack house as soon as my shift ended. It was still early and Amanda wasn't awake yet, but I couldn't leave. Walking away felt impossible. I asked if I could stay and wait for her, and the guard at the door agreed. An hour later, the Alpha called me in."

My spine stiffened in response to the memories: the anticipation I felt walking down the hall, the confusion when I didn't see Amanda in his office, and the cold, hard look in the older man's eyes as I stood in front of him.

"Amanda was still asleep, but somehow, he'd guessed the situation. Maybe I had a lovesick look about me, I don't know. He demanded to know what business I had with his daughter. His Alpha authority compelled me to answer, and I didn't really want to hide it anyway. I told him we were mates and that she was willing to accept me. I promised to do whatever I needed to in order to be worthy of her. I just kept talking, and when he didn't say anything, I spoke some more. Finally, I ran out of words and the silence that followed chilled me to the bone."

Jasper shivered next to me, as if he could feel it too. "What did he say?"

I swallowed hard before forcing the words out. "He told me that I was nothing and no one, and he ought to have me executed for daring to think I would ever be a suitable mate for his daughter."

Jasper sucked in a breath. "Shit."

"It gets worse. He accused me of trying to use Amanda to improve my ranking in the pack. He claimed I was manipulating her somehow, that she would never agree to accept me on her own, and he said that unless I agreed to stay away from her and never mention our mate bond again, he would exile us both from the pack."

As someone who knew the consequences of exile personally, Jasper blanched. "He threatened to exile his daughter?"

"Not just that." Bile gathered in the back of my throat but I forced it down once again. "He promised to put a bounty on her head. He would rather see her dead than mated to me, and the bounty would only be for *her*, not for me. So that if she were killed, I'd have to live with knowing it was because of me."

"Fuck," Jasper breathed. "That's insane. I can't believe the Alpha said that."

"I didn't want to believe it either, but nothing about him at that moment suggested he didn't mean it. I couldn't call his bluff. I just couldn't put her in that danger. So, I agreed to his terms, and he added one more condition."

Jasper guessed it easily. "You couldn't tell her what he said."

"Right."

For a minute or two, we walked in silence again, the calmness of the forest at complete odds with the pounding of my heart inside my chest.

"If it were only my life at risk, I wouldn't have hesitated, but how could I protect her against assassins with no pack, no friends, no money? I couldn't take the chance, so I agreed to all of his conditions, and she's hated me for it ever since."

"You have to tell her," Jasper urged. "She deserves to know the whole story."

"She does, but I'm afraid..."

I trailed off, my throat closing up one more time.

"I'm afraid she won't believe me. It's his word against mine, and she has no reason to give me the benefit of the doubt. I need to earn her trust first, to prove myself to her, and then I can tell her. Does that make sense?"

Jasper grimaced, kicking at a stone with his foot as he stepped. "I see your point, I do, but I still think she needs to know. If for no other reason than because it's another potential person who means her harm. Her father gave up the pack, but maybe he's not beyond hurting her to take it back again. If he was willing to kill her before, what's stopping him now?"

An icy cold shiver slithered through my entire body. *Fuck.* I hadn't considered that.

Could her father be the one who planted the necklace in her mother's jewellery? Did he know about the genie? Would he use Kalo to get rid of his own daughter?

"We need to get back to the pack house," I announced, and before Jasper could respond, I broke into a jog, determined to get to Amanda's side before anything else could go wrong.

Chapter Sixteen

~Amanda~

Before calling Kalo in to speak with me again, I took a moment alone in my office to reflect on the task ahead of me. *Maybe Kalo will turn out to be a friend,* Calista said, but she failed to take into account the fact that I had very little experience with making friends. Oh, I had a wide social circle, to be sure; as the Alpha's daughter, everyone in the pack knew me and was friendly with me, but close friends I could be truly myself with? Those had never been easy to come by.

From my desk, I walked over to the large window overlooking the lake and mountains. Despite the cool autumn air and rapidly-darkening sky, a few children played on the beach, chasing each other with sticks in some kind of game they'd invented. Bracing myself to the cold, I cracked open one of the window panes, letting the noise of their cheerful shouts and shrieks drift up to me along with the blast of chilly air.

Vague memories flickered in the back of my mind at the sound, memories that were mere fragments rather than fully-formed scenes, of playing and laughing with other children when I was very young. That was before my mother's multiple miscarriages and the gradual acceptance that I would be my parents' only child. Almost overnight, I went from being a carefree, doted-on child to a commodity that needed to be protected at all costs. Reading in the library replaced running around outside and my tutors took the place of the budding childhood friendships I'd only just started.

Small talk, I could do. Pleasant dinner conversation with the upper ranks of any other pack? All in a day's work. But getting someone to open up to me on a personal level remained a skill I never mastered. With Savannah, I'd made some progress, but that had much more to do with her general openness than any action I'd taken.

No one would ever use the word 'open' to describe me.

Still, with my pack's safety and perhaps even my life on the line, I would have to try.

Closing the window again, I headed towards the fireplace to brush off the chill. The logs crackled quietly, the embers burning red as they maintained a steady heat. With the poker, I shifted the wood to give it some new air, allowing the flames below to breathe, and watched the dancing colours for a moment. The golden glow reminded me of Kalo's eyes, and I wondered, now that we knew a little more about him, if that glow represented his true, non-corporeal form. Could he change his appearance to any form he liked? Had he always been a genie, or were genies 'made', the same way species like vampires were?

The more I dwelled on the subject, the more my curiosity grew, and it occurred to me that letting my genuine interest show by asking Kalo those questions directly might be the best way to begin.

Please bring our visitor to my office, I instructed my staff through mind-link, and a few minutes later, Kalo once again appeared at my door.

"Come in. Have a seat by the fire."

He followed my instructions, pulling his chair a little closer to the fire's warmth. "Your pack members have done a good job of keeping me occupied, but I'm hoping you're ready to continue our negotiations now."

Despite myself, I found myself smiling at how easily he'd seen through our attempts to distract him. "I am. Now that I know your species, I think our conversation will be much more productive."

For just a second, he went unnaturally still, as if his consciousness had left his physical form, but he quickly covered it with a short, forced laugh. "I doubt that you've figured me out quite so quickly."

"Then you underestimate me, Kalo. And apparently, I've underestimated you too. But perhaps you can forgive me since I've never met a genie before."

A beat of silence passed, and another, with only the fire's gentle crackling filling the space between us. Kalo's golden eyes blazed into me so fiercely, I thought they might quite literally erupt.

But then, to my surprise and great relief, a dazzling smile flashed across his face.

"I must congratulate you, Alpha Amanda. Most people I meet don't have the imagination to make such a leap. Even when I tell them, they don't believe me. It gets awfully tiring trying to convince someone of the very essence of your being, and I truly appreciate you saving me the trouble."

Although not what I expected, his reaction opened the door to further enquiries, and I walked straight through. "Is that why you wouldn't tell me right away? Or are you not supposed to until I make a wish? Are there rules that govern how you interact with people? I have so many questions."

His smile widened as he let out a deep, throaty laugh, showing off his bright, white teeth. "I would be very happy to talk about this with you at length, but first, we really should secure your border. When your captain took me to the lookout point, I noticed a small gathering to the south that I suspect is intending to make an incursion into your territory tonight. With the sun setting soon, it's imperative to shore up your defenses as soon as possible."

He continued to smile at me, but my lips pulled down into a frown. Troy hadn't said anything about seeing people beyond our borders that afternoon. Could he have forgotten to tell me about it during our conversation about Kalo? Or did he not mention it because he was involved in the plot against me? The trust I had started to put in him over the course of the day suddenly felt premature.

As before, Kalo seemed to read each of my thoughts in my expression. "Oh, the captain couldn't see them. I'm blessed with powers of observation far beyond most other species. The gathering wouldn't have been visible to a werewolf from our vantage point."

My breath came a bit easier at knowing Troy hadn't done anything wrong, but that didn't mean I fully believed Kalo either. "In other words, he can't corroborate that any threat exists, and I just have to take your word for it."

"Not at all." He extended his hand towards me. "Now that you know what I am, there's no need to hide my other skills either."

My eyes darted between his offered hand and his face, trying to read his intentions. "What skills?"

He smiled once more, almost wistfully that time. "Trust me, Amanda. Just this once."

Trust him. *Get to know him.* Perhaps by doing the former, the latter would follow? Tentatively, I reached out and placed my hand in his.

The floor fell out from under me.

Colours and lights flashed past until, with a start, I realized I stood at the lookout point, Troy beside me. Beside *Kalo*, actually, because the eyes I looked out from didn't belong to me.

What the hell? Was I inside his mind? Was this a trick? An illusion?

"Look," a voice echoed around me, coming from nowhere and everywhere all at once. "In the distance, to your right."

I looked, squinting even though I didn't seem to have eyes of my own at that moment, and the view appeared to zoom in. Distant smoke curled over the tops of the trees, just barely visible, with flashes of movement below.

When the view zoomed out again, seeing the world more normally, none of what I'd just noticed could be seen.

A second later, I was back in my office, landing in my chair with a heavy thump, though my body had never moved at all. My stomach heaved, and Kalo immediately knelt at my feet, a gentle hand on my back.

"Lean forward and focus your vision on one spot. The nausea will fade."

Again, I did as instructed, and slowly, the motion sickness eased. With my stomach settled, I sat back up and Kalo took his seat next to the fire again, as calm and unflustered as always.

"What just happened?"

"You saw what I saw," he confirmed. "Activity in the woods, not far from your border. You could send your forces in, but you don't know what kind of weapons they have, or if they're merely a distraction from a larger attack. It would be much more efficient to enhance your entire border, which I'm capable of doing."

If it was a trick, it was a damn good one, and I didn't particularly like the idea of gambling that he might be bluffing. "And that would be the first of my wishes?"

"Yes. And I know it's uncouth of me to keep reminding you of the time pressure, but I really wouldn't wait too much longer if I were you."

I glanced up at the clock above the mantle, calculating the time left until sunset, but before I could respond in any way, the door to my office burst open and Troy stormed in.

Chapter Seventeen

~Troy~

Amanda's startled eyes met me from her seat near the fireplace. A quick inventory of her suggested she hadn't been harmed, at least not yet, but I didn't miss the annoyed look that flickered across Kalo's face. Apparently, he didn't appreciate the interruption but I didn't give a shit about what he wanted. I had to talk to my mate.

"What is it? Has there been an attack?" She got to her feet at the same time that I reached her, and it took every last drop of self-control I possessed not to pull her into my arms. To protect her or to reassure myself that she was okay, I couldn't be sure. Maybe both.

"The borders are quiet, but I need to talk to you."

Kalo stood as well, his golden eyes fixed on me. "We're in the middle of something."

"It can wait," I growled.

"I really wouldn't advise it. If I had to guess, the attack will come within the next half hour."

My scowl deepened. "There's no way you can possibly know that unless you're involved in it somehow."

"There's no way *you* could know it, but I have abilities you don't possess."

"He may be right," Amanda interjected calmly, and we both turned to her. "Kalo showed the encampment to me. It seems an attack is imminent."

"And I will protect you from it if you wish me to do so," he prodded.

"At what cost?" I demanded.

"That's a good question." Amanda's head cocked slightly to the side as she surveyed the genie. "Now that we don't need to tiptoe around what you are, why don't you tell me your price? I'm willing to negotiate if it's something I can provide."

He made a visible effort to relax, the annoyance fleeing his face and a serene, calm expression taking its place. "Certainly. My price is very simple. You may wish for anything you choose for your first two wishes and for the third, you must wish for all wishes to be undone. It's as simple as that."

Amanda's confused expression met mine and a second later, her voice echoed in my head. *That's it?*

It seems too easy. There has to be a catch.

Out loud, she addressed Kalo. "How does that help me? I could wish for you to protect my borders, but when that wish is undone, we end up getting attacked anyway?"

"Not necessarily. The final wish doesn't reset time. When you wish for me to protect your land, I'll do so. From the time of your first wish to your last one, you have three days. Use those days to install other defenses or call for reinforcements and you'll be fine when mine vanish."

A little time would come in handy, but I still didn't trust him. "This is what you ask every time you help someone? Why?"

Those strange near-glowing eyes turned back to me. "I told you earlier that there's something I would like to undo, a wish that I made myself a long time ago. If you wish for *all* wishes to be undone, it will include mine. It's the only thing I truly want."

"And no one has ever made that wish?" Amanda sounded incredulous. "If you still need it to be done, that means no one else agreed?"

His shoulders lifted in an almost-indifferent shrug. "Many say they will, but when the time comes, when they've seen the true extent of my power, they don't want to lose what they've gained. Or they think of something else they must have with their final wish. It's almost like a kind of madness comes over them. I can't explain it, but no, no one has ever fulfilled this request."

"How many people are we talking about?" I wondered.

"Around eighty, give or take, over thousands of years."

Eighty. For a stunned moment, neither Amanda nor I said anything as we digested that. A handful of people being overwhelmed by greed or selfishness, I could understand, but eighty? There had to be an angle we weren't seeing.

Amanda recovered herself first. "I have no problem with that price. Truthfully, I wouldn't wish for anything at all if I had the choice, but I understand that now that I've summoned you, we must complete this transaction."

"Precisely so. But forgive me for saying that I don't believe you have nothing to wish for."

His eyes darted between the two of us as if he could sense the bond between us.

Hell, with all his powers, maybe he could.

"Make your choices wisely and we can all be satisfied. I'm at your service."

With a flourish of his hand, he made a small bow just as Devon's voice rang out in my head.

All men to the southern border, now!

One glance at Amanda confirmed she hadn't heard it. Her focus remained entirely on Kalo, so Devon must have only linked with the border team.

I reached out to him directly. *What's going on?*

Foreign wolves approaching. Dozens, I'd guess. We can't see them yet but we can smell them. They'll be here in a matter of minutes. Where are you?

At the pack house. Stand by.

I closed the link by force before he could protest and turned to Amanda. "Alpha, there's a group approaching the border. Potentially a big one."

Kalo would have been justified in gloating, but he simply bowed his head once more. "Say the word and you're all safe."

In Amanda's stricken gaze, I could read the debate that must have been taking place inside her head, wondering exactly what words she should use, how this might backfire and whether or not we truly had a choice at this point.

In the end, she put the pack's safety first, exactly as I would have expected her to.

"Kalo, I wish for you to seal our border, allowing no one in or out until I say otherwise. The seal should allow water and air to get through but no living beings and no weapons of any kind."

His lips stretched into a smile. "As you wish."

Taking a step back from us, he lifted his hands, and we watched in fascination as his fingers began to glow the same golden hue as his eyes.

To me, he said, "Tell your men to make sure they're inside your border by a few feet to be safe."

I relayed that message to my team and once they'd all confirmed they were in place, I nodded at the genie. "Ready."

A ball of light began to build between Kalo's glowing fingers, growing bigger and brighter until, with a bright flash, it completely disappeared. I shielded my eyes and Amanda did the same, only gradually lowering our hands and letting our eyes readjust.

"Is that it? Is it done?" she asked just as Devon's voice once again sounded in my head, breathless with disbelief.

Holy shit. Fifty wolves just came out of the trees and ran for us, but when they reached the border, they bounced right off it.

A second later, another curse followed.

Fuck, there are people behind them, and some of them are armed. Everyone take cover!

I couldn't hear the sound of gunshots but it almost seemed I could, holding my breath until Devon spoke again.

The bullets bounced off too. What the hell is going on?

At last, I responded. *The Alpha bought us some time. The border is safe for now, get everyone back to headquarters and I'll explain. We can keep a skeleton patrol tonight.*

Whatever good or bad qualities the genie had that we still needed to discover, one thing was clear: his magic was the fucking real deal.

Chapter Eighteen

~Amanda~

As Kalo's built-up magic exploded, bursting through us on its way to do his bidding, a surge of pure power rushed through my body. Like an orgasm, almost, but far more intense than any I'd ever experienced. It left me flushed and heated, every nerve on edge, but I did my best to maintain my composure as I addressed Kalo.

"Is that it? Is it done?"

"Why don't we ask your captain?" he replied, his golden eyes glinting in satisfaction as he held his hand out towards Troy. "What do your men say?"

Troy didn't say anything for a moment, his eyes glazed over as he communicated with his team through mind-link, but when they cleared, he nodded. "It worked. Wolves and bullets were repelled. I've called everyone back so we can start working on a more permanent plan. The clock is ticking, right?"

"Right," Kalo confirmed. "Starting now, you have 72 hours to make your other two wishes. I suggest you make your second wish very carefully. Now, if you don't mind, that took a great deal of energy on my part, and I believe dinner is almost ready."

It was, but I couldn't think about food. My mind raced with everything that had just happened - primarily, how I'd just entered into a deal with an honest-to-goddess *genie* - and the weight of the decisions that still needed to be made.

How would I protect the pack when the magic ended? What should I do with the second wish?

It finally fully dawned on me that the being in front of me could do *anything* with his magic, and all I had to do was ask. The flush of power that came with that recognition swelled so strong inside me, I almost didn't know what to do with myself.

Somehow, Troy seemed to notice my indecision and took control of the situation. "I'll have someone come and accompany you back to the dining room," he told Kalo. To me, he bowed his head. "Stay here, Alpha. I'm going to speak to Beta Savannah and Jasper for a few minutes and I'll be right back."

Too giddy with the possibilities of this new situation to come up with a better plan, I didn't object, sinking back into the chair by the fire while Troy took Kalo from the room.

Think of all the good we could do with power like that, Cinder said in my head as soon as we were alone.

I know. I wonder how far it goes. Could I heal my mother? Or go even bigger and wish for a cure for all diseases?

Some kind of special ability, like always knowing when someone's lying to us, she suggested.

Superpowers! I agreed, laughing out loud at the idea. *Ever wanted to fly?*

Why stop at flight? We could have them all.

It would make us invincible.

Unstoppable, she agreed. *We could rule all the wolves, not just this pack.*

We tossed more ideas back and forth before a sobering thought penetrated my flights of fancy.

Whatever I wish for will be undone with the final wish. It makes it all useless.

Not if you used the final wish for something else. Then you could have two wishes.

Her words almost instantly sobered me. This was what happened to the other people in my position, wasn't it? They got drunk on the magic inherent in their wishes and the power it represented. This was the danger.

On an intellectual level, I understood that, but resisting the allure wouldn't be easy.

Why did *all* wishes need to be undone? Couldn't I wish for something good with my second wish and then simply wish Kalo's past wish undone, not mine? There had to be a way around it; I could almost feel it lurking at the corners of my mind. I just needed it to come into focus.

Having completely lost track of time, I jumped when Troy reappeared beside me. I didn't even hear him enter the room but as soon as I tracked his movement from the corner of my eye, his scent hit me full force, as it always did.

His head bowed once again, shielding his features from me. "Alpha, please come with me."

Still distracted with finding a solution to the problem I set myself, I got to my feet and followed him without question. "I need to speak to Savannah again. With the phone lines down, we can't reach Calista and Felix, but she might be able to help me brainstorm ideas of what to do with my second wish."

"Of course," Troy agreed easily. A little *too* easily, I might have noticed if I'd been paying closer attention. "I've asked them to meet us at a secret location so we're not disturbed."

I nodded, not fully absorbing what he said until we stepped out the back door of the pack house where an idling ATV sat waiting, a large trailer attached behind it. Night had completely fallen, blanketing the forest in darkness. Maybe I imagined it, but with the protective wall Kalo put in place, it felt quieter than usual. Clouds covered any stars above, adding to the blackness.

What time was it? How long had I been sitting in my office? And why were we leaving the pack house?

For that matter, why hadn't there been a guard at the back door?

I took a step backwards as Troy turned to me. "What secret location? I'm not going anywhere. We agreed this morning that I would stay in the pack house where it's safe until we understood the situation fully."

His jaw set into a firm line, determination flaring in his pale brown eyes. "I need you to trust me, Amanda. You're safer with me."

"*Alpha*," I corrected him, taking another step back. If I turned and ran, I might be able to make it back to the door before he caught me. He had size on his side, but I could be fast when I needed to be. My eyes darted left and right, looking for the patrol that should be circling the pack house perimeter. Where the hell was my security team?

I need help at the back door, I announced through mind-link to the pack house staff, but in the moment I used to make the link, I lost my advantage. Troy closed the distance between us, slapping something hard on my wrist before yanking the other one to join it.

Handcuffs. *Silver* handcuffs.

Hello? Is anyone there? Savannah? Jasper? I tried again, but the silver severed my ability to link to my pack. Nothing got through.

"I'm sorry," Troy said even as he produced a leather strap that he tied around my mouth, cutting off my actual voice as well as my internal one. "I know this looks bad but there isn't time to explain. We need to go now."

With no further attempt at an explanation, he picked me up with one arm and carried me to the trailer at the rear of the ATV. Lifting the lid, he placed me inside, and with the silver weakening my ability to move or even reason, I could barely offer any resistance. My pitiful attempt at struggling made absolutely no difference to him and when the lid closed above me, plunging me into complete darkness, I shouted in frustration against my gag.

I take back anything nice I ever said about him, Cinder mumbled, sounding barely conscious herself. *What the fuck?*

I had no idea, and as the world began to move beneath us, I had even less idea where we were going or why. Whose side was Troy on? Was he really taking me to safety as he said, or had I lowered my guard too much with someone who had only ever let me down?

Chapter Nineteen

~Troy~

If I ever had a chance of winning Amanda over, gagging her and shoving her into a trailer certainly didn't help my cause. Though it shouldn't be possible, I could almost feel her fury radiating through our unconsummated mate bond as I drove the ATV away from the pack house and into the forest. A few members of the pack lifted their hands in greeting as I drove by, unaware that their Alpha was bound and gagged just a few feet behind me.

I had a good reason for doing it. Whether or not I could convince *her* of that remained to be seen.

At the end of a dirt road, out of sight and earshot of any other building, Jasper's house appeared through the trees. He and Savannah lived in the pack house, not far from Amanda's suite, but this house still belonged to him as well. Unknown to all but a few people within the pack, the basement contained a 'safe room' originally constructed by Jasper's grandfather to withstand an attack or natural disaster. When Jasper was framed for kidnapping, the children were found in the room, where the thick metal walls not only offered protection but muted any attempts at communication by mind-link.

It sounded like exactly what I needed.

Slowing to a crawl, I steered the ATV behind the house where it wouldn't be immediately visible to anyone passing through the area and took a deep breath before cutting the engine and opening the trailer lid again. Although I'd done my best to prepare for the look of anger and betrayal in Amanda's eyes when we came face-to-face again, it still cut deep.

"We're here," I told her as calmly as possible, reaching in to lift her out of the narrow box. It wouldn't have been comfortable in there for her, but it didn't appear to have harmed her either. The silver weakened her so much that she could barely stand on her own, so I slung an arm around her waist to hold her steady while I let us into the empty house.

An area rug in the hallway covered the trap door entrance to the basement, so I propped Amanda against the wall while I opened it up. She knew making a run for it would be impossible so she didn't even try, and the fear that filtered into her expression when she saw the dingy staircase leading down into the ground hit my heart like a thousand pin pricks all at once.

"You're safe here," I promised again, though I could tell my words held little comfort for her. Actions spoke louder, and I'd have to do my best to prove to her that I had her best interests at heart in bringing her there. Wrapping my arms around her and ignoring the way she stiffened at my touch, I carried her down the cement stairs and to the door at the bottom. A keypad gave us entry, and once inside, I fumbled around for the light for a long moment before realizing I couldn't find it while still holding onto Amanda.

In the darkness, I stumbled forward until my shins hit what had to be the bed frame, and I placed her down as gently as possible before returning to the door, finding the light switch, and swinging the heavy metal door closed behind us. The lock clicked into place, the sound stark and cold in the silence.

The light was dim to conserve power, and even with my enhanced wolf night-vision, it took a moment for my eyes to adjust.

Not that there was a lot to see. Besides the single bed that Amanda sat on, a small pantry area with canned food and some basic cooking utensils took up one side of the room, a small stack of books and writing paper on a small table sat on the other side, and a tiny bathroom lay beyond a secondary door at the opposite end from where we'd entered.

'Primitive' might describe the space best, designed for survival and not much more.

And for that night, at least, our temporary shelter.

"Whmm shh ihhm sh?"

Behind her gag, I couldn't make out a word Amanda said, but now that we were safely cut off from the world, we no longer needed it. From my pocket, I withdrew the key to the silver cuffs and removed them from her wrists. Her posture straightened as soon as they were gone, and she reached behind her head to untie the gag over her mouth herself, her eyes blazing in indignation.

"What the hell do you think you're doing?" she demanded in a tone so sharp, it could cut glass. "Do you *want* to be exiled?"

Without waiting for an answer, she pushed past me and strode to the door we'd just entered through. When she attempted to pull the handle, though, it didn't budge an inch. Her fingers ran over the cold metal, looking for a keyhole, before her eyes fell on the keypad on the wall next to it.

Huffing in frustration, she spun back around. "Give me the code."

"I can't. Not yet."

"Give me the code *now*."

With no silver muting her power, the Alpha power in her tone hit me hard. I staggered back, my head bowing beneath the weight of my inherent desire to obey her, and my mouth pulled into a twisted grimace as I fought the nearly unbearable urge to give in.

"Not yet," I managed to grit out again.

Amanda prowled towards me, her eyes glinting black as her wolf hovered just beneath the surface. "If you don't let me out right now, you'll spend the rest of your life in prison."

The power emanating off her, power fed not only by her natural abilities but also by her anger, was the most intense I'd ever experienced, perhaps even stronger than that morning in her father's office all those years ago. I gave in to it then, but not because of the force of his will. His threats secured my agreement instead, and strangely, remembering the last time an Alpha had turned his full strength on me gave me the push I needed to resist Amanda now despite every drop of my blood begging me to submit.

"If it keeps you safe, I'll gladly give up my freedom. You can lock me up as soon as we know you're out of danger."

She stared at me for a long moment, eyes boring so deep into me, it felt like she could see straight to my soul.

When I still didn't give in, she turned away with an angry sigh. The Alpha authority that had been assaulting me dropped too and I gasped in relief, sinking down onto the bed when my knees trembled too much to hold me upright.

"Where are we?" she demanded, her tone still cold and hard even without the display of power.

That much, I could tell her. "Jasper's house."

Her head twisted back towards me. "How do you have the code?"

She wouldn't like the answer, but I wouldn't lie to her either. "He gave it to me. He knows we're here."

Betrayal filtered into her expression, dislodging a little of the fury that had been dominating it. "Does Savannah know too?"

"No. At least she didn't when I left. How long Jasper can keep it from her, I'm not sure."

That news mollified her a little, but only a little. Anger still radiated from every inch of her posture, from her broad stance to the arms folded tight across her chest.

"I can't reach anyone by mind-link."

"No, and neither can I," I acknowledged. "The room dampens communication. No one will look for you here."

Curiosity fought with mistrust across her beautiful face, but eventually, the curiosity won out. "Who would be looking for me?"

That was the main thing I needed to tell her, and now that she finally seemed willing to listen, I didn't hesitate.

"Whoever's collaborating with that pack outside our border. We don't know who's behind it yet but one of Jasper's men overheard a call placed from one of the satellite phones in their office. It went to a cell phone just outside our territory and the person told their contact on the other side that they would 'secure' you and force you to lower whatever protection had been put in place. They said they knew exactly where to find you in the pack house, that you would be staying there all night and they had contacts among the staff to get to you. Jasper apprehended the man, an unranked wolf who's obviously just following orders, and his team will be questioning him right now to find out who he's working for. In the meantime, I had to get you out before whoever's in charge made their move."

Amanda took a moment to absorb all of that, turning the information over in her head in her usual methodical way. "Why didn't you just tell me that instead of abducting me like a lunatic?"

"I didn't know how much time we had or if anyone might be listening in. If they were, our departure needed to feel calm and unhurried. Jasper called the security staff away from the door just long enough for us to leave. No one saw you go, so they may still make their move and Jasper will have people on hand at your office and your rooms in case anyone tries to break in."

When she didn't argue with any of that, I added one more thing.

"Besides, making the wish with Kalo seemed to affect you. I saw the change in you, and I didn't know for sure if you were even still in your right mind."

As I might have expected, she took that in the worst possible way. "Now you think I'm crazy? Is that why you felt entitled to manhandle me? Or is it simply because I'm a woman? You wouldn't have done the same thing to my father, I bet."

"No. I would have let him get captured."

That unexpected response took a little of the wind from her sails, but only for a second before she changed course. "I don't even know whether any of this is true or if you simply brought me here because you're jealous."

"Jealous of what?"

"Of Kalo. He's an attractive man." I bristled at her acknowledgement of it, even as I tried not to react.

She could read it on my face though, just as well as I could read her. Emboldened by my reaction, she went on.

"He's charming. Powerful. You've been on edge around him since he arrived, more than anyone else, all because you're afraid I might be interested in him."

She wasn't entirely wrong, but if she thought I would kidnap her over a man, she truly didn't understand me at all. "I've never stopped you from pursuing another man before, no matter how much it hurt. You're free to make your own decisions, always, unless your safety is at stake, as it is now."

"How much it hurt?" She scoffed as she repeated the words back to me. "You don't strike me as the emotionally fragile type, Troy. Inappropriately possessive, sure, but hurt? That's a stretch."

My jaw clenched hard as I fought to bring myself under control before answering her. "I'm speaking of the physical pain, actually, but if you think it doesn't affect me emotionally, you're wrong."

For the first time since we arrived, Amanda faltered, confusion flickering across her pretty face. "What physical pain?"

"The pain I feel through our mate bond whenever you're with another man."

Her arms slackened and her lips parted in surprise as she stared at me in a mix of disbelief and horror. "You... you feel that?"

Did she really not know? Her confusion seemed genuine. "Every time."

For a long moment, neither of us said anything, our eyes locked across the small distance that separated us.

Since she didn't seem to know what to say, I explained it a little further, as much as I understood it. "Our bond still exists even if we haven't accepted it. Physical contact with someone else is a betrayal of that bond, that's just the way it works. And yeah, it hurts. Physically, emotionally, you name it."

Her mouth opened as if to make a reply before closing again. A long blink, and another, her lips opening and closing twice more before sound finally came out. "But... but I've never felt anything like that."

"No. You haven't."

I let those words hang in the air between us, knowing that they didn't need any elaboration. She would figure it out on her own that she'd never felt that pain because there had never been any betrayal. Since the moment I first saw her in that moonlit forest and she said she wanted to be with me, I had never even *thought* of any other woman.

Amanda swallowed hard, her eyes never leaving me. "I didn't know," she whispered after another minute of silence. "I didn't know you would feel it. I didn't do it on purpose."

Honestly, I wasn't sure if that made me feel better or worse. I'd always imagined in those moments that she would have thought of me, relishing the pain she caused. At least she hadn't been that malicious, but instead, it meant she hadn't thought of me at all, and that was one more blow I didn't need.

My mouth had gone dry, making it difficult to swallow. "I didn't know either, not until the first time it happened. I don't know anyone else who's kept their bond so long without accepting or rejecting it. I had no one to ask."

"Fuck." She dropped her head, rubbing her hands over her face as if she could scrub the idea from her mind. "I'm sorry, Troy."

I hadn't expected an apology, hadn't ever felt she owed me one, but now that it had been said, it meant more to me than I thought it would. "I'm sorry too. For all of it."

That didn't require any further explanation either, and when Amanda's hands fell back to her sides and she looked back up at me, she looked younger than before. Sadder, perhaps, but a little less guarded too.

"Is there something we can eat here? I'm a little hungry."

The words were a peace offering, and I accepted them in that spirit, putting the conversation we just had behind us. "Let me see what I can put together."

Chapter Twenty

~Amanda~

There weren't many places to sit in the small, enclosed space, so when Troy got up from the bed and moved to the corner with the food supplies, I took his spot on the mattress to keep out of his way and take a minute to gather my thoughts.

He felt it? Cinder whispered in my head, horror in her tone. *Every time?*

Guilt swelled in my chest again, just as it had when Troy first said the words. I had no idea he would feel pain through our bond when another man touched me. That happened with marked wolves; everyone knew that, but we hadn't marked each other. We never accepted our bond so it never even crossed my mind, especially since I never felt anything on my end other than the aching emptiness from being apart from him.

But now I knew I hadn't felt it because there'd been nothing *to* feel. For seven long years, he'd been celibate, and though he hadn't specified whether that was because no other woman caught his eye or because he didn't want to cause me pain, it didn't really matter. I could still remember the hungry look in his eyes the night of my first shift when we spoke to each other. He'd been attracted to me then, without a doubt, so his abstinence in the intervening years didn't stem from a lack of interest in sex.

No, only one conclusion made sense: for seven long years he was alone *because of me*.

No. I quickly shook my head at the thought. Not only because of me. It was because of him too, because he wouldn't defy my father to claim me but also wouldn't let me go. He wouldn't have had to suffer if he'd rejected me. He chose to hold on.

Even though it caused him pain.

Fuck, what was I supposed to do with that information? I couldn't tell if I found it sweet or insane, endearing or psychotic.

"Have your cooking skills improved at all since your visit to the Okanagan?"

Troy's question pulled me out of my head and I blinked twice, forcing myself to concentrate on his words. When I glanced over, he was on his knees, looking through a stack of cans and smiling over at me.

"I didn't realize you witnessed that debacle."

His smile vanished at the coldness in my tone, and I winced. That sounded more dismissive than I meant it to, and more than that, the words were a lie. I knew he was there. I always knew when he was nearby.

"I mean, I hoped you'd blocked it out," I amended, offering a hesitant smile of my own. "The smell was bad enough to cause temporary amnesia."

A retreat with some of the other future pack leaders in the region had included a cooking class in a winery in the hills above Kelowna. My father had sent me there to sniff out potential matches for an alliance, but while all the other young men and women produced edible results, mine somehow managed to be both undercooked and burnt at the same time, emitting an odour that quickly emptied the room. Sensitive werewolf noses found the aroma offensive.

As part of my escort team, Troy stood near the door with the other staff, watching as I did my best to flirt with the future Alphas in attendance as I'd been instructed. After the cooking class, however, no one seriously considered me as a potential partner. The men who had seemed interested before that suddenly found themselves too busy for a private discussion before the retreat ended.

"The whole thing was stupid," I complained, my cheeks heating in embarrassment as the scene played out again in my mind. "No Alpha or

Luna is going to be cooking for the pack. They could have given us a more useful activity."

"Most people think cooking is a fairly useful skill," he replied, and I could have sworn he was actually teasing me. "Didn't your mother ever teach you anything in the kitchen?"

"Never. My father didn't think I should concern myself with it. He said it was beneath the Alpha's daughter, and his word was law. Nobody dared to go against him."

Troy understood that better than anyone and his shoulders tensed at the mention of my father. But a second later, he took a deep breath, pushing back to his feet with two cans in his hand. "Well, it's never too late to learn. Come on over, Alpha."

The idea of learning how to cook in the ridiculously small 'kitchen' was ludicrous, but honestly, what else did I have to do with my time while we were locked up there? I got to my feet and took three steps to bring myself into line with him.

Troy pulled out a utensil from a box on the shelf to his left. "This is a can opener."

I fixed him with my best unimpressed glare. "I'm not *that* useless."

"Alright, alright." He seemed to be holding back a smile as he handed me the opener and one of the cans. "Go ahead and open that."

I'd seen people use a can opener before. On TV, maybe? It looked simple enough then, but when I tried to attach the device to the top of the can, it kept slipping off without actually piercing the top.

Troy let me struggle for a minute or so before intervening. "Do you want a tutorial?"

"Yes," I admitted through gritted teeth. "Don't do it, just show me how it works."

Taking the can from my hand, he placed it down on the narrow counter space before wrapping his hand around mine, the one that held the can opener. Sparks instantly sizzled up my arm, sending a wave of heat and excitement through my body that I did my best to ignore.

Shifting to stand behind me, he placed his other hand on top of mine to guide it into place.

"This metal disc is what's going to open the can, so you need to position it along the lip's edge, just here. Squeeze it together to get a good grip."

The opener made a satisfying *pffft* sound as the disc pierced through the lid.

"Now that it's hooked, use the knob to rotate it around the top."

His hand moved over mine, twisting the handle as the metal drew a perfect circle around the can's lid. When it had completed the full rotation, the lid detached with a sharp snap.

"Good." Troy abruptly dropped his hands from mine and Cinder whimpered in my head, already craving his touch. "Now, open the other one on your own."

I didn't get it hooked quite as smoothly as he had but I did eventually get it, and when I smiled up at him in satisfaction at completing my task, he was gazing down at me with an expression so full of longing, of *admiration*, that Cinder let out another needy mewl.

I cleared my throat as I placed the opener down. "Now what?"

"Now, we make soup."

The cans we'd opened contained a condensed cream of celery soup and evaporated milk, which Troy explained needed to be mixed together and heated. He stood back and let me handle it, providing prompts when necessary as I set up a saucepan on the hot plate and stirred the milk. Soon, gentle bubbles had formed in the thick, creamy liquid and a pleasant aroma, not at all offensive, filled the small space.

Under his supervision, I poured the soup into two bowls and we each took one and a spoon and returned to the narrow bed to sit and eat.

"Not bad for your first meal," he said as he lifted a steaming mouthful to his mouth.

"It barely counts as cooking," I protested even though I did feel rather stupidly proud of it.

Troy's smile suggested I wasn't fooling him. "My stomach says it counts."

Wanting the attention off me, I shifted it to him instead. "Where did you learn to cook? Did your mother teach you?"

"My aunt did. I never knew my mother."

My spoon stopped halfway to my mouth. "What do you mean?"

I'd seen him with an older woman before at pack events. They hadn't seemed particularly close, but I'd seen them together often enough that I assumed it must be his mother.

"Just what it sounds like. My mother left the pack when I was young and left me with my aunt. Apparently, my father came from a neighbouring pack and I was the result of a drunken hook-up. He was never interested in me but she kept trying. She went to see him when I was two and never came back. I don't know what happened to her."

"Goddess, Troy. That's awful."

How did I not know this about him?

How much more was there that I didn't know?

He gave a half-hearted shrug as he put another full spoon into his mouth. "I came to terms with it a long time ago, as best as I could. When I turned 18, I went looking for her. I knew the pack name, the Battle River pack, but not my father's name and no one there would talk to me. The trail went cold pretty quickly. I'd like to know if she's still alive, but I don't think she is. If she were, I think she would have come back. I'd like to think so, anyway."

My throat tightened so much that even swallowing the soup became difficult.

"My aunt raised me. She never had children of her own, never wanted them, but she made sure I had what I needed. Taught me to take care of myself."

It wasn't hard to read between the lines of what he said: it seemed she provided what he needed physically, but little more.

He'd basically raised himself while I was the pampered, spoiled Lota who couldn't even open a can of soup without help. Did he think I was as much of a liability as the men at that retreat had? Was that why he wouldn't take a chance on me when my father forbade our mating?

No, that didn't make sense. If he truly thought me beyond help, he would have just rejected me, not hung on all these years.

Something didn't add up, and perhaps the time had finally come to hear his point of view on the whole situation.

"Troy."

He immediately stopped eating when I said his name and put his spoon down, giving me his full attention.

"Tell me what happened when you spoke to my father."

Chapter Twenty-One

~**Troy**~

For years, I'd been waiting for this opportunity. *Years.* I'd imagined it in multiple different locations and scenarios, though I never imagined the two of us locked into a small underground bunker together.

The setting didn't really matter. What was important was that Alpha Warren's threat no longer hung over us and Amanda seemed open and willing to listen to my side of the story. When I told Jasper about it just a few hours earlier, I said I wanted to earn Amanda's trust first before asking her to trust me on this, but now that she'd asked me about it outright, putting it off any longer didn't feel like the right decision.

For the first time, it felt like she might actually give me a chance to explain.

I started slowly, picking my spoon back up and taking another mouthful of soup before speaking in a subtle attempt to ensure she continued to eat too. It worked; my mate mimicked my action, swallowing her spoonful of soup while I did the same.

"I came to the pack house that morning like you told me to. I asked for you, but you were asleep. I said I'd wait, but before I got a chance to see you, your father called me in. He'd already guessed why I was there."

Amanda nodded stiffly. "I suppose it didn't take a genius to figure it out: a man turning up out of the blue, asking for me right after I got my wolf. I had hoped to warm him up to the idea a little first. I didn't mean to oversleep."

That sounded dangerously close to an apology, one I'd never felt entitled to. She hadn't done anything wrong that day.

"The first shift takes an awful lot out of you. I should have anticipated you would need more sleep than usual, if I'd thought about it logically. Logic didn't factor into it, though; I just wanted to see you."

Her head dipped, hiding her eyes from me, but not before I caught a flash of something that almost looked like regret in them. "What did he say?"

This part of the conversation, I'd never looked forward to. How did you tell someone their own father threatened to kill them? True, she'd recently overthrown that very father to take control of the pack, but that hadn't been personal. Whereas the things he said about her were as personal as they could get.

I might have been tempted to gloss over it, but after what Jasper suggested that afternoon about her father potentially still working against her, it had only become more important for her to know the whole story.

To buy myself a few more seconds to figure out how to phrase it, I lifted the bowl of soup to my lips and finished the rest of it. Canned cream of celery soup had honestly never tasted so good as it did knowing that my mate had made it for me.

Amanda didn't drain hers like I did but she did raise her spoon to her mouth again, her eyes still downcast as she waited for me to speak."First, he spent some time disparaging me, calling me an unranked bastard, among other things."

Her head lifted at that, indignation clear in the tightening of her eyebrows. Seeing her get angry on my behalf instead of *at* me made such a welcome change that I almost laughed.

"I mean, if we're being pedantic, my parents weren't mated, so I'm technically a bastard, and my mother had no rank within the pack. If my father had a rank, I don't know what it is. I don't consider being unranked or a bastard an insult. Those things are facts which are out of my control."

She let out a frustrated huff. "I'm sure his tone made it an insult."

"Oh, absolutely. You'd have thought I committed the worst crime any werewolf ever had because, aside from being an unranked bastard, I also had the nerve to be mated to you. Which we all know I had total control over."

My sarcastic tone drew a reluctant, rueful smile from Amanda. "I'm sorry he spoke to you that way."

I shrugged, not wanting her apology for that either. "You didn't choose your family any more than I chose mine."

She hesitated for a moment, thinking that over before nodding to herself. "Then what?"

"Well, he believed that we were mates, which was something, but he said there was no way you would have agreed to even entertain the idea of accepting me. I must have manipulated you in some way. When I told him you were capable of making your own decisions, he assured me I was wrong."

It hurt to see the way she winced at those words, but there were worse to come so I pushed ahead.

"He ordered me to stay away from you and never tell anyone we were mates or we would both be exiled."

Her jaw clenched, her fingers tightening around the handle of her spoon. The movements were subtle but I'd spent so long studying her, I could have written a thesis on what each move meant. "You already told me that."

And it wasn't enough, Hunter reminded me. He'd kept silent for this entire conversation so far, but he chimed in now with the encouragement I needed. *You need to tell her the rest. It's time.*

"That wasn't all he said."

A small flaring of her nostrils, a slight incline of her head. More signals, more unspoken communication that I understood on a cellular level. She wanted to hear more.

"He said that once we were exiled, you'd be dead to him, and he'd make sure you were dead to everyone else too. He swore he'd put a bounty on your head. He swore he'd kill you."

I paused there to let the words sink in, taking no pleasure in the way her cheeks paled, her blinking turning more rapid.

When I thought she'd absorbed it, I carried on. "Only you would die, though. He'd give strict orders to leave me alive. I would have to watch you die, feel the mate bond rip apart inside me, drown in the agony of it, and know that I was responsible for all of it. His description of it was very... *vivid.* He'd put some thought into it."

A grimace pulled at my lips as she continued to stare at me, not speaking a word.

"I didn't know what to do, Amanda. I had no idea how I could protect you. I'm not rich, I don't have any important friends or connections. Outside the pack, I could have offered you a basic existence but no true protection. How could I ask you to risk your life for me? I didn't want to. The thought of losing you, even then, even when our bond was only hours old, devastated me. I would have rather seen you happy with someone else than cold in the ground because of me."

Her tongue slowly moved across the seam of her lips. No doubt her mouth had gone dry just as mine did every time I thought about her father's ultimatum. "Why..."

Her voice cracked but she cleared her throat and tried again.

"Why didn't you tell me any of this before?"

"He made me promise not to. He made me promise not to say a word about why I couldn't accept you. He said you'd find my unwillingness to fight for you unforgivable and cut yourself off from me without the need for any further intervention. If you ever said another word about me to him after that day, he'd assume I told you and he'd carry out all his threats just the same. Now, you know him better than I do, and maybe you're going to tell me he didn't mean any of that and he exaggerated to scare me, but I couldn't take that chance. I *couldn't,* not when it came to you."

Taking a deep breath, I leaned back in my chair, my heart thumping heavily in my chest. I actually did it. After all this time, I finally disobeyed the Alpha's orders, and now, I could only wait and see if my mate believed me.

Chapter Twenty-Two

~**Amanda**~

The picture Troy painted of my father as he described their conversation on that long-ago morning should have felt completely alien to me. After all, what kind of father, what kind of *Alpha*, would threaten the life of his only child and heir?

It *should* have felt completely alien, but I'd be lying if I said I didn't recognize bits and pieces of the man I'd grown up both respecting and resenting in his description.

In fact, the longer I thought about it, the clearer the picture became, until I wanted to claw at my temples to scratch it from my mind forever.

"My father never forgave me for the fact that I wasn't a boy."

Although I didn't mean to speak the words aloud, they came out anyway. My head felt too full, too tight to keep them inside.

Keep going, Cinder urged. *Be honest with him. Let your guard down, just a little.*

"If I had a brother, maybe my father would have felt differently, but more children never came. I was all they got, and I wasn't what he wanted."

Troy's hand twitched where it rested on the mattress between us, as if he wanted to reach out to comfort me but didn't dare to. My own hands had started to tremble, so I placed the soup bowl I still held down on the floor, folding my hands over my lap in an attempt to steady both them and my nerves.

Gathering all my strength, I raised my head and looked into my mate's eyes.

"He could have named me as his heir outright. It might have taken some persuasion to convince the pack to accept it, but he had two decades to make his case. He never even tried."

The emotions in Troy's gaze were exactly the ones I had the right to expect from a mate *and* from my father: support, concern and protectiveness. His jaw shifted, teeth grinding as he forcibly held back whatever words were on the tip of his tongue. He wouldn't interrupt me while I talked this all out; without a word, he made that crystal clear.

"I convinced myself he only wanted what was best for the pack. They would resist a female Alpha but rally behind a male one, whether that turned out to be my mate or whoever he chose as his heir when I left the pack. His decision didn't reflect on me as a person; it simply came with the territory of being an Alpha and the responsibility he bore."

Troy's jaw clenched so tight, I thought his teeth might crack.

"I told myself that, but deep down, it felt like a rejection. It made me cautious about opening up to other people who might reject me too. I threw myself into learning diplomacy and understanding how to represent the pack's interests, since that's where I could bring value. All of that was ingrained in me from a very young age."

When was the last time I spoke about myself this way? I didn't even know where half of it was coming from. My subconscious, maybe, or possibly from Cinder herself? I only knew that now that I'd started, I wanted to keep talking, wanted to say the words out loud so they were no longer my burden to bear alone.

"So, when you refused to fight for me, it felt like the same thing all over again. It felt like you decided I wasn't worth the trouble and you never even tried. And my father knew I would feel that way because he'd conditioned me to feel it. He told you I'd find it unforgivable because deep down, he knew I'd never forgive him either."

I could almost have been impressed by my father's manipulation if it weren't at my own expense.

Troy sucked in a long breath before he finally dared to speak. "Does that mean you believe me?"

"I don't want to." The words came out soft and quiet in the calm, demure way of speaking I'd adopted whenever I wanted to hide how I truly felt. "It would be less painful to think you were making it all up but it's that detail, the fact that he told you I wouldn't forgive you, that rings so true, I can't pretend that you're lying."

He swallowed so hard, I could hear his throat working. "Do you think he was bluffing?"

Again, I wanted to. Inside me, the little girl who looked up to her father and thought he was the smartest, bravest man in the whole world begged me to state with confidence that my father would never toy with my life that way.

But he was also the man who traded me for an alliance and, when it didn't work out, demanded Vaughan's pack send his sister to us instead, treating both of us as possessions. The man who allowed experimentation on his own pack members when it suited his purpose.

There were sides to him that ran darker and deeper than I'd realized until even just a few weeks ago.

Did I think he was bluffing?

"No. I don't think he was."

Troy's exhale sounded so ragged, for a second, I almost thought he might be crying. But when our gazes locked again, his eyes were dry and achingly earnest. "You don't know what it means to me to hear you say that. So many times over these years, I wondered if I threw it all away for nothing. If it could have been different if I'd just taken the chance."

I could almost feel his relief in my own chest, along with a hollow pain I recognized all too well. In its emptiness, a little voice whispered 'what if'. What if he *had* taken the chance? What if things had been different for us?

Was it too late to find out?

"Why are you telling me all of this now? My father's been gone for weeks now."

He nodded, as if he approved of the question, and his weight shifted ever-so-slightly towards me on the mattress. "I wanted to tell you right away but… well, you were still so angry with me. You had a lot on your plate, and it didn't seem like the right time."

I could read between the lines well enough: what he actually meant but was too polite to say was that I'd been a stubborn bitch who wouldn't listen.

Told you so, Cinder hummed.

"And why tell me now?" I pressed, still trying to see the big picture. "Is there really a threat at all or did you make it up to lock me in here with you so I'd have to listen?"

Troy's eyes glinted with that same protective edge as before. "The threat is real. Having the chance to spend time with you alone was a happy byproduct of keeping you safe. And the main reason I told you now is *because* of that threat and because of Kalo."

"Kalo?" I repeated the genie's name in surprise. "What does he have to do with it?"

"You said the necklace that summoned him was in your mother's jewellery but she didn't recognize it," he reminded me. "What if your father put it there? What if he's trying to set you up to fail?"

The suggestion landed on my already-cracked heart with a heavy thud. Once again, I wished I could deny the possibility and proclaim my father would never do that, but after everything we'd just discussed, defending him would be laughable. Of course he could have planted the necklace. He had the opportunity *and* a motive, since I'd technically deposed him and taken over his pack.

He never wanted me to be Alpha. Now that I was, would he stoop as low as sabotage to take the position back?

How far would he go?

And by making my first wish, had I fallen right into his trap?

Chapter Twenty-Three

~**Troy**~

I'd never felt the kind of undiluted rage that flowed through my body when Amanda outlined how her father treated her. As if she were inadequate, or unworthy.

How could he not see the incredibly strong woman that I did every time I looked at her?

"He might be responsible for the necklace," she conceded, still mulling over my last words. "It makes as much sense as anything else I've come up with. If it was left in my mother's jewellery intentionally, with the goal of binding me to the genie, it had to be someone who knew it would cause me harm and wanted that to happen. My father fits that criteria."

Though she kept her tone neutral and analytical, I didn't miss the tightening of her lips or the flash of pain that crossed her eyes so quickly that most people wouldn't have noticed. She was putting on a brave face, playing a part like she always did. Being so strong that no one would notice the hurt underneath.

But I saw it.

I always had.

"He's lucky he's not in the territory right now," I growled, the palms of my hands pressing into my thighs so I didn't give into the urge to punch the concrete wall. That wouldn't accomplish anything, hurting me more than anything else, but I needed to put that energy *somewhere*. "Now that he's not my Alpha, he'd find out exactly what I'm capable of."

One of Amanda's manicured eyebrows rose, a ghost of a smile dancing over her lips. "Oh, really?"

"You don't think I could take him?" My chest puffed out on instinct, my muscles rippling beneath the fabric of my shirt, jumping with anticipation at even the thought of getting my hands on the man who'd denied me the greatest blessing of my life for far too long.

"I think it's easy to say when we're locked up and he's thousands of miles away." She leaned back, her hands on the mattress behind her and that faint almost-smile still hovering over her mouth. "Talk is cheap."

Was she *trying* to rile me up? "As Alpha, he hid behind the power of his bloodline and his authority over the pack. Man-to-man, he wouldn't stand a chance."

Again, my muscles flexed almost out of my control, and Amanda's eyes dropped to the taut sleeves stretched over my biceps. "You are awfully... large... for an unranked wolf."

She wasn't the first to make that observation. Among werewolves, the highest-ranked men were usually the tallest and strongest, genetic traits passed down in their bloodlines. But occasionally, there would be exceptions and I'd always been the biggest one in my class, in my training program, and now in my unit.

Something in the way she said it made me pause, though, and when her eyes flicked up to mine, just for a second, amusement danced in those gorgeous brown depths.

"You're teasing me," I realized, a little too late.

"The conversation was getting a little too depressing," she confirmed, tossing her head back so that the long, brown waves of her hair hung down so far, they almost touched the mattress. "I don't want to talk about my father anymore. I don't want to think about any of it, not right now."

This side of her was new, at least to me. With the air somewhat cleared between us, the past finally on full display even if neither of us had brought up what it might mean for our future, the tension that always existed between us eased. Some of the weight that hung over my heart for seven years had lifted, and I had to guess she felt the same. She seemed lighter, almost buoyant. A little giddy, even.

As soon as I stopped to really let the conversation we'd just had sink in, I felt it too.

In the weeks since her father left, we'd gone in circles, spinning our wheels, her trying to push me away and me resisting. Now, we could put that to one side and suddenly, the path ahead seemed full of new possibilities.

I forced my body to relax as I mirrored her pose, leaning back until my face came into alignment with hers. A few feet still separated us but after years of seeing her only from a distance, it felt like nothing. "So, you'd rather talk about my... size?"

The deliberate pause before the final word made it clear that it could have multiple meanings and Amanda grinned, obviously pleased I'd decided to play along. Fuck, she was beautiful when she smiled. Instantly, the tug towards her, always there in the background, grew stronger.

"I can think of worse things to discuss," she said, her eyes still gleaming with that teasing playfulness.

"I can also think of better things," I countered. "Wouldn't want to get you all worked up when we might be called back at any minute."

I held my breath for a moment after the words left my mouth, not sure if I'd pushed things too far, but she simply laughed, her head tipping back again, drawing my attention to that gorgeous cascade of thick hair. If she had any idea how many times I'd wondered what it would feel like to run my fingers through it or wrap it around my fist, she'd probably have me committed.

"I'd be more worried about *you* getting worked up," she replied, casting a meaningful glance towards my lap where the bulge in my uniform cargo pants had definitely grown over the last minute or so. "It's a little more obvious for you than for me."

This little game she'd started was quickly moving into dangerous territory. The air sizzled between us, thick with electricity, and for the first time since that very first night when we found each other, it actually seemed possible that it might ignite.

"I don't know about that," I shot back, my voice thick with building lust. "Visually, it might be more obvious, but don't rule out the sense of smell."

To prove my point, I inhaled deeply and nearly groaned when I caught the faint aroma I'd been hoping for, just behind her delicious mate scent.

She was getting fucking turned on.

Rather than looking embarrassed or uncertain at my discovery, Amanda held my gaze steadily. "It doesn't take much at this point. It's been a long time for me."

"I know." The words were so throaty, they barely sounded like English. Based on the last time I felt the agony of her pleasure at another man's hands, she hadn't had sex for eleven months and twelve days. That *was* a long time, but not nearly as long as it had been for me.

Regret flashed across her beautiful face as she absorbed that response, and I could have kicked myself for throwing the equivalent of a wet blanket onto the growing heat between us. However, just as quickly as the mood dipped, Amanda pulled it back up, raising her chin a little higher.

"Well, how about you let me take care of that before it becomes an even... bigger... issue?"

Again, her eyes moved to my lap, and my bones turned liquid. Did she actually mean she would...?

Holy fuck, Hunter breathed in my head, sounding just as awed and hopeful as I felt. How the hell did we get here? It seemed like a fucking dream.

There was just one little problem with that scenario, which I realized as soon as some of the blood that rushed to my dick gradually returned to my brain.

"There's no world in which my mate gets me off before I do the same for her."

Amanda's eyes widened in surprise, either at my declaration or my tone, I couldn't be sure which. Maybe both.

But a moment later, a slow, devilish smile spread across her lips. "Who says it has to be one or the other?"

Chapter Twenty-Four

~Amanda~

I didn't actively decide to proposition my mate. His macho declarations about fighting my father to protect my honour, or whatever he thought it would accomplish, were kind of cute, but the way his muscles rippled with tension tipped the scales from cute to sinful in mere seconds.

Once I started looking at his body, I couldn't stop. Over the past seven years, I'd done everything I could to avoid looking at it, pretending not to notice the way his broad chest and sculpted ass filled out his guard's uniform anytime we happened to be in the same room. With those same assets within arm's reach, they became a lot harder to ignore, especially when the anger and resentment I felt over his past actions began to recede.

He was a damn fine specimen of a man, locked in a small space with a woman who hadn't been touched in far too long. Who could blame me if I pushed things a little further than I intended?

Be careful, Cinder warned in my head. *This isn't a one-and-done scenario. He's our mate.*

I knew what she meant. Each touch between us would mean more than it did coming from any other person. If we gave into the rising heat between us, it would have consequences. Messy, potentially destructive consequences depending on how everything played out. Just because I believed what he told me about his conversation with my father didn't mean that seven years of hurt and loneliness simply disappeared.

It *did*, however, open up new possibilities, and one of those was to finally indulge in some physical pleasure with the one person who had the ability to make my body light up in a way no other man ever would. People always said nothing compared to a mate's touch, and suddenly, I couldn't wait to find out if they were right.

For his part, Troy seemed to have lost the power of speech when I suggested a little mutual enjoyment, and I had to laugh at the way his mouth hung open, jaw slack, looking like he might begin to drool at any second.

"You said you haven't been with anyone since that night," I reminded him, my tone softening in recognition of the sacrifice he'd made on my behalf since discovering we were mates. "But I assume you're not a virgin?"

His lips pressed back together as he swallowed hard. "No. Things were pretty... open... in my training program."

My mind flashed to the trim, fit women on the guards team, their muscular bodies in stark contrast to my softer one, and an irrational flash of jealousy seared across my chest. I had no right to be jealous, not when we hadn't even met then, and certainly not when he'd forsaken any pleasure of his own once we did, but it didn't change the fact that the idea of him touching or being touched by another woman irked me.

It made me want to stake my claim, to make sure that any memories he might harbour from those times paled in comparison to what I could do for him, and the feeling startled me with its intensity. When I agreed to take Vaughan as my mate, I hadn't cared one bit if he'd been with other women before me.

When the hell did I become so possessive?

As if he noticed my hesitation, Troy leaned closer to me and flashed me a teasing grin. "We had to shift in front of each other all the time, so being shy wasn't an option. And what can I say? The ladies liked what they saw."

The line couldn't have been any lamer and he knew that. He did it on purpose to keep things loose, and it worked: I laughed, my jealousy fading into the background as lust once again took over.

I leaned closer too, our faces now only inches apart. "Don't hype it up too much. You don't want me to be disappointed."

Both amusement and naked desire flashed in his stunning eyes. "I'm not worried."

A simple statement, but the confidence with which he uttered it made my pulse quicken. The throbbing between my legs that had started up as soon as we started talking about his body kicked into an even higher gear. "Put your money where your mouth is, soldier. Show me."

His gaze held mine a moment longer, years of yearning and unfulfilled need condensed into seconds of scorching heat, before he reached down to the black belt wrapped around his waist. My eyes dropped down to watch as, with one hand, he undid it and, with a snap of his wrist, pulled it completely free from the loops of his pants.

My thighs immediately clenched. *Why the fuck is that so hot?*

My fingers itched to reach over and help, to feel the bulk of that bulge beneath the black fabric for myself, but I forced myself to sit still and watch as he pulled down the zipper and roughly tugged down both his pants and underwear, yanking them down to his knees as his cock finally came into view.

He was right. He definitely didn't have anything to be worried about.

As he leaned back to resume his previous position, hands on the mattress behind him and body half-reclined, his hard, thick cock lay rigid against his stomach, dripping a few drops of pre-cum onto the fitted black t-shirt he still wore. Veins lined the length of it, drawing trails I ached to follow with my fingers or my tongue.

I didn't even realize *my* mouth had fallen open until he laughed, a deep, rich sound that rumbled from his chest. "No snarky comeback, Alpha?"

For some reason, him calling me 'Alpha' at that moment caused my brain to temporarily short-circuit. I could only blink up at him in a stupor until I regained control of my body and snapped my mouth shut.

"I guess you're not *all* talk," I conceded, trying to keep some control over the situation as I got to my feet. "Lie down. Prop yourself up with the pillow."

Troy frowned up at me, his handsome face torn between eagerness to please me and his masculine pride. "I told you I'm not letting you..."

I cut him off before he could finish. "You said you wouldn't come before I did. Well, we'll just have to see who's faster, won't we?"

Before I could second-guess myself, my hands went to my own pants, undoing the button and pulling down the zipper. The way Troy's breath hitched at the peek I gave him of my lacy black panties gave me the ego boost I needed to go the rest of the way, kicking off my heels and pulling off the pants and panties all at once. When I'd stepped out of them and tossed them to the side, Troy's focus hadn't shifted from the smooth skin between my legs.

I preferred being waxed, for myself rather than for any man, and if I ever worried my mate might not like it, those doubts vanished in the heat of Troy's stare.

"Lie down," I instructed again. "I need somewhere to sit."

At last, realization about what I intended to do dawned on him, and he immediately abandoned his protests, shifting his body horizontally onto the narrow, twin-sized bed. Due to his height, his feet hung off the end and his upper half was at a 30-degree angle, his shoulders against the wall in order to fit. The bed definitely wouldn't fit both of us lying side-by-side, but that didn't matter. I didn't intend to lie next to him.

Doing my best to ignore the way my heart pounded in anticipation, my whole body tingling with excitement, I stepped towards the head of the bed and turned around. With my back to his face, I rested my hands on his firm abdomen for support. Before I could even lift one leg, Troy's strong hands gripped my hips, giving me the feeling of flying as he lifted me up and positioned me over his chest. My knees rested in the crook of his elbows as I wiggled forward until his cock lay just below my salivating mouth.

"Are you ready?" I asked, trying to sound flirty and in control, but the words came out breathy and almost desperate.

"No," he breathed out from behind me, the exact same mix of need and excitement in his tone. "But I'm not going to fucking stop."

Neither was I. "First one to come loses," I teased, even though I could already feel the wetness gathering between my thighs. Just the thought of his mouth on me had my body throbbing.

I didn't say what the winner got. I didn't have to. We both knew it didn't matter.

All that mattered at that exact moment was the feel of his cock in my hands as I lifted him to my lips, and the earth-shattering cascade of sparks that lit up between my legs when he pulled me down onto his face.

Chapter Twenty-Five

~**Troy**~

It had to be some kind of dream. Maybe Amanda knocked me out with the saucepan while making soup, or maybe I simply fell and hit my head. It didn't seem possible that after all these years of waiting, years of dreaming what this moment might be like but knowing I would never have it, I was finally going to get a chance to taste her. A chance to know even a fragment of the pleasure we'd both been denied for so long.

It felt too good to be true, but as my fingers pressed into the soft skin of my mate's hips that hovered just above my face, I inhaled deeply, almost drowning in the scent of her arousal mixed with the delicious headiness of her unique mate scent. If this was just a dream, I didn't ever want to wake up.

My tongue had just connected with the soft skin between her legs when her lips slid over the head of my cock. My chin jerked up, something between a gasp and a groan rumbling in my chest, and my grip tightened around her hips.

Amanda's warm laugh filtered through the pounding in my ears. "You okay there, big guy?"

Fuck. As if the sparks from her lips weren't enough, hearing her call me 'big guy' while she held my cock in her hand sent a shiver of unfiltered lust straight down my spine. If she kept that up, I was going to come before she even got started.

No, I instructed myself forcefully, pushing the desire back down the way I'd trained myself to do every time I laid eyes on her over the past seven years. This was one game I did not intend to lose.

Refocusing on the tantalizing vision above me, I abandoned all thought of taking my time exploring and dove straight in instead. If she wanted to play dirty, I could definitely play dirty. My tongue swiped along her slit, following her mouth-watering scent straight to its source, and I thrust my tongue deep inside with no further warning.

That time, Amanda was the one who gasped, her body tensing above me. I only pulled her down harder, burying my face in her warmth completely as I licked along her inner walls, plunging my tongue as deep as it could go and swirling it around to lap up as much of her as possible.

If heaven had a taste, this would be it. Nothing could have prepared me for how good it would taste, and smell, and feel, and I already knew I'd be craving her on my tongue again as soon as we were done.

A strong jolt of desire interrupted my thoughts, all the blood in my body temporarily diverting down to my groin. Stroking me with her hand, Amanda's tongue swirled over my balls, the sensation equally unexpected and fucking electric.

"Goddess help me," I muttered, tilting my head back for a deep breath and the chance to gather myself before diving back in. I could have sworn Amanda laughed again, but it quickly faded when my tongue swiped up from her hole and found her clit instead.

Her moan vibrated through her body, setting my nerves on fire in return. Hips rocked against my face, just enough to show me where she wanted attention, and with all the enthusiasm of a starving man sitting down to dinner, I gave it to her, my lips and tongue nipping, caressing and sucking on her until she moaned again.

A second later, my entire body froze as her warm, wet mouth enveloped my cock. Instructions between my brain and body short-circuited, pleasure overriding every other rational thought. My grip on her shifted from holding her in place to holding on for dear life as she pulled me down into a pool of fulfillment I'd never known. I wanted to drown in it, to let go and let her take control, until I remembered she needed to come first. I *couldn't* forget that.

I lost track of time as control shifted back and forth between us. Every time I thought I might be getting her close, her tongue found another sensitive spot on me, or her hand tugged me in just the right way, and I lost my ability to function. I teetered on the edge, my body begging for release while my mind resisted, and based on the way her thighs trembled on either side of my face, she couldn't be far off either.

I knew exactly how stubborn she could be, but I could hold out just as long.

I just didn't want to anymore.

Lifting her slightly so I could take another breath, gasping for the air my lungs had been denied while I was buried in her, I offered a compromise.

"I'm so fucking close, Alpha. If you let go, I will too."

I couldn't say why I called her Alpha at that moment. Maybe because she had the upper hand, literally, being the one on top of me. Or maybe because she'd always held full control of my heart, since the moment our wolves recognized each other. Either way, her body shuddered above me at my words.

"O-okay," she stuttered out, another sign that I'd been doing my job right. "Together. Don't let me down now."

My growl vibrated the bed beneath us. "Not a fucking chance."

With that, I took one last breath and pulled her back down onto my waiting mouth. Sparks travelled the length of my cock as she took me in deep, the head of my cock touching the back of her throat. My hips thrust upwards by themselves. Hers bucked in response, her wetness sliding over my face as I feasted on her, ravenous for the prize I knew was coming.

When she began to tremble beneath my fingers once more, I groaned again, low and deep. That noise seemed to finally push her over the peak and her thighs contracted, hard, around my head. As soon as the first taste of her release hit my tongue, I let go too. My soul disconnected from my body, the sweetest ecstasy flooding me from head to toe.

I thought I was ready, but I was wrong.

Holy fucking hell.

Everything disappeared, nothing left in the world but me, her, and the deepest, truest satisfaction I'd ever known.

Gradually, my consciousness returned, and I realized I was still holding onto Amanda's hips so tightly, she'd probably have bruises in the morning. Forcing my body to obey, my grip loosened, and she immediately lifted herself off me, letting a rush of air back into my lungs.

I immediately missed the feel of her on my face. Breathing was nice, sure, but given the choice between the two, I'd take her pussy every time.

Amanda's breaths sounded shorter than before as she lay her head against my thigh to catch her breath, and the gesture somehow felt more intimate than anything else we'd just done.

Like I told her, I'd had sex before. There had been no emotions involved, just young, horny werewolves looking for a physical outlet. It felt good in the moment and as soon as it ended, I never thought about it again.

This, though... this would linger in my memories for the rest of my fucking life. Which made the next words either of us chose to say extremely important.

Just as I cleared my throat to say those words, to declare my undying devotion to her, or maybe just tell her how incredible that had been and how I already wanted to go back for seconds, a loud beeping sound filled the room.

Amanda immediately scrambled off me, her eyes wide. I caught just a glimpse of the shadow of her pleasure before it vanished beneath a wave of confusion. "What was that?"

I didn't know, but the next sound made it a lot clearer. An intercom crackled to life, static noise followed by the unmistakable voice of Beta Savannah.

"We're coming in. You've got five seconds to make sure all your clothes are on."

Chapter Twenty-Six

~Amanda~

"Shit!" I whispered as I stood up and ran to grab my pants from where I'd discarded them on the floor. Five seconds didn't give me enough time to make myself presentable, assuming Savannah meant her warning literally. I didn't regret what Troy and I just did, especially with the pleasure of my orgasm still reverberating through my body, but I didn't exactly want it to be public knowledge just yet either.

"I'll stall," Troy announced, standing up and yanking his pants back up. He'd only pulled them down, not removed them entirely, so he could hide the evidence much more quickly than I could. Wincing only slightly, he tucked his cock back into his underwear and zipped his pants up, striding over to stand in front of the door right as the lock clicked open.

His large body blocked the view into the room entirely when the door pushed open, buying me a few more precious seconds to make myself presentable as he greeted my Beta.

"What happened? Did you find out who was behind that phone call?"

"Let me in and I'll tell you," Savannah instructed, and when the large man didn't move, she huffed in frustration. "Why are you being weird? You didn't tie her up or anything, did you? I was joking about putting your clothes back on."

I slipped back into my shoes, double checking that my pants were done up before I sat down on the bed and did my best to look unflustered. "Let her in, Troy. I don't think Savannah's a threat."

My tone sounded no different than it had that morning, cool and detached, and when Troy looked back over his shoulder, I could see the appreciation in his eyes for my ability to slip into my Alpha role when needed.

Not everyone noticed the effort it took, and his acknowledgement of it, however small, made me feel a little more seen than I had before.

He stepped aside, letting Savannah enter, and my Beta burst into the room with the same energy she brought to every room, her curls bouncing around her shoulders as she moved. I thought her mate might be with her, since we were in his bunker, but she'd come alone.

"Jasper's still at the pack house, keeping an eye on everything," she explained, as if she'd heard my thoughts. "We haven't made any progress on figuring out who's been working with the attackers."

"Why are you here, then?" Troy grumbled, not being rude, exactly, but clearly annoyed that there hadn't been an earth-shattering reason for interrupting our intimate moment.

Savannah sent a withering glare in his direction. "Maybe I just wanted to make sure you weren't taking advantage of the situation." She paused, sniffing the air before her eyes narrowed. "Why does it smell like sex in here?"

Fuck. A werewolf's sense of smell could really be *too* sensitive sometimes, and of course Savannah would point it out.

"That's the soup," I offered in explanation. "I tried my hand at cooking and I don't have a lot of experience."

Her nose scrunched in dismay. "Remind me not to let you cook for me anytime soon."

Troy tried to stifle his laugh and ended up choking on it instead, leading to a coughing fit that he had to turn away to finish.

Changing the subject seemed like the best course of action. "You came here for a reason. What is it?"

"Oh. Right." Straightening her shoulders, she switched back to business mode. "A team from the Crimsontooth pack is here to assist but they can't enter the territory because of the barrier in place. Do you want to lower the barrier now, or should we tell them to find somewhere else to spend the night?"

Confusion creased my brow as I processed that information. "Why are they here? They would have had to leave home hours ago, and we haven't asked them for help yet."

Her expression turned sheepish as she offered me a half-hearted shrug. "I might have alerted Vaughan to the situation this morning, after Kalo's arrival. I didn't ask him to send help yet, but apparently, he decided to take matters into his own hands. I'm sorry, I didn't mean to overstep."

If anyone had overstepped, it was Vaughan, but given the circumstances, I couldn't fault his foresight. If we hadn't had Kalo's help, his men might truly have been needed.

Troy's whole body stiffened at the sound of my former fiancé's name. "The Alpha's here?"

"Not personally. Leo, his Gamma, is leading the team. Their orders are to help us however we need them to. The men at the border post can speak to them through the barrier, but they can't come in and our men can't go out."

That was what I'd asked Kalo for in my wish, and although it seemed inhospitable to deny our allies entry, I didn't feel ready to lower the barrier yet, not when we hadn't resolved anything. The Crimsontooth warriors would help but they didn't make us invincible.

"Please ask them to find somewhere to spend the night. There's a motel in the nearest human town that should have room this time of year. I'll cover any expense. They can come back in the morning and hopefully we'll have a clearer picture of our needs by then."

"Sounds good," Savannah agreed, and with that settled, her eyes swept over the interior of our small hideout. "This place really is tiny."

"It's cozy," I agreed, keeping my eyes on her so I didn't accidentally catch Troy's gaze. I could imagine his smirk, remembering just how *cozy* we'd been with each other just a couple of minutes earlier. "Are we free to go now?"

The way Savannah grimaced gave me my answer even before she spoke the words out loud. "Jasper wants more time to investigate, and he thinks your absence might draw the conspirators out. Embolden them to make a move. He thinks you should spend the night here."

My eyes immediately fell to the narrow bed I sat on, not nearly big enough for both me and Troy unless one of us was on top of each other.

"I'll keep watch," Troy immediately offered, sensing my thoughts as he often seemed to lately. "You can rest, Alpha."

"I'll come back in the morning, as soon as Jasper gives the okay, and bring you some fresh clothes then," Savannah offered. "Do you need anything else in the meantime?"

I shook my head. "We have the essentials here and making too many trips back and forth, even if this is your house, could attract suspicion. I don't love being cut off here, but I understand the reason for it. What about Kalo?"

She shrugged. "I gave him a guest room at the pack house and unlimited access to the kitchen, and he seems as happy as a clam. Jasper has a guard posted outside the door, for all the good that'll do, and he'll meet with you in the morning."

It sounded like she had everything under control. "Alright. Thank you for handling all this. We'll regroup in the morning and figure out what to do next."

The Beta bid both of us good night, shooting Troy one more warning look before she left, as if reminding him not to push his luck, and the door clicked shut behind her when she left. The electric whirring of the lock confirmed we were once again shut in, and this time, Troy entered an additional code into the keypad.

"That'll stop anyone else from coming in from outside, even if they have the code," he explained with a wry smile. "I didn't think it would be necessary before, but now..."

He trailed off, and my skin instantly began to tingle under the heat of his gaze. We had at least eight more hours locked up together in the small room with no distractions, no interruptions, and the pull of our mate bond that had only grown stronger since I got a taste of the kind of pleasure he could give me.

Could we make it through the whole night without this growing spark between us becoming an inferno?

Chapter Twenty-Seven

~Troy~

Amanda couldn't have looked any more inviting, sitting on the bed in the small underground bunker, her cheeks still a little pinker than usual thanks to the orgasm I'd given her. Did Savannah really buy Amanda's excuse that the scent of our mutual pleasure still lingering in the air came from our dinner instead? Based on everything I knew about the Beta so far, she didn't seem that naive, but she might honestly believe that Amanda disliked me so much, anything would be more likely than the fact that I'd had my face buried between her legs mere minutes earlier.

I still had a hard time believing it myself, even with her delicious taste lingering on my tongue.

And as much as I wanted to do it again, as much as I wanted to spend every moment of the time we had locked away from the world exploring and enjoying every inch of her, there was something I needed even more.

"You're not going to ask me to reject you again, are you?"

The question flew from my mouth like an arrow, and I could see the exact moment it reached my mate. She swayed slightly to the side, absorbing its weight, and the desire I'd seen building in her eyes dimmed.

Fuck. "I mean, I don't expect you to fully accept me either, not tonight, but I need to know if what we just did meant something to you."

Her eyebrows rose, not as far as they could go, but enough that I knew those words hadn't landed right either. She said so much with the smallest movements. "Because I regularly have meaningless sex? Is that what you mean?"

Hunter growled in my head, not at her but at me for my clumsy phrasing. "That's not what I meant. It's just... I've been waiting for that moment for seven years. For a chance to please you. But I know that your feelings towards me over that same time have been... considerably more mixed."

One corner of her mouth quirked in acknowledgement, so I carried on.

"You have my heart, Amanda. You have my loyalty and my commitment and my body too. All of it is yours, whenever you say the word, and I'll do whatever it takes to prove that to you. I know it'll take time. I'm not going to assume that just because you gave me access to your body, your *incredible* body..."

My breath stuttered as my eyes drank her in from head to toe, my mind mingling what it saw with the memories we'd just created together. On the one hand, that memory was good enough to last me a lifetime, but on the other, I wanted so much more.

"...I know it doesn't mean that you're ready to give me the rest yet. What I'm trying to ask, very badly, is how you're feeling about what just happened?"

Amanda humphed out a sigh, but the tension in her face relaxed as she leaned back. "Then just say that next time."

"I'll try." I offered her a smile as I sat back down on the bed too, keeping a bit of space between us. "You make me nervous. I'm doing my best."

The admission took her by surprise, a startled laugh my reward for my honesty. "How do I make you nervous?"

"Are you kidding?" It was my turn to give her an incredulous look, my eyebrows raising in disbelief. When she just stared back at me, curious and clueless, I shook my head. Apparently, it wasn't a joke, so I laid it out for her. "The first time I saw you, I thought you were an angel. Literally."

Her eyebrows scrunched together. "The night of my birthday?"

She was so lost, I had to smile. "No. I'm talking about the very first time I saw you. It was a big pack celebration, one of the few my aunt let me attend. There were games and competitions, and because I was bigger than most kids my age, I won a bunch of ribbons. I was 12 years old, so you would have been around 8, I think? At one point, the Alpha came out on the balcony of the pack house, where we could all see him, and you walked out to join him wearing a shiny white dress that sparkled in the sunshine."

Recognition warmed her beautiful brown eyes. "I remember that day, and that dress. I hated it because I couldn't play any of the games in it. I'd been listening to the staff talk about all the fun things they were planning all week, and when the day arrived, I just had to stand there and wave."

"I waved back at you," I admitted, feeling rather foolish admitting it since I knew even then that she hadn't noticed me. Why would she have? "And I asked my aunt if she saw the angel too. I didn't know that someone so beautiful could be real."

Her lips parted in a way that made it almost impossible not to lean over and kiss her, but I forced myself to continue the story instead.

"My aunt slapped the back of my head and told me not to be so stupid. You were the Alpha's daughter, and that was the closest someone like me would ever get to someone like you."

She winced at the words, just as I had done on that day.

"After that, any time there was an event where you might be there, I found a way to go. I never got too close, just hung out in the back so no one noticed me. But any glimpse of you I could get always made me feel better for a long time afterwards. It reminded me that beauty existed, even when things got rough."

Her brow lined with concern at the last part, but I didn't want to talk about my childhood right now. I'd much rather focus on her.

"For years, I lived off those glimpses, admiring you like a piece of art, something to be appreciated from a distance, completely out of reach, but then came the year of the canoe races."

Amanda groaned, her eyes closing in dismay. "That was so embarrassing."

I wouldn't have used that word. Eye-opening, certainly, at least on my end, but she had no reason to be embarrassed.

The pack's top warriors and ranked members raced across the lake in canoes while the rest of us watched from shore and cheered. As Lota, 17-year-old Amanda had the job of presenting the winner with his trophy. She wore a beautiful, pale-yellow sundress, shining as brightly as the sun itself in my view. Her hair was beautifully styled, her makeup perfectly done. But when she went to step back after presenting the prize at the end of the dock, she accidentally caught the edge of the platform and went tumbling into the water.

I could still feel the way my heart had crawled into my throat, every second until she resurfaced like an eternity. I even stepped forward to run into the lake myself from my spot on shore, but my fellow recruits in the training program held me back.

When she broke the surface again, the men on the dock pulled her back up, everyone breaking into relieved applause to see the Lota still safe and sound, but I found it even harder to breathe than before. Her once-flowing yellow dress, now damp, clung to every new curve of her body, the fabric almost see-through and revealing the clear outline of the lacy garments she wore beneath it. With her hair slicked back and the powder on her face gone, she looked somehow even more beautiful.

Up until that moment, I'd still only seen her as the angel I first imagined her to be, but in that moment, she became real to me.

"My father was furious," she added, her eyes casting downwards. "He said I'd made a spectacle of myself."

"You did," I agreed and when her eyes snapped back up in indignation, I smiled softly at her. "The most beautiful spectacle I'd ever seen. And you didn't look embarrassed, if that helps. You handled it so well, it didn't seem awkward at all."

She'd made a joke I'd been too far away to hear, but from the way the men on the dock all laughed and relaxed, I could tell she'd said something to set them all at ease. It was a skill I'd seen her use many more times since then, but that was the first time I saw the diplomat she would become.

"After that, I stopped going to pack events to see you," I confessed. "Not because I admired you any less, but because once I saw you as an actual person, not some kind of demi-god, I realized my aunt had been right all those years before. We might live in the same pack, but I would never really know you, and it hurt less when I didn't think about it. I didn't see you for months after that, not until the night of your birthday."

"When we found out we were mates," she whispered, and I nodded solemnly, hoping she could understand, even just a little, why that moment had been so momentous for me. It wasn't just finding my mate, it was that *she* was my mate, the woman I'd watched growing up from afar and never dared to dream would ever look my way. She was *mine*.

Until she wasn't.

Until I had to let her go.

And that was why, even after the intimacy we'd just shared, I needed to hear her say the words. I needed her to tell me that there was still some hope that someday, we might share more than that.

That she would claim me as hers, since I always had been.

Chapter Twenty-Eight

~**Amanda**~

Listening to Troy recount episodes from my past from his viewpoint felt a bit like seeing myself through a funhouse mirror: the events were recognizable, but distorted from my own recollection.

He was right that I hadn't seen him wave back to me on the balcony. My attention had been focused on the large group of children my own age, the ones who got to run around and play without me. Similarly, I hadn't noticed anyone on the lakeshore who looked concerned for my safety when I fell in the water after the canoe race. Everywhere I looked, I only saw people trying not to laugh. Several of them failed.

For me, those moments had been framed by the weight of my father's expectations and the narrow role he'd defined for me. When I looked out over the crowd, I envied the anonymity they had, the ability to blend in and go about their day without having each movement scrutinized.

But over time, as I took on more responsibility within the pack and got to interact with others at all levels of our society, I came to understand that while our challenges might be different, no one had it easy. And with each glimpse into his own past that Troy shared with me, my empathy for him grew.

Time and time again, he'd been confronted with his supposed lack of worth. His aunt had driven it home in dozens of little ways, I could tell just by reading between the lines of the things he'd told me. And my father? Well, my father had stated it outright, accusing him of wanting to use our connection for his own benefit, since he clearly didn't matter on his own.

Time and time again, people had underestimated him. Failed to see his potential.

But not the goddess. When she matched us, she must have seen something in him that others had failed to.

Or perhaps she saw something in *me* that no one else did.

Maybe she saw that I needed someone who would be strong enough to suffer the indignities my father dished out, loyal enough to protect me even when he couldn't claim me, and patient enough to wait for me when faced with what seemed like impossible odds.

Maybe she knew that those traits would impress me far more than any bloodline or rank ever could.

"What would you have done if that day had gone differently?" I asked him, casting my mind back to the morning after my 18th birthday when I'd hurried down to my father's office to talk to him, only to have my heart broken. "If we'd been able to talk to my father together, like I wanted, and if he'd agreed to our mating, what would have happened next?"

Troy's expression softens into wistfulness, his lips caught in a tug-of-war between a smile and a frown. "I would have asked to see your room."

I let out a soft snort. "Typical man."

His smile won the fight, mischievousness sparking in his pale brown eyes. "Not for that, although sex definitely would have been on the agenda for that day. A lot of it."

The way he stated it, calm and certain after the orgasm he'd just given me with his tongue, made my limbs go weak. I didn't doubt for a second that he meant it.

"First, though, I would have wanted to know more about you, and I have a feeling that your bedroom would have been the best place to start then. See what book you were reading. What you chose to put on your walls, and what keepsakes you held onto. I would have asked you to tell me about each of them so that through them, I could start to know *you*. Not the angel. Not the Lota. Just Amanda."

Damn it. How did he know exactly the right thing to say?

All the men my father considered mating me to never bothered to actually get to know me. They were more concerned with how I could benefit them, and although I had come to accept the transactional nature of an arranged mating, it still stung when our conversations inevitably settled around *their* ambitions and needs rather than mine.

When Vaughan came to pick me up and take me back to his pack, he never asked to see my room. He never asked much about me at all, even before he met his fated mate upon our return.

"Where did you live? Back then, I mean."

His big shoulders lifted in a shrug. "Same place I do now: the border team barracks. I moved in there after I completed my training. Before that was the training barracks."

"Do you have your own room?"

"Now I do, as captain. Back then, I had a bunk in a shared room, same as in training. So, if we were going to have sex that day, it would have been in your room."

His grin, half-goofy and half-smoldering, had me smiling back out of instinct. "I've never shared a room with anyone. It must have been an adjustment for you coming from your aunt's house. I assume you had your own room there."

The way his lips pulled a little tighter let me know my assumption had been inaccurate even before he said the words. "Well, I slept on the couch and no one else was in the room, so I guess that counts as my own room?"

"You slept on the couch? The whole time you were growing up?"

He looked down, which he only ever did when talking about his past, I'd noticed. Whenever we talked about me, he stared straight at me as if he were drinking in every word, afraid of missing a drop, but when the subject shifted to him, he avoided my gaze, as if the emotion I might see in those expressive eyes of his would betray him.

"It was quite comfortable when I was little. When I got taller, it suited me less. By the time I signed up for training, moving to the barracks felt like luxury."

Based on the way he didn't even fit in the bed we were on now, I couldn't imagine him trying to sleep comfortably on a sofa.

"I have money saved up, though," he added, his tone turning slightly defensive. "Now, I mean. I've put aside most of what I've earned since I started working. I could buy a house. It just doesn't make sense when it's only me. The barracks suit me fine."

I heard the words he didn't say: he didn't need me to house him or provide for him. If we were to accept each other now, he would move into the pack house, naturally, but he didn't *need* to. What he wanted from me went far beyond the material benefits being my mate would bring.

Something was missing in that equation, though. "What are you saving the money for?"

If he'd put all the money he earned away rather than buying a house, and he knew that if we somehow ended up together, he wouldn't need to buy one for me, what did he plan to do with it?

His eyes slid away again, avoiding putting his vulnerability on display. "I wanted to have enough saved up that if the opportunity ever came up again to defy your father and take you away, I would be in a better position to protect you."

Fuck. Tears stung at the corner of my eyes, sharp and uncomfortable. "Is there anything you've done in the past seven years that *wasn't* about me?"

Slowly, his eyes raised, trailing over my body in a way that sent heat spreading to every extremity, until our gazes locked. "Not a damn thing."

The bond tugged at my chest, pulling me towards him, and he leaned forward in perfect sync. Our noses brushed, my eyes closing at the delicious sparks that lit up my skin, and his soft breath whispered across my lips.

Earlier, we gave each other pleasure, but it had been almost entirely physical. Quenching a need, giving in to temptation. This felt different as I inhaled his scent, held my breath, and kissed my mate for the very first time.

Chapter Twenty-Nine

~Troy~

If having Amanda sit on my face had been heaven, I didn't know what to call the way I felt when she kissed me. It felt just as good but more grounded somehow, more deeply rooted, like vines were digging beneath my skin and tying the two of us together.

She tasted even better than she smelled, and her scent had always been mouth-watering. With every soft press of her lips and every tentative swipe of her tongue, I simultaneously wanted to savour each second and devour her whole.

I'd kissed other women before, but I'd never had a kiss like this.

In the back of my mind, a little voice tried to remind me that we still hadn't fully defined what any of this meant, but deep down, I didn't care enough to stop. If she only gave me that night, I would rather have it than nothing at all.

But more than that, I didn't think Amanda would toy with me that way. She knew how I felt, she knew what I'd been through over the last seven years, and though she might not have said the words, her kiss felt like an answer anyway.

An answer that said *I see you.*

I want you.

And even if that wasn't quite *I accept you* or *I love you*, for now, it was enough.

Her soft lips moved from mine to trace a line down my jaw and onto my neck, sending a shiver of pure pleasure through me. How could such a light touch feel so fucking good?

When she reached the neckline of my black uniform shirt, she paused. "Can you take this off?"

Almost before she finished speaking, I had the hem of the shirt gripped tight in my hand, ripping it over my head without a moment's hesitation. Amanda's giggle lit up the whole room, filling it with lightness and joy. She so rarely giggled, at least not when I was around. Around others, her laugh was always controlled. Polite. But as my shirt flew across the room, her shoulders shook with amusement, and my chest swelled with satisfaction.

I wanted to hear that laugh every day for the rest of my life.

Her eyes still dancing as they held my gaze, she leaned forward to place a kiss on my bare shoulder. A groan rumbled in my chest, the sparks from the touch of her lips on my skin stoking my growing need higher with each passing second. My cock hardened, demanding attention, but I ignored it to watch her move in a lazy line across my shoulder and down to my pecs, leaving a trail of light kisses and licks in her wake.

In all the times I'd imagined what being with her would be like, my fantasies centred primarily around the pleasure I would give her. I didn't spend much time picturing her exploring *my* body, but now that we were actually there, it didn't seem strange at all. Of course she would be a little dominant; Alpha blood ran through her veins, giving her a natural authority. Pack instinct willed me to submit to her while my mate instinct urged me to take control. The twin desires pushed and pulled against each other, leaving me on edge and utterly at her mercy.

Thankfully, once she'd completed a full traverse of my torso, she sat back up and arched an eyebrow at me. "Do you want a turn?"

"Fuck, yes."

My throaty growl earned me another smile, and I hardly dared to breathe as she reached down to unbutton the pretty blouse she wore. Inch by inch, her delicate skin came into view, along with the lacy black bra that matched the panties she wore. My mouth watered once again as she pulled the shirt off entirely and leaned back in open invitation.

I wasted no time diving in. My tongue found the hollow at her collarbone, licking a wide circle before my teeth nipped at her skin. Her soft sigh drove me on further, laying wet, hungry kisses downwards until I reached the swell of her perfect breasts. I kissed her over the bra first, my teeth finding her already peaked nipple through the fabric. When she gasped in surprise, my fingers slid beneath the fabric and pulled it down, exposing the pretty pink bud to me so I could suck it into my mouth completely.

"Troy." She moaned my name as her thighs pressed together, her body shifting on the bed and the scent of her arousal in the air growing stronger.

So much for taking things slow. The sounds and smell and taste of her were too much, and before I even knew what I meant to do, I had the zipper of her pants pulled down and my hand plunged between her legs, beneath the damp panties there and straight to her clit.

With another growl, I switched to her other breast, sucking and licking the nipple while my fingers rubbed at her clit. Amanda's head fell back, her hips pressing forward to grind against my hand, responding to my eager pace with equal urgency.

"Oh, fuck," she gasped, one hand knotting in my hair and pressing my face even harder against her breast. "That's... so good. The sparks... you... fuck!"

Her body contracted with her orgasm, her back arching and her thighs tightening around my hand. I eased the pressure but kept rubbing her through a small wave of aftershocks, her body vibrating with residual pleasure.

"Amanda." My voice seemed to have dropped an octave as I rasped her name. "I want to be inside you so fucking bad."

I didn't phrase it as a question, but I knew she'd hear the unspoken query anyway. I didn't carry condoms with me, because why the hell would I? On top of that, everyone knew mated pairs were more fertile. I had no idea if she used any kind of birth control, so the decision about whether or not we went any further that night rested entirely with her.

To my immense relief, her gorgeous brown eyes met mine with steely resolve. "I want that too. We don't need to worry; I'm taken care of."

Thank the fucking goddess.

Almost as fast as I'd gotten rid of my shirt, I stood up and ripped off the rest of my clothes. There was no giggle from Amanda this time, just a hurried shimmy as she pulled her pants the rest of the way down, kicking off her shoes once again. When I turned back to her, we were both fully naked, and despite the driving desire that made it difficult to think with anything but my cock, I took a moment to simply admire the incredible work of art in front of me.

She was flawless. Soft and curvy, her skin smooth and waxed, her inner thighs glistening with her wetness and her nipples still pebbled and taut. Her hair, usually so carefully styled, had pulled loose, strands curling over her bare shoulders. Pink flushed her cheeks and her eyes flared with need.

I couldn't imagine anything more beautiful.

"I hate this bed," I grumbled by way of apology as I sat back down. I would have loved to be on top, to let her lie back and lose herself while I ravished her, but it simply wouldn't work in the space we had. Instead, I reached over and pulled her on top of me, twisting her body so that she faced me, her thighs straddling my pelvis. When she sat down, her wet pussy sliding against my hard cock, we both moaned.

No, it wasn't the way I'd imagined it, but it was still perfect, and when she lifted her hips and reached between us to grab hold of me, lining me up to her entrance, the world seemed to stop.

And when she sank down on top of me, taking me inside her for the first time, my life was finally complete.

Chapter Thirty

~Amanda~

I couldn't stop the moan that rattled from my throat when I slid down onto Troy's thick, hard cock. I didn't *want* to stop it. For the first time in my life, I wanted to throw propriety to the wind and give into the primal instincts coursing inside me.

Because this wasn't any man. This was my *mate.*

My mate inside me, and nothing in the world had ever felt so right.

It looked like he agreed, since Troy's head fell back as I slowly pushed myself back up on my knees, my inner walls stroking along his full length until only the tip of him remained inside me. When I let myself fall down again, slamming onto his lap, he muttered a curse, his arms tightening around me to hold me in place.

"Fuck, that feels too good. You're going to make me come in about two seconds if you keep doing that."

My fingers ran through his short hair, my nails scraping lightly against his scalp. "Is that a challenge?"

He lifted his head to find me smiling at him, and groaned. "Make that one second. Your smile could set me off on its own."

Funnily enough, I didn't think he was lying.

"Guess it's a good thing werewolves have such a quick recovery time, then," I consoled him before I raised and lowered my body on his cock again, harder and faster than the first time.

In truth, it took more like thirty seconds until he lost control, but I didn't mind. Seeing him mindless with pleasure beneath me sent a thrill of power surging through me. I didn't stop my movements when he came, especially since he stayed hard afterwards, his body almost immediately beginning the build to a second orgasm. Thank the goddess for werewolves' healing ability.

Not that he let me have *all* the fun. As soon as he regained full awareness, his fingers slid between us and found my clit, rubbing me in just the right way while I rode him. Sparks sizzled along my skin and deep into my core, the pleasure building higher and harder than I had ever experienced before, and when I tumbled over the peak of my own orgasm, he was right there with me.

The next time started slower, more sensually, punctuated by deep, lingering kisses and fingers trailing across all of our exposed skin, until eventually need took over and he held me tight by my waist as his hips thrust off the bed, his cock pumping into me hard enough that I saw stars when I came a second time.

By the time I finally crawled off of him, a little sore but perfectly sated, his cum dripped down my thighs and a thin layer of sweat covered us both.

"I could do that all night," Troy confessed, his smile dazed and satisfied, and his half-hard cock suggesting that wasn't entirely a lie. "But you need to rest. We don't know what tomorrow will bring."

"I don't want to think about that right now," I murmured, sounding exactly like the spoiled princess people often saw me as, and Troy laughed.

"Good. You don't have to. Come on."

With a tenderness that warmed my heart, he helped me to the tiny bathroom in the bunker, cleaned me up with a warm washcloth, and found me some clean, loose-fitting clothes to sleep in. I tried to reach out to Cinder in my head to see how my wolf felt about all this, but she didn't reply. She must have gone into the same lust-drunk post-coital state I had. All I wanted was to curl up in my mate's arms and sleep for the next week.

Unfortunately, when Troy walked me back to the small bed and got me settled beneath the covers, I was quickly reminded that wouldn't be possible.

"There has to be a way for you to sleep too," I said, punctuating the sentence with a long yawn. "What if you lie down first and I get on top of you?"

He chuckled, his light brown eyes shining with a light I'd never seen in them before. Or maybe only once before, that night in the moonlight when we first met. "With you on top of me, sleep would be the last thing on my mind. Don't worry about me. I've had plenty of training to prepare me for way less comfortable situations than this. My priority is taking care of you."

When was the last time I'd felt like someone's priority? I honestly couldn't remember, but once again, I believed that audacious statement to be true.

"Wake me after a few hours and we can switch places," I instructed, but my voice held none of its Alpha authority. My heavy eyelids closed and I fell asleep wrapped in the warm certainty that someone really did have my best interests at heart.

The smell of coffee woke me up some time later, though with the lack of natural light in the bunker, I had no idea how long I'd slept. Raising my head from the pillow, I could see Troy's large frame in the small kitchen space, steam rising from the recently boiled kettle and two mugs that sat on the narrow counter.

"What time is it?"

His head snapped up at the sound of my voice and even in the dim lighting, I could see the circles under his eyes. He clearly hadn't slept at all. "Nearly eight. I expect the Beta to return soon."

Eight? That meant I'd slept for at least nine hours, and I couldn't remember the last time I'd slept so long or so deeply.

It's because he fucked you to sleep, Cinder hummed in my head, sounding rather well-rested herself.

Charming, Cin.

She might have a point, though. Maybe my good sleep owed itself to the way the ache in my chest had eased, the ache caused by my unfulfilled mate bond. The ache that had been my constant companion for the past seven years. It wouldn't vanish entirely until we marked each other, but after our physical union the night before, it seemed temporarily satisfied. On a scale of one to ten, it barely registered.

"You were supposed to wake me up," I reminded him as I swung my legs over the side of the bed and stretched my arms over my head. For such an uncomfortable bed, I felt remarkably refreshed after the night in it.

Troy ignored that comment, stepping out from behind the counter to hand me one of the mugs. "Have a drink and then go use the bathroom to get ready. I'll make something for breakfast."

I wanted to protest, to tell him that I could take care of us since he'd spent the whole night watching over me, but he was right that Savannah would be on her way any moment. The real world called us back and I had to be ready to answer.

I redressed in the previous day's clothes, fixing my hair and makeup the best I could with the limited supplies available, and returned to the main room to find toast and scrambled eggs waiting.

"There are eggs in the pantry here?" I asked in surprise.

"Powdered eggs," Troy explained, wrinkling his nose. "Not great, but better than nothing."

He said nothing about what happened between us the night before and I didn't either, unsure of exactly *what* to say. Were we together now? Did I want to be? Should we put our relationship situation on hold until the rest of our current mess got sorted out?

Unsure where to begin, I simply took the plate he offered me and we both took a seat on the bed again, a bed that he'd already remade with military precision.

We had just taken our first bites when a buzzing sound rang out in the small space. Troy placed his plate back on the counter and walked to the door, entering the code to open it to our visitor. Unsurprisingly, Savannah was the one to burst through the door as soon as it was open.

"I'm here to spring you out!" she announced triumphantly, buzzing with energy. She'd clearly already had her morning coffee. "Jasper has two wolves under arrest back at the pack house, the guards want to run their defense plans by you, Kalo wants to know what your second wish is and Leo's calling every five minutes to see what you want him to do. Come on, we can get you a decent breakfast back at the house."

She snatched the plate from my hands before I could protest, tossing Troy's efforts into the trash, as if nothing that had happened during our short lockdown together mattered anymore.

That wasn't the case though. It mattered a great deal, and I needed to figure out exactly how much my world had shifted before Troy and I addressed the subject of our future together.

First, however, I had a pack to run.

Squaring my shoulders, I got to my feet and followed Savannah out of the bunker, back to all my responsibilities and problems, with Troy keeping watch at my back.

Chapter Thirty-One

~**Troy**~

I was a coward.

Nothing else explained why I didn't press Amanda for an answer on how she felt about us after our night together in the bunker. I had the opportunity when she woke up looking well-rested and satisfied, easily the most beautiful sight I'd ever seen. I could have asked her while she got ready and I made us breakfast, before the real world crashed back in.

But as I kept watch all night, my imagination went into overdrive. The bunker's emergency lights cast long, wavering shadows on the walls, painting Amanda's face in a soft, golden glow. Her breathing was slow and steady, her lips slightly parted, and every rise and fall of her chest felt like both a promise of what could be and a reminder of the destruction she could wreak on me with just a few words.

I'd spent years pretending I could live without her, convincing myself I didn't need what I knew I'd never have.

Last night shattered that illusion.

The thought of losing her after having a taste of everything I'd ever wanted felt like tearing open my own ribs and exposing the raw, beating heart beneath. I'd rather live in hope a little longer than face the possibility that she might not feel the same.

So, I didn't ask. I let the moment pass me by, and as we walked back to the pack house with Savannah keeping up a steady stream of chatter about what we'd missed overnight and what Amanda would be required to do that day, I kept my eyes and ears trained for any sign of danger, and my feelings shoved tightly down into the box where I'd kept them locked up for the past seven years.

For now, I would focus on keeping her safe, protecting the territory, and helping her find a way to navigate the bargain with Kalo.

When all that was finished, maybe I'd find the courage I lacked and ask her for the commitment I was dying to make.

Security had been increased around the pack house, I was glad to see, and everyone seemed on edge. With communications down and the possibility of an attack looming over us, it made sense that tensions ran high. However, I didn't miss the relief in the eyes of the people we passed when they saw their Alpha safe and sound, and I hoped Amanda saw it too.

A lot of people believed in her and were happy that she was the Alpha. They wanted her to succeed. She needed to remember that whenever the negative voices got too loud.

In her office, Jasper sat at the meeting table with maps and documents laid out in front of him. The scent of fresh coffee filled the air, much better-smelling than the instant stuff I'd prepared in the bunker, and Amanda poured herself a cup before turning to me.

"Do you want one, or do you want to get some rest?"

That was a positive sign. She'd never offered me a drink before.

"I'll take a cup, please."

Even though she'd offered it, her lips pursed in disapproval at my response. "You should sleep."

"I'll sleep when we're all safe."

Letting the matter drop, she poured another cup and handed it to me. Sparks flickered where our fingers brushed, and I caught the ghost of a smile on her lips before she took a seat at the table next to Jasper.

Savannah's eyes darted back and forth between the two of us during the short exchange, narrowing on me as she sank into the seat across from Amanda. "What happened between you two last night? You're both acting... different."

Amanda ignored the question as she leaned over one of the maps on the table. "These are the locations of the attacking packs?"

Jasper nodded. "That's right. Leo and his men from the Crimsontooth pack flew some drones over the area last night and got the intel for us."

While he pointed out the camps and their estimated numbers, I slowly circled the perimeter of Amanda's office. The air felt heavier than it had the day before, charged somehow. A faint, almost metallic tang lingered in the air beyond the coffee's aroma. The walls, the furniture, even the soft hum of the lights seemed unchanged, yet a whisper of unease crawled over my skin.

I cut off Jasper's explanation of our would-be attackers' forces mid-sentence. "Savannah said you arrested two men last night. Who are they?"

All eyes moved to me, Savannah's narrowed while Jasper simply looked startled by the interruption. He turned to Amanda, looking for guidance on whether to answer me or continue their conversation.

I assume you have a good reason for butting in? my Alpha's voice asked inside my head, her tone a little sarcastic but not without affection.

That was new too.

I do. Sorry, but I think we should focus on that first.

She nodded at Jasper, her hand gesturing towards me. "Go ahead and answer him."

Having his orders, Jasper smoothly switched gears, pulling out two personnel files from the stack of papers in front of him and showing them to Amanda.

"Our security cameras picked up this man, Travis, one of the house security guards, letting this man, Curtis, into the house through a back entrance. Curtis doesn't have clearance to be in the house without an invitation, and even if he did, we had implemented a lockdown after you and Troy left. Everyone thought you were in your room and no one should have been going in or out unless they went through the main doors."

"What's Curtis' role in the pack?" Amanda asked, picking up the photo of the man and studying it closely.

"He works in the medical centre and had two syringes on him, filled with an unidentified liquid. So far, he's refused to tell us what they are or why he had them."

My chest tightened at the thought of anyone attempting to inject Amanda with something, and Savannah's scowl indicated she felt the same, especially after her own recent brush with medical experimentation.

"I'd be happy if I never saw another needle again," she declared.

"Who are they working for?" I pressed. "If they were trying to get to the Alpha, whose orders are they following?"

Jasper gave me a frustrated shrug. "We don't have those answers yet. My team is interrogating both men but they're not giving up much. It confirms there *is* someone plotting against the Alpha though, at least as far I'm concerned."

It proved it to me too, and to say I didn't like it would be a huge understatement. I continued to prowl the room, sniffing and scanning everything my eyes fell on, searching for the source of my uneasiness.

"Is there a connection between them and the person you caught trying to make an external call? What do they have in common?"

"I actually might have the answer to that," Savannah volunteered, and based on the intrigued look Jasper gave her, that came as news to him too. "I was searching through the former Beta's records this morning, and I found payments made from his expense account to all three of these men, plus a few others. I think they were working for him unofficially."

"Informants?" Jasper wondered aloud.

"Maybe," Savannah agreed. "Or just doing tasks he didn't want recorded under his official records."

My eyes moved to Amanda who had been listening carefully while reviewing the information in the men's files. "Does the former Beta have reason to move against you?"

She huffed out a frustrated sigh. "Well, he quit when I assumed the role, so he's definitely not a fan of mine. And I know over the years he made some attempts to have his son named as my father's heir if I mated into another pack, but my father always resisted."

That sounded like a hell of a motive to me. "So, with your father gone, if you were removed too, his son would be next-in-line?"

"In his mind, perhaps."

"And maybe some of the other, more traditional members of the pack," Jasper suggested, giving me a nod of approval. "It's a good place to start. I'll bring the former Beta in for questioning."

As my thoughts lingered on the man who had held the Beta role for my whole life, my eyes moved to the wall that separated his former office, now Savannah's, from the room we sat in, and that was when I saw it.

A flicker of movement, and the thing that was different.

A small hole in the wall that I'd never noticed before, and the small cylinder that protruded through it.

The barrel of a gun, aimed straight at the back of Amanda's head.

Time collapsed. One moment, I was processing the tiny gleam of metal; the next, my body was already in motion. My pulse pounded in my ears, a war drum with only one message: *Protect her. Keep her safe.*

"Troy, what are you..." she started to ask, but before she could get the question out, a sharp crack rang out through the room and something hot and sharp and heavy sank deep into my chest.

Chapter Thirty-Two

~Amanda~

"Get down!"

Before I could react to the order or the loud bang that preceded it, Jasper yanked me off my chair, throwing me to the ground and beneath the table. My breath hitched as I hit the hard floor, the force of the movement jarring my ribs. Savannah joined me from the other side, her eyes wide, as Jasper shielded my body with his own.

"That didn't come from the window or the door," he panted. "Where the hell are they?"

A sickening realization slammed into me. "The walls. There's a secret passage from this room. Someone must be in the passage."

My father designed it that way when he had the current pack house built thirty years earlier. Most of the house was connected with a narrow passage between the walls of each room, kept secret from all but those with the highest clearance.

When I helped Jasper and Savannah against Kyle a few weeks earlier, we made use of those same passages, so he immediately understood what I meant.

"Where's the entrance from this room?"

"Next to the fire. There's a switch behind the portrait of the first Alpha."

"Got it. Stay here."

With that, he dashed away to give chase to our would-be assailant while Savannah called after him to be careful. My breath came in shallow pants, my entire body coiled so tight I thought I might snap.

Someone had just tried to kill me. Inside my own office, a place that should have been safe. My pulse roared in my ears, drowning out everything else... until I saw *him.*

A body lay sprawled on the floor, face-down and motionless.

Troy.

My stomach plummeted, the world tilting around me as my brain connected the dots. He bolted forward just before the noise, practically leaping from where he stood to the spot directly behind me. He saw something. He tried to protect me.

No. *No, no, no.*

I scrambled forward, still on my hands and knees, but Savannah's hand clamped down on my shoulder. "Jasper said to stay here. You might still be in danger. I'll go."

To hell with that. "He's my mate. Let go."

Cinder's authority infused my words, merging with my own, and Savannah's hand immediately dropped as she blinked over at me in surprise. I'd have to explain it to her later, but for now, I could barely breathe past the crushing weight on my chest.

"Troy?" I croaked, my throat raw as I reached him. "What happened?"

His head was turned away, his face obscured, but when I placed a trembling hand on his shoulder, he groaned, a soft, pained sound that sent ice down my spine. He moved slightly, just enough to turn his face toward me, and my breath caught.

His skin had gone pale, the color drained from his lips, his expression unnervingly slack.

"You're okay," he breathed out, his voice weak but filled with relief.

A sharp pang of fear shot through me. "I'm fine. What's the matter with you?"

I tried to turn him but could barely budge his solid frame. His body felt limp and unresponsive, and I made no progress until Savannah appeared beside me, helping to roll him onto his back. He landed with another groan.

Immediately, my eyes dropped to the dark spot on his black t-shirt, a thick, spreading stain. My fingers instinctively went to the spot, and when I lifted them, they came away red.

My stomach twisted violently and the world blurred at the edges.

"Get a doctor, now!" I ordered Savannah. She didn't hesitate, her eyes clouding over as she put out the call. My hands pressed down on his chest, desperately trying to stem the flow of blood, but it kept coming, warm and thick between my fingers. The metallic scent of his blood stung my nose. His pale eyes locked onto mine, heavy-lidded with something I couldn't name. "Is it silver? Does it burn?"

His head moved an inch downward in a barely perceptible nod. "Silver, yes. Doesn't burn. It's... numb."

Fuck. That didn't sound good at all. Not only was he losing blood, the bullet doing who knew what to his internal organs, but the silver could be leaching into his bloodstream, weakening him more by the second. Werewolves had incredible healing ability, but the silver would prevent it. That bullet needed to come out of him. *Now.*

We might not be able to wait for the doctor.

"Get me Kalo!" I barked at Savannah and she bolted from the room without question or comment, confirming she saw the severity of the situation as well as I did.

That didn't make me feel any better.

When I looked back down, Troy's eyes remained fixed on me, still with that odd, wistful expression. "Thank you. For last night," he whispered. "I'm glad we... had that."

The words sent a spear through my heart.

No. We were not saying goodbye. Not now.

"It won't be the last night. I promise," I choked out, my voice shaking as I pressed harder against his chest.

A faint, ghost of a smile touched his lips, but just as quickly, it vanished. His beautiful brown eyes dulled, his gaze turning unfocused, as if he were staring at something past me.

"Troy?"

My voice cracked as I pushed down harder with my hands. My fingers turned white from the pressure.

"Troy! Look at me."

My plea echoed through the room as agony erupted in my chest, white-hot and all-consuming.

This wasn't the dull ache of our incomplete bond. Something ripped through my chest, shattering and exploding inside me. A raw, primal scream tore from my throat, a sound that I'd never made or even heard before.

"Alpha!" Strong hands gripped my shoulders, trying to pull me back. "Where are you hurt?"

I blinked through the haze of agony and found the doctor kneeling beside me. "Not me. I'm okay. He's been shot. The bullet is silver; it needs to come out."

The room spun as more people flooded in, cutting open Troy's shirt to get to the wound underneath.

So much blood.

So little movement.

"We have no pulse," someone said.

No.

"Get the bullet out!" I repeated, Cinder's agony joining mine in a guttural growl. "He'll heal if the bullet comes out."

The doctor's grimace felt like another tear across my heart, but he nodded at the paramedics with him. "Start CPR. We'll move him to the operating room."

They obeyed, one beginning rhythmic compressions on Troy's chest while the others prepared him to move, but I could read it in all their faces. My body said the same thing.

He was already gone.

At last, Savannah blew back through the door, physically dragging Kalo behind her. The genie's golden eyes quickly surveyed the scene in front of him, understanding dawning immediately, before they landed on me.

In three smooth strides, he was at my side. "What do you wish?"

My hands clenched into fists. "Bring him back. Now."

His grimace reminded me of the doctor's. "It's not that easy. Some things are beyond even magic. If he's truly dead…"

But he's not, Cinder howled in my head. *He can still heal. He's strong. He'll fight.*

She was right. We just needed that damn bullet out.

"I wish for you to remove the bullet from his chest. Take it out and he'll heal himself."

Kalo bowed his head, and just like before, a warm glow began to build between his hands. Energy crackled in the air, stealing all the breath from my lungs as I waited, before erupting around us.

I felt no rush of power this time, no dreams of glory.

Only desperation.

It had to work. *It had to.*

I crawled back to Troy's side, pulling back the hands of the paramedic performing CPR, and sure enough, a moment later, a silver cylinder bubbled up out of the open wound. I snatched it from his skin, ignoring the way silver burned my skin, and tossed it away.

"Start the compressions again," I ordered the paramedic. "Don't stop until I say so."

His eyes flicked to the doctor but he didn't contradict his Alpha as he resumed his movements, pressing down on Troy's chest to keep the blood moving through his body.

This time, I felt it. With each pump of his hands, the pain in my chest receded. The broken bond began to stitch itself back together until it pulled taut, and Troy's chest rose with an inhale.

"We have a pulse," one of the paramedics breathed.

A sob tore from me, relief and fear and all the emotions of the last few minutes escaping in one desperate exhalation. Colour began to return to Troy's face, and I glanced back over my shoulder at Kalo with a whispered, "Thank you."

He nodded in acknowledgement but worry lined his brow and tight lips, and it took me a moment to realize why.

I only had one wish left, a wish he wanted me to use to undo every wish made before. But now that my wish had saved my mate's life, how could I possibly wish it undone?

Chapter Thirty-Three

~Troy~

One moment, I could have sworn I was dying. The next, something hard pushed against my chest and the numbness that followed the silver bullet lodging in my heart disappeared.

Now, everything fucking hurt.

"Troy." Amanda's hands cupped my face, sending a pleasant tingle of sparks across my skin that helped to ease my discomfort, at least a little. Even if she hadn't spoken, I would have known the touch came from her. Nothing had ever felt as good as her hands on me did. "Can you hear me?"

"I hear you." My tongue felt heavy, the words ill-formed, but she didn't seem to care. Her fingers trembled against my face as she rested her forehead against mine and I never wanted the moment to end.

But someone else spoke up, a voice I didn't recognize. "Alpha, we should take him to the hospital and monitor his recovery there."

"No," I pushed out, doing my best to ignore the pain in my chest. I still had no idea how I survived but I knew one thing for certain: I wasn't going anywhere while someone was trying to kill my mate. "No hospital. I'm okay."

"You are most certainly not okay," Amanda contradicted, and for a moment, I feared she would actually try to send me away. "But you can recover here as well as in the hospital. Take him to the guest room at the far east end of the second floor and set a guard outside the door. Do whatever you need to make sure he's stable and comfortable and I'll be there shortly."

My hand reached blindly for hers. I still hadn't managed to force my eyes open. Thankfully, she found me instead, her soft hand slipping into the grip of my rougher one. "I'm not leaving you."

"Yes, you are," she replied, overruling me again. "You're no good to me right now anyway."

The words could have been harsh if spoken in her usual businesslike Alpha tone, but a vulnerability seeped through them instead, robbing them of any sharp edges. It only hit me then that she must have believed I was dying as much as I did, and her sending me away now wasn't meant to be a punishment.

It was fuelled by fear.

Her breath skated over my cheek as she leaned closer. "I'll be there soon, I promise. I just need to deal with a couple of things and then we'll regroup and come up with a plan. Will you go along with them quietly, please? For me?"

There was no way I could say no to that.

More voices appeared on my other side, and solid hands lifted me off the ground and onto some kind of stretcher. The bumpy movement as they carried me through the pack house stirred up a wave of nausea to go with each jolt of pain, but the stinging meant healing, so I gritted my teeth and bore it without complaint.

In the room, I finally managed to crack open my eyes while two of the pack's paramedics moved me onto the queen-sized bed. My shirt had been cut away and blood smeared across my chest above the wound where the bullet must have gone in.

How did it come out, though? No pain on my back suggested I had no exit wound, and the rapidly healing hole in my chest wasn't big enough for the medical team to have gone in to extract it. But it *was* gone. I wouldn't still be drawing breath otherwise.

A doctor followed behind the two paramedics and began checking me over while I resisted the urge to scratch at the itchy, healing wound. "You're healing very fast," he noted, frowning down at the blood pressure monitor in his hand. "Faster than I would expect in these circumstances. Do you have any ranked-wolf blood?"

"Not that I know of." I'd never seen this particular doctor before and didn't feel like getting into my family background with him when I had more pressing questions. "How did you get the bullet out?"

He let out a soft snort. "You'll have to ask the Alpha about that. I'm not entirely sure what happened."

What the hell did that mean?

"I'm going to give you a mild sedative," he continued, pulling a small bottle of pills from his bag. "It will help you sleep and you'll heal even faster."

"You just said I'm healing fine," I protested. "I don't want to sleep."

You need to, though, Hunter said inside my head, speaking up for the first time since the gunshot. Silver affected him even more than me, and I was glad to hear his voice, even if it sounded a little weaker than usual. *You didn't sleep all night and you just got shot. How can we be at our best when Amanda needs us if we're exhausted?*

I hated when he was right.

Reluctantly, I took the pills the doctor offered and swallowed them down. One of the paramedics cleaned my chest and placed a bandage over the already-healing wound, and the other one pasted some electrodes to my chest to monitor my heart while I slept. I kept my eyes open as long as I could, clinging to consciousness so I didn't miss anything important, but eventually, I couldn't fight it anymore and I let sleep take me.

When I woke, a couple of hours had passed, based on the sun's position in the sky. I noticed that first, followed quickly by Amanda's presence in the room. Her scent infused every breath I took, and my nerves were calm in the way they only were when she was near. A desk that hadn't been there when I fell asleep now sat against the far wall, and she sat behind it, facing towards me, her head bent down over an electronic device. Its light bathed her face in a warm glow, accentuated by the sunlight through the window, making her look utterly angelic.

Even more than usual.

"Hey," I croaked out, and her head immediately snapped up, her body already halfway out of her chair before her expression softened into a smile.

"Hey." She strode over to me and picked up a glass of water from the bedside table, offering it to me. "Have a drink. You sound parched."

I pulled myself up to a sitting position before taking the glass from her. The cool liquid quenched the dryness in my throat in no time, feeling almost as good as anything I'd ever put in my mouth.

Almost.

"How long have I been out?" I asked as she took the empty glass from me. My hand went to my bare chest and the bandage there. A bit of blood had soaked through, but the pain beneath it felt like little more than a scratch. The electrodes were gone; the doctors must have decided they weren't necessary.

"A couple of hours," she confirmed. "Are you still tired?"

Her hand returned to my face, just as it had in her office, and once again, the trail of sparks left by her fingertips soothed me better than any amount of rest could.

"No, I'm fine. Where's Jasper? What happened to the shooter? Did you get him? What about the former Beta? Is he..."

I started to pull the covers back as my questions multiplied, but Amanda grabbed them from me and firmly tucked them back around me. "I'll tell you everything, but only if you stay in this bed. Deal?"

She held my gaze, her blazing brown eyes daring me to contradict her, but even without her Alpha authority, I would have given in. My ability to say no to this woman was pretty much non-existent

"Deal," I grumbled, bowing my head in acceptance before I locked eyes with her again. "How are you?"

Amanda threw up her hands in exasperation. "Would you stop worrying about *me*? You're the one who almost died."

That reminded me I still had questions about that too. "Speaking of that: how am I *not* dead?"

The way her eyes immediately slid away from mine gave me a warning that I wouldn't like the answer. Still, I didn't expect the words that came out of her mouth.

"Kalo saved you. I wished for it."

For a long moment, I could only stare at her, the implications snapping into place piece by piece in my head. She had used one of her chances to wish for anything in the world to save my life. That had to mean she cared enough about me to at least want me alive, and she must have been convinced I would die in order to use her wish that way.

But Kalo had made it very clear that anything she wished for would have to be undone, or things would end badly for her.

She'd bought me a reprieve, but possibly only for a matter of days, the same way she held off the attacking packs to buy us more time.

And at the end of that time, if it came down to a choice between her life and mine, there could only be one decision. I would never let her put herself in danger to save me, and from the pain and uncertainty written across her beautiful face as she watched me put it all together, I knew that she knew it too.

"I'm going to bring Kalo in here now that you're awake," she told me, doing her best to sound in control despite the way her voice wavered. "It's time to figure out exactly what he wants and why."

Chapter Thirty-Four

I could read every expression in Troy's eyes as I filled him in on what happened. The confusion over how he survived gave way to concern over me using my second wish, and ultimately, to resignation.

A resignation that meant if he had to die to keep me safe from whatever curse the genie might put on me, he would.

But I didn't let him die that morning, and I didn't intend to do it in a couple of days either. There had to be another way. We just had to figure one out.

Only a few minutes after Troy was taken from my office earlier, Jasper returned, out of breath and harried. "I didn't catch him," he growled, clearly frustrated with himself. "As soon as I slid the door open, he ran. I could smell him, but he obviously knew his way through the passages better than I did."

Savannah threw herself into his arms, not paying any attention to the sweaty state of him. "You could have been killed! I might kill you myself if you keep risking your life that way."

Rather than pointing out the irony in that statement, I gave Jasper a nod of acknowledgement. "If you hadn't gone after him, he could have kept shooting. You saved all of us."

His eyes scanned the rest of the room, empty now other than Kalo who stood by the window, his face turned towards the sun as if trying to absorb its rays through the panes of glass. "Is Troy okay? Where is he? Why is Kalo here?"

"Troy will be fine. He's been moved upstairs to one of the rooms that's not connected to the secret passage network. I've arranged for a guard outside, so no one should be able to get to him there. Jasper, I need you to bring in the Beta, as we discussed. Along with the evidence Savannah found tying him to the men in holding, he's one of the few who would have knowledge of the hidden passages. It can't be a coincidence."

He bowed his head, separating himself from his mate's embrace. "Yes, Alpha. I'll keep you updated through mind-link if that's alright, since comms are still down."

"That's perfect. Savannah, I need you to take over my scheduled meetings for today along with keeping in touch with the team from the Crimsontooth pack. Reassure the pack as much as possible that it's business as usual."

Her curls fell in a curtain around her face as she bowed in acceptance. With my adrenaline still high from the near miss and the emotion surrounding Troy's shooting, I must have been exuding more Alpha authority than I realized. Normally, she wouldn't feel the need to bow to me. Making a conscious effort to slow my breathing, I turned to Kalo last.

"I'll need to speak with you this afternoon, once I've had a chance to review the situation outside our borders. Don't go too far."

Though he wasn't compelled to bow like the others, the genie dipped his head anyway, charming as ever. "Take the item you initially used to summon me. Say my name while touching it and I'll come to you."

Well, that made things easier. We could have saved some time that morning if I'd known I could call him at will.

Some of the staff moved a small desk into the room where Troy slept, and I set up there with the necklace to one side and my father's defensive plans on a tablet for me to review along with the map of troop positions Jasper had prepared for me. If our mole *was* the Beta, I had to assume all of our defensive tactics were compromised, so I reviewed them not with the idea of using any of them, but as a guide of what *not* to do so we could keep our enemy guessing.

When Troy woke, I abandoned that work, and now, with his blessing, I returned to my desk and picked up the necklace. "Kalo? I'm ready for you."

Not even thirty seconds later, a knock sounded at the door, and the guard in the hall poked his head in. "Alpha? There's a man here to see you."

"Let him in, please."

The genie strode in, still wearing the same clothes from the day before. Did he own any others, I wondered? Where would he keep them? Where did he live? In the stories I'd heard, genies lived inside lamps, but I summoned him with a necklace, not a lamp.

I still had a lot of questions.

Starting with this one: "What's to stop you from simply appearing in the middle of this room when I summon you? Why knock on the door?"

He shrugged in his effortlessly elegant way. "It tends to unnerve people when I appear out of nowhere. But if you'd prefer it, I can do so going forward."

I gestured towards the armchair on one side of Troy's bed. "Well, now that you're here, have a seat. I'd like to talk to you."

While he sat, I perched on the edge of the bed where I could see both men clearly.

Troy gave Kalo a grudging nod of acknowledgement. "I understand you saved my life."

"No, Amanda did that," Kalo corrected graciously. "I'm simply the tool she used."

"And you couldn't have refused?" I asked.

"Only if you asked for something impossible, such as raising someone long dead. But anything else you ask for, I'm obligated to give you. Which is why I must remind you that your final wish is of the utmost importance. Do not make it impulsively."

I heard the implication, that my other two wishes *had* been impulsive, and perhaps he was right. In the heat of the moment, I managed to stave off disaster both times with Kalo's help. Now, I needed to think long-term. Strategically.

And to do that, I needed to understand the man in front of me much better than I currently did.

"Where do you come from, Kalo? Are genies born with their abilities, like werewolves, or are you made?"

His shoulders tightened just a little, his hands clenching around the arms of the chair he sat in. "I thought you asked me here to discuss your final wish."

"I never said that." I pushed myself further back onto the bed and pulled my legs up, crossing them in front of me. Hopefully, by relaxing my own posture, I could help to set him at ease. "I'd like to talk about you."

"Wouldn't you rather…"

"The Alpha asked you a question," Troy interrupted. "I think she would rather you answer it."

It felt strange to have someone backing me up like that, but kind of nice too.

Kalo acceded with another incline of his head. "Very well. Genies are made. I'm not sure where the first one came from, but any others I've encountered were once human, as was I."

It was hard to imagine the man in front of me as human. Although he had the form of one, the same as Troy and I did, his golden eyes gave him an otherworldly air, especially when coupled with the gracefulness imbuing each movement. As a human, he must have been much more… ordinary.

"When were you human? How long ago?"

"Around 5000 years ago."

Holy shit, Troy's voice breathed in my head, like he was whispering in my ear.

Not what I expected, I had to agree.

"Where did you live?" I asked next. He didn't look like the indigenous people of this part of the world, and his answer confirmed it.

"Mesopotamia. What you now call the Middle East."

I cast my mind back over anything I'd learned about that part of the world in the time period he was talking about but came up almost entirely blank.

"So, you're immortal," Troy concluded. "And you've just been wandering around the world for 5000 years?"

Kalo's head tilted to the side, a gesture I was coming to learn meant 'no', just as his bowed head signified 'yes'. "I'm here only when I'm summoned, only for the three days it takes to complete the wishes. So, although I became a genie 5000 years ago, I have only actually experienced a handful of years in total since then."

That must be incredibly disorienting, experiencing massive leaps in time each time someone new summoned him.

Troy, however, saw a flaw in that explanation. "Wait a minute. You said you spoke to some werewolves in town the night before the Alpha summoned you, but now, you only exist when summoned?"

Kalo's head bent, showing his agreement. "I said that because it would be easier for you to understand. When I am summoned, I… know things. I'm not sure how to explain it. I can speak whatever language the person speaks, and I understand things about their life and their nature. It's part of whatever magic takes place during the summoning."

Troy posed another question before I could respond.

"Where do you go between these summonings? What happens to you?"

Kalo spread his hands in a universal gesture of uncertainty. "Your guess is as good as mine. I am simply not here. I don't feel the passage of time or space. I leave one place and arrive at another."

It sounded like a rather lonely existence to me. I knew how power could cause division, and Kalo's power exceeded anything I'd ever encountered before. "Do you have any friends?" I blurted out.

Troy's eyebrows drew together in confusion at my question, but in my mind, it was an important one.

Kalo also seemed taken aback, his eyes dropping to the floor as an almost wistful smile pulled at his lips. "No. Not for a long, long time."

"Do you like being a genie?"

Slowly, his golden eyes raised again until they locked with mine. "No. Not for a long time."

I had a feeling that would be his answer, and I also had a strong gut instinct about the next question I needed to ask.

"If I wish for all wishes to be undone, like you requested, what happens to you?"

His gaze held mine, silence filling the space between us for several long beats. He seemed to be debating his response, deciding what response to give me, but when the answer came, it carried the ring of truth. "If everything I've ever used my power on is undone, my power disappears. I will no longer be a genie."

That had to be it. The reason he so desperately wanted me to make the wish. "And you want that?"

"More than anything," he confirmed, eyes still fixed on me. "I want it to be over, and you have the power to end it. You're the one who can finally set me free."

Chapter Thirty-Five

~Troy~

Finally, we were getting somewhere with Kalo, and I had to take a moment to marvel in appreciation at my mate's tactics. I didn't know why she started asking him about friends, but it turned out to be an insightful question, leading us straight to the heart of the matter.

Kalo didn't want to be a genie anymore. That was his motivation, while ours remained protecting Amanda and the pack. With that information, we could move forward with finding a way to satisfy everyone.

Amanda didn't look ready to celebrate yet, though. Her lips pursed thoughtfully as she watched Kalo, absorbing everything he just said.

"What if I simply use my last wish to wish you free of your power?" she asked. "We wouldn't have to undo *all* the wishes."

That sounded good to me, but Kalo immediately shook his head. "It doesn't work that way. As long as any trace of my power remains in this world, I stay bound to the necklace. Someone did try it once, a couple of hundred years ago. He wished for my freedom, but when I tried to grant his wish, the magic wouldn't come. Later, I spoke to another genie and found out why. Undoing all the wishes is the only method proven to work. It's the only thing that can stop the cycle."

"And what happens to you when your power is gone?" I couldn't help wondering. "Do you become human again? Mortal?"

Kalo's hands curled into fists for just a moment before he forced them loose again. "I believe so, but to be honest, I don't know for certain. Perhaps it will kill me."

He shrugged as if it didn't matter much to him one way or the other, and Amanda's frown deepened. "Death is better than living as a genie?"

"Yes," Kalo answered without hesitation. "I have power beyond anything else I've ever experienced in this world, but I have no control over it. No control over my own destiny. Not to mention that the power is... cursed."

While he was in such a talkative mood, I wanted to know more about that as well. "The people who make wishes through you die," I summarized bluntly. "Why?"

Kalo's shoulders stiffened in a defensive reflex. "It's not intentional on my part. Something in the magic twists the final wish in ways that harm the wisher. But if you wish my power gone, it can't hurt you."

He turned back to Amanda, his eyes imploring.

"It's the only way to protect yourself. You'd be helping us both. You *must* make this wish."

I could tell she'd listened carefully to every word, but Amanda never rushed into anything. She would take her time, thinking things over and examining every angle before she made a decision.

At least, she *hardly* ever rushed into things. Using her second wish to save my life was a spur-of-the-moment decision, but what drove her to do it, I still didn't fully understand. We'd connected in new ways during our night together in the bunker, but was it love? Acceptance of our bond? Those words still lingered unspoken between us. There were moments when it felt so close, I could almost taste it, but then her guard would rise again and I'd be left wondering if I only saw what I wanted to see.

"Have you never explained this to anyone else?" she asked Kalo. "It seems logical enough to me."

Kalo raised a weary hand, waving it across the empty space in front of him as if he were conjuring memories of a past we couldn't see. "I have tried. People always think they'll be the exception. Power is addictive, and the draw of the magic is strong. You felt it too with your first wish, I know you did."

Amanda's eyes slid over to me, as if she were embarrassed to admit the truth in front of me, but I gave her a nod of encouragement. I had noticed it too, the out-of-character fixation that took hold of her after the first wish, and I didn't blame her for it.

What would I wish for if I could have anything in the world?

I didn't even need to think about it.

"I did," she agreed. "But Troy taking me away helped me to refocus, and after the second wish, I didn't feel it again. I'm clear-headed now, I'm fairly certain, and I understand what you're saying."

She paused there, her gaze moving to the window as she thought things over. Kalo and I both waited in silence for her to continue.

"I have another 48 hours to make the final wish, correct?" she asked, and Kalo nodded in agreement. "And if I make the wish you want me to, the shield over the land will disappear and Troy will die."

Her voice caught on the final word, sending a sharp stab of regret through my still-healing chest. Causing her pain was quite literally the last thing in the world I ever wanted to do, but I might not have any choice.

Kalo, however, had a slightly different interpretation. "Remember what you wished for. I didn't bring him back to life. That's outside my ability."

That was news to me. When she told me what happened, she said that she wished for him to save me. Apparently, the wording was important, so I asked her to clarify. "What was your wish?"

"I wished for him to take the bullet out of your chest," she replied slowly, considering each word as she said it. "It was making it impossible for you to heal."

My response came out just as carefully. "So, if the wish is undone, the bullet goes back into my heart."

My eyes flicked to Kalo for confirmation, and he nodded. "How fast it would kill you, I can't guess, but it wouldn't be immediate. There would be a chance for you to remove it another way."

For the first time since Amanda told me what she did, hope flickered inside me. Maybe there was a way for us both to survive this?

Amanda looked far from certain about it, though. "It all happened so fast," she whispered. Her gaze locked onto mine, but she wasn't looking at me; she was looking *through* me, back to that moment. Her lips parted as if she wanted to say something else, but no words came. Then, she swallowed hard. "It's a miracle you survived, a miracle I'm not sure the goddess will repeat."

"But it's a chance," I argued softly. "And it's the only real choice you have."

As far as I was concerned, our path was now clear. We had forty-eight hours to prepare. Two days to figure out a way to get that bullet out of my chest before it killed me. Two days to reinforce the pack's defenses before the shield fell. Two days to ensure Amanda didn't regret her choice.

Two days for me to spend with my mate, in case that was all the time we had left.

Chapter Thirty-Six

~Amanda~

"This has been very helpful," I told Kalo, my fingers grazing over the necklace I still held in my hand. Even with the genie right in front of me, the urge to touch it was strong. An ancient magic, without doubt. "You're free to go for now, and I'll call you back when I need you."

His head dipped in acknowledgement but he didn't immediately rise from his seat. "There is one other thing. The shield that you put in place around the territory will remain until either you ask me to remove it or until you wish the magic undone. However, I do have some... leeway."

Troy leaned forward curiously and I did the same, trying to read the genie's meaning in his golden eyes. He'd been forthcoming with us, and my gut instinct told me everything he'd said was true. He wanted freedom, even if it meant death. For that, he needed me. He had no reason to double-cross us. "What kind of leeway?"

"I could create a temporary opening in the shield for my own use. If something else were to slip through at the same time, it wouldn't affect your wish in any way."

Troy caught on to the implication quicker than I did. "You mean we could move reinforcements in?"

Kalo's lips curled in approval. "Precisely. If they were gathered outside your territory at a specific time and place and I happened to create an opening, it wouldn't break any magical laws."

Very interesting, Cinder murmured in my head. *If he can bend the rules for that, maybe he can do something to help Troy too.*

Perhaps. I knew I needed to think about it, but every time I imagined that moment, the sharp gasp of pain, the warmth of his blood seeping through my fingers, the way his eyes had gone unfocused, it felt like a knot tightening around my heart. Could I really watch it happen again? Could I risk losing him for good?

"Amanda?" Troy's head cocked to the side as he said my name, making it clear I'd missed something.

"Sorry. What was that?"

"I said that Savannah could ask the Crimsontooth wolves to meet us at the border along the beach. It should be far away from the attacking packs camped in the forest."

"Agreed. That's the best entry point. I'll have her make the call and we can take Kalo there to let them in."

"*I* can take Kalo there," Troy corrected. "You need to stay where it's safe."

I wanted to argue that apparently, I wasn't even safe in my own office so I might as well make myself useful, but he had a point. With at least one would-be assassin still out there, I didn't want anyone else putting themselves in danger's way on my behalf.

So, I didn't argue, agreeing to my mate's suggestion instead. "If you're feeling up to it, I'll leave you to coordinate that with Savannah."

Surprise flickered in his light brown eyes. He'd expected me to put up a fight, but when he realized I was entrusting him with this important task instead, his chest puffed with pride. "I feel absolutely fine. I'll go and find her now."

He barely spared a glance for Kalo as he sprang out of bed and headed to the door, intent on his mission.

That half-smile lingered on Kalo's lips as he watched him go. "Werewolves really do have extraordinary healing ability. Hard to believe he was practically dead just a few hours ago."

That was exactly what I wanted to focus on now that Troy was gone. "This 'leeway' you have with your magic... is there a way to use it to help Troy when the bullet returns?"

Any hopes my wolf might have planted in that regard immediately withered when I saw the regret that flashed across Kalo's face. "When the wish is undone, my magic will be gone," he reminded me. "If I'm still alive, which isn't guaranteed, I won't be able to do anything."

Damn it. That would have been too simple, I supposed. "Alright. I'll call you when we're ready to bring the others in."

This time, Kalo rose from his seat, bowed to me, and disappeared right before my eyes.

That *was* kind of unnerving.

With Savannah and Troy occupied and no news from Jasper about the former Beta's whereabouts, I reached out by mind-link to the doctor who had treated Troy earlier. *I need to speak with you as soon as you can spare the time.*

On my way, Alpha, he immediately replied.

Less than ten minutes later, the guard once again knocked on the door, admitting the doctor. I had returned to my temporary desk, and he took a seat in the same armchair that Kalo had previously sat in, leaning forward in anticipation.

"What do you need, Alpha?"

As succinctly as possible, and leaving out any talk of genies and wishes, I explained how magic had removed the bullet from Troy's chest, but that the effect was only temporary. All too soon, we were going to be facing a scenario where the bullet would return to its previous position, except now we wouldn't even have the external wound guiding the way.

When I'd completed my overview of the situation, I got to my reason for asking him there: "If we have Troy in an operating room, ready to go, will you be able to remove the bullet again before it kills him?"

The doctor leaned back in his chair, blowing out a long breath. "We'd have a good shot at it, certainly." He winced as the words came out of his mouth. "No pun intended."

My mother always said doctors had to have a dark sense of humour to survive in their chosen profession, so I didn't take any offense. "What are the odds of survival?"

The doctor hesitated before answering, and that alone sent my heart skittering. Finally, he exhaled. "It's hard to say without knowing exactly where the bullet will land, but I'd put it at fifty-fifty."

Fifty-fifty. A coin flip that might go either way. The pounding of my heart grew heavier. "Is there any way to improve those odds?"

Again, his face scrunched with discomfort at having to deliver an answer he knew I wouldn't like. "If we knew exactly where the bullet would be, then yes, but I don't have any way of knowing it. Based on his rate of healing, scans are unlikely to show anything. Even if we opened him up right now, I don't think we'd see any scarring."

Something about the way he said '*his* rate of healing' stuck out to me, as if it were different in some way to the norm. "What's special about Troy's healing?"

"It's extraordinarily quick. I asked if he had any ranked wolf blood, but he didn't think so. I haven't seen anyone in the pack heal that fast besides your father."

Interesting, Cinder chimed in again. *He doesn't know who his father is. Maybe he **does** have ranked blood.*

Anything was possible. The last day had taught me that much, if nothing else.

"I was actually going to ask him if I could run a DNA check against a new wolf genetic database," the doctor continued. "It might show if he has a connection to any of the dominant bloodlines in the area. It could be useful for him to know, but I need his permission."

It could be useful indeed, but after the conversation we had the night before about his family, I suspected Troy might not be on board. He clearly didn't have much respect for whoever his father might be, especially given his mother's disappearance, and I couldn't blame him for that.

However, if there were even the slightest chance that knowing more about his family's medical history could help keep him alive over the next few days, it needed to be explored.

"Go ahead and run the test. I'll authorize it."

The doctor bowed his head. "Certainly, Alpha. And with your permission, I'll call together some of my colleagues with the most experience in open-heart surgery, to get their perspective on the bullet extraction operation."

"Please do. I'll check in with you tomorrow. Thank you."

He got to his feet, bowing once again, and no sooner had the door closed behind him than another voice echoed in my head, this one belonging to Jasper.

I've got Beta Chad. Bringing him to the cells now.

My pulse spiked, adrenaline kicking in. Finally, something was going our way. *Excellent. I'll meet you there.*

Chapter Thirty-Seven

~**Troy**~

I found Savannah in her office with an additional guard posted outside her door. *Good.* Amanda might have been the assassin's target, but we needed to keep security tight until the situation was under control.

The Beta was on the satellite phone when I got there, but she beckoned me inside without even taking a breath. Her office was smaller than Amanda's but decorated in a similar, masculine style. Redecoration hadn't been at the top of anyone's priority list with everything else going on, but the tastes of the previous Alpha and Beta didn't suit our new leadership team at all. "That's as much as I know right now, Vaughan. I'm not keeping things from you; I simply don't know any more."

My shoulders stiffened at the Crimsontooth Alpha's name, and the motion didn't escape Savannah's attention. She shot me a knowing glance before rolling her eyes at whatever the man on the other end of the line said.

"You're the one who put Leo in charge, and he and I are handling it. Let us do our jobs and stick to doing your own!"

Although I couldn't hear his verbal response, the low rumble of his growl vibrated through the handset.

Savannah cut him off mid-sentence. "Look, someone just arrived to give me some news. I have to go."

She hung up without saying goodbye, tossed the phone onto her desk, and sat back in her seat with a sigh.

"Do you have any brothers, Troy?"

"No." I'd always thought I would have liked a sibling, or several, but this didn't seem like the best time to bring that up.

"Consider yourself lucky," she grumbled, exhaling one more time before shaking her irritation away. "Do you actually have news? I just said that to get rid of him, but I'd love to hear something good. Sit down."

"Actually, I do." After lowering myself into the seat across from her, I relayed the conversation Amanda and I just had with Kalo about bringing the Crimsontooth warriors onto our land, and Savannah immediately perked up.

"That's fantastic. It'll be much easier for them to help in planning our defense if they're here. Can I tell them to come now?"

"Whenever you'd like. I'll give you the coordinates for where we'll make the crossing."

With me there to answer any questions, she called the Crimsontooth Gamma at the hotel where he and his men had spent the night and shared the news with them. They estimated they could arrive at the crossover point in a little over two hours, and we made plans for Savannah and me to meet them there along with Kalo.

When she hung up once more, we were both energized from the shift in momentum and our new plan. It felt good for us to be on the same side rather than fighting against her suspicion like I had for the past few days.

Savannah stated as much outright, casting an appraising glance over me. "You're not so bad when you're not creeping on Amanda."

Having been warned about the Beta's bluntness, I did my best not to take that personally and answer her in kind. "And you're not so bad considering your brother is an idiot."

Her lips parted in surprise, a couple of beats passing as she stared across the desk at me. Just when I thought I might have gone too far and opened my mouth to apologize, she cracked a smile.

"I'll let that go this time because he *was* just being an idiot, but in the future? I'm the only one allowed to badmouth him."

I held up my hands in surrender. "I'll never understand how he let Amanda go, but since I'm glad he did, I won't say any more on the matter."

She huffed a laugh. "He let her go because he found his fated mate. I would think that you of all people would understand what it's like to try to resist something written in your bones."

My heart panged at the memories of those seven long, lonely years. "You have no idea."

Hearing the desperation in my voice, Savannah studied me carefully, as if really *seeing* me for the first time. "No, I really don't. How either of you fought against it all this time, I can't imagine. I'm also not sure which of you is more stubborn."

"Maybe that makes us a good match," I offered, giving her a smile meant as a peace offering. I couldn't tell her what transpired between me and Amanda the night before, partly because it was private between us and partly because I still didn't know what it meant for us going forward, but if nothing else, I hoped I could convince the Beta that I had Amanda's best interests at heart, always.

Once again, she seemed to read my mind. "You were very brave taking that bullet for her."

Brave wasn't the word I would have used. "I did what I had to do. For my Alpha and my mate."

She couldn't argue with that. "And what happens if her wish is reversed?"

"The bullet goes back into my heart." I said it evenly, as if it was a simple fact. Maybe it was. But the idea of it sat heavy in my chest; not so much the hot, searing pain I'd have to endure again, but the thought of being permanently separated from my mate.

Still, given the choice, I knew what my answer would be, and my voice remained steady as I spoke it out loud.

"I'll take it gladly if it saves her and this pack."

The tight nod she gave me felt almost like approval. "Well, we'll try to make sure that doesn't happen. If I learned anything from meeting my own mate, it's that sometimes, you have to make the impossible happen. Maybe I can..."

She didn't get to finish that thought as the guard outside the door knocked once before opening it a crack and sticking his head through. "Beta? Your mate has just let me know that he has a prisoner down in the cells. He asked you to join him when you're free."

My heart rate instantly picked up. Did he catch whoever tried to kill Amanda? Or the former Beta? Any possibility of getting to the bottom of the danger to Amanda was good news to me.

Savannah's eyes met mine, filled with the same determination. "Shall we?"

That simple question marked another small act of inclusion that meant a great deal to me. If Savannah could learn to trust me, and if Jasper and I could be friends, maybe the idea of Amanda accepting me wasn't as impossible as it once seemed.

For the first time in my life, it felt like I was finding my true purpose and my true place in the pack.

Now, I just needed to find a way to survive long enough to make it count.

Chapter Thirty-Eight

~**Amanda**~

Savannah and Troy arrived at the landing outside the holding cells in the pack house basement just before I did. Troy's sharp gaze immediately swept over my shoulder, checking for my security detail. Any other day, I would have chided him for being overprotective, but considering he'd taken a bullet for me that morning, the concern seemed justified. And I *had* brought my guard, though now that I had Jasper and Troy there, I dismissed him.

"You can wait for me at the top of the stairs. Make sure no one else comes down."

"Yes, Alpha." He bowed his head before nodding once to Jasper and disappearing back up the staircase.

The scent of damp concrete and old metal hung in the basement air, nothing like the fresh pine scent of the main floors. Most of the pack never set foot down there, but for me, it was becoming an unfortunately familiar place.

"Where did you find him?" I asked Jasper, my head jerking towards the door that led to the cells where Beta Chad had been taken. "Did he put up a fight?"

"He left his wife and youngest children behind to try to throw us off the trail," Jasper explained, his nose wrinkling in distaste. "They claimed he wasn't home but we found him cowering in the closet in the master bedroom. Seems like your move to seal the border disrupted his plans. He'd been hoping to get away and meet up with the attacking packs by now."

Fury prickled along my skin. Beta Chad had been my father's closest friend and a pseudo-uncle to me, although never a particularly affectionate one. My father trusted him, and though Chad made it clear when he resigned that he didn't support me taking over, I never thought he would betray us like this.

Even if he didn't feel he owed *me* his loyalty, he should have respected my position.

"What did you do with the rest of his family?" Troy asked, his voice tight with restrained anger.

"The ones at home are under house arrest, but his eldest son is still unaccounted for."

That son being the one Chad had always wanted to be Alpha. It stood to reason he was part of this plot, too.

"Alright, let's see what he has to say for himself."

Jasper punched in a code, and the door to the cells unlocked with a metallic click. On the other side, another guard waited, and he inclined his head at my approach.

"Wait outside until we're done," Jasper instructed.

Only when the door closed behind him did I turn to face our prisoner.

Chad stood in the centre of his cell, arms crossed. Despite his incarceration, his posture remained defiantly straight, his expression unreadable. His hair, once a deep brown, had started graying at the roots, the colour fading like his former influence. He was still in excellent shape for his late forties, a man who had spent his life training for battle.

His gaze settled on me, and a slow smirk tugged at his lips.

"You're looking well, Amanda," he said, the words pleasant but his tone laced with disdain.

"That's *Alpha*," Troy snapped from behind me. "And she *is* well, no thanks to you."

Chad barely spared him a glance. "And you've got yourself a new guard dog, I see."

Cinder growled in my mind, the vibration of her anger thrumming through me. *That's our mate he's talking about.*

Yes, and if I tell him that, it puts a great big target on Troy's back, I reminded her. My father had gone to great lengths to keep Troy's identity as my fated mate hidden, and although I never expected that to work in our favour, right now, it did. As long as someone was trying to kill me, Troy's anonymity was an advantage. *We need to stay calm. He's trying to provoke us.*

"We have reason to believe you've been plotting against this pack and its Alpha, Chad." Just as he had, I deliberately left off his title. Normally, former Betas retained the honorific as a courtesy, but he had forfeited that right. "I would think very carefully about your next words."

He didn't take my advice.

"Actually, I don't think I have to worry about that at all." His smirk widened. "You can't prove anything, and even if you could, it's only treason while you're in charge. Since the clock started ticking the moment you pulled that little stunt with the border, I'd say your time is running out."

A chill settled deep in my bones as his words sank in. "What do you think I did to the border?"

"I don't think *you* did anything," he sneered. "I bet a very special 'friend' did it for you."

"You planted the necklace!" Savannah gasped, pointing an accusing finger at him. "You knew about the genie. You set her up."

Chad chuckled, feigning innocence. "I'm sure I don't know what you're talking about."

He wanted to play games, but I refused to take the bait. He'd all but admitted it. "Where did you get it?" I demanded instead. "Was my father involved?"

Behind me, Troy tensed. Even without looking, I could feel the shift in his stance, the way his body locked up at the question. It was like my body had a radar for his, tracking his every move.

Chad scoffed. "Your father is the reason we're all in this mess. If he'd listened to me and named my son as his heir, you wouldn't have been able to stage your little coup and make the Ravenstone a national laughingstock."

"That sounds dangerously close to treason," Jasper said, his voice edged with steel. "Care to rephrase?"

For the first time, Chad's smirk faltered, his jaw tightening. "Fine," he muttered. "I don't know about any necklace, but if I did, I'd say your family isn't the only one with heirlooms."

My pulse steadied with his response. If I was interpreting it right, he meant the necklace hadn't come from my father. That was one small comfort. He might never have supported me, but at least he didn't want me dead.

Since that answer didn't change the bigger picture, however, I moved on, watching Chad's expression closely as I asked my next question.

"Speaking of your son, where is he now?"

His eyes glinted with something dangerously close to triumph. "None of you will see him coming."

Savannah turned to me, shaking her head. "He's obviously with the attacking packs. This guy is terrible at keeping secrets."

She wasn't wrong; Chad had given away plenty, but it didn't necessarily make him careless.

He was talking because he truly believed my fate was sealed. He didn't know about undoing the wishes. He didn't know it could all still change.

And that overconfidence might be exactly what we needed to give us the edge.

"I've heard enough," I said, turning my back on the cell. "Jasper, keep questioning him. Let me know if he says anything useful."

"That's it?" Chad taunted as I walked away. "You're even weaker than I thought."

"We'll see about that," were my parting words as I left the cell with Troy close behind me. Chad might think he had already won, but I was just getting started.

Chapter Thirty-Nine

~Troy~

I followed Amanda back up to the second-floor guest room serving as her temporary office, staying two steps behind her until the door closed behind us. As soon as it clicked shut, I wrapped an arm around her waist, spinning her to face me and pulling her tight against my body. Her wide eyes locked onto mine for half a second before my lips found hers, and sparks exploded in a sharp burst between us.

"You were so strong just now," I muttered between kisses, both of us gasping for air as our lips parted. "So in control. It's so fucking hot."

I'd thought so every time I watched her take charge, every time she owned the moment with her unshakable authority and iron will, and that day, the feeling was even stronger. Watching her command that room, standing firm even as betrayal stared her in the face, did something to me. It made me want to kneel at her feet and fight to the death for her in the same breath.

Knowing I might not have much time left, I finally let myself show it.

To my relief, she didn't resist me. In fact, she clung to me just as desperately, kissing me back with just as much hunger, her body pressing into mine as if she needed me to anchor her. The bond between us urged us forward, raw and relentless.

"I liked having you there," she confessed breathlessly, her fingers twisting in my shirt. "You gave me strength."

That might have been the single best thing I'd ever heard in my life.

A growl rumbled in my chest as I lifted her from the ground, my hands sliding beneath the backs of her thighs. In three steps, I had her against the edge of her makeshift desk, my fingers already at the zipper of her pants.

"Someone might... need us," she tried to protest even as her hips lifted off the desk to help me pull the fabric down.

"They can wait. This can't."

When I had her bare enough to spread her legs, I dropped to my knees, inhaling her sweet scent like I needed it to live. How I'd gone without it for so many years, I'd never understand.

Any further protests she might have made died when my tongue connected with her clit, tracing a circle around it in a slow, deliberate pattern. "Goddess!" she gasped, her head falling back as she surrendered herself fully to the pleasure in store.

The contrast between the powerful Alpha she'd just been and the woman unravelling for me now sent a rush of heat through my veins. It vibrated beneath my skin as my tongue dragged lower, plunging into her warm pussy, and filled me with triumph that she trusted me with this side of her, the one she rarely let anyone see.

If I really was going to die in a couple of days, any time *not* spent with my face between her legs seemed like an utter waste.

However, as much as I wanted to savour her, she didn't need slow and teasing right now. She needed release, so I worked her with purpose, drinking her in with every greedy swallow, every roll of my tongue drawing her closer to the edge. Her knuckles whitened as her fists clenched, the peak of her pleasure growing closer and closer.

"Let go, Alpha," I rumbled against her skin. "You've earned it."

Her thighs clenched around my head as she shattered, her cries muffled by her own fist as she bit down on it. I kept licking and swallowing every drop of her wetness like I could live off the taste of her alone. It would have to sustain me until the next time we could steal another moment together, whenever that might be.

When she finally slumped against the desk, breathless and glowing, I pressed one last kiss against her trembling inner thigh before standing.

"Damn," she murmured, her flushed face tilting up to meet my gaze. "You really shouldn't be able to do that so fast."

"You needed it fast. When it's time to go slow, trust me, I can take all fucking night."

Her thighs clenched again as I pulled back with a reluctant smile.

"I should go find Savannah and Kalo. The Crimsontooth men will be ready to come through the border soon."

"You don't want me to take care of that first?" she asked, glancing down at the noticeable bulge in the front of my pants.

I exhaled a short laugh. "I'm used to self-denial. But if you're offering to take care of it later, it'll give me something to look forward to for the rest of the day."

We hadn't discussed where either of us would be sleeping that night. Depending on what still needed to be done, I might not be sleeping at all again. But when Amanda nodded, something warm flickered in my chest.

"I'll make sure I get a chance to return the favour," she promised, a teasing glint in her eye. "As soon as things are settled for the night."

"In that case, the sooner I get going, the sooner I can come back."

I leaned down, brushing my lips over hers in a kiss far softer than the first. Her taste still lingered on my tongue, mingling with the sweetness of her kiss in a perfect, intoxicating blend.

"Do you want me to clean you up before I go?" I murmured, the words full of heat even as I pulled back.

Her smile that time was different, new and tender. "I think I can handle it. Be careful out there, all of you. If anything seems off, do *not* open the border."

I didn't miss the flicker of frustration in her eyes. She hated staying back, hated being away from the action, but I was glad she didn't push to come with us. With her in danger, I'd be completely unable to function.

"We'll be careful, I promise." I hesitated, then added, "I'll check in with you as soon as we're back."

I stepped back, giving her the bow I owed to my Alpha, as if I hadn't just had my face buried between her legs, and turned for the door.

"Troy."

My name, spoken softly, stopped me in my tracks.

I turned back, meeting her gaze over my shoulder. "Yes?"

"We'll talk tonight too. As soon as we get a chance."

My pulse stuttered, my wolf stirring restlessly in my head. From her tone, I knew she meant talking about the future, about what came next for *us*, assuming we both survived the next few days.

And I had no idea whether I should be looking forward to that conversation or dreading it.

It seemed I would have to wait a little longer to find out.

Chapter Forty

~**Amanda**~

To keep from going crazy while I waited for the others to return from the border, I had to find a way to keep myself occupied. As it happened, I had an idea of how to do that, even if it wasn't the most pleasant thing I could think of.

First, I carefully inspected the room to make sure no changes had been made in my absence. No hidden listening devices, no cameras, nothing out of the ordinary. I hated being paranoid in my own home, not being able to trust even the most basic security, but after the things the former Beta had said, I had to take precautions. The things I was going to be discussing weren't for anyone else's ears.

Once I satisfied myself that nothing had been altered, I had the security team bring me the satellite phone Savannah had been using, and I placed a call of my own to her former pack.

"Alpha Vaughan, please," I requested when the pack office picked up. "It's Alpha Amanda from the Ravenstone pack."

The woman did her best to hide her surprise, but a little of it still bled through in her reply.

"I'll see if I can get him for you, Alpha. Please hold."

I hadn't called the Crimsontooth pack directly since my ignominious departure. All contact with Vaughan and the others had gone through Savannah, allowing me to avoid any awkward interactions with the pack that I would have helped to govern if things had worked out just a little differently.

Even though I understood why Vaughan made the choices he did, the memory of being cast aside still burned. I'd spent years trying to prove my worth to my father and to the entire pack, and I'd returned in disgrace, like I had some kind of defect. Maybe someday, his rejection wouldn't sting anymore, but that day hadn't arrived yet.

"Amanda?" Vaughan's gruff voice echoed through the phone a few moments later. "What's going on? Did something happen to Sav?"

I should have anticipated he would jump to that conclusion. Why else would I be calling instead of his sister?

"She's fine, don't worry. I'm calling about something else."

He exhaled a heavy breath, the line crackling beneath its weight. "Fuck, you scared me. What can I do for you, then?"

Curiosity underpinned the question, along with a touch of guilt. Vaughan knew as well as I did that I'd been treated poorly in our brief relationship, and he'd done his best to be a good ally to us since then. His guilty conscience might persuade him to be more indulgent of my request than he otherwise might have been, and I wasn't above using that to my advantage. Not when it came to the reason I called.

"I was thinking about the meeting we had with your leadership team, back when the sasquatches were attacking your pack. How everyone in the room worked together to come up with a solution, putting the needs of the pack first."

"What about it?" he asked, clearly not on my wavelength just yet.

"I'm working on building a similar council here, starting with Savannah and Jasper, but it's still a work in progress. I don't know yet who I can fully trust, but I have a problem that I could really use some help brainstorming about. So, I wondered if I could borrow some of your pack's best minds for it. Including your mate."

The word stuck in my throat a little, but I forced it out anyway. As an expert on most supernatural things, Calista's input in particular would be invaluable.

"You're actually in luck," Vaughan answered, sounding relieved that some advice was all I wanted. "I have Callie, Felix and Evalina with me right now to talk about something else. Will that work?"

"Evalina?" I knew Calista and the pack's Beta Felix, but the last name was unfamiliar to me.

"Felix's new mate," he explained. "She's a fairy, so she might not understand everything we're talking about, but she also might bring a completely unique perspective to things."

Genies *and* fairies? What next?

"That would be great. Thank you."

I could make out some muffled conversation but no actual words as he spoke to the people in the room with him. Soon, his voice returned, further away than before but still clear. "You're on speaker now. Go ahead."

As clinically as I could, I explained what happened that morning when Troy got shot, the wish I made to save him, and my conversation with Kalo about undoing all the wishes.

"Fascinating," Calista stated when I'd finished my account. "Previously, I wouldn't have thought genies could feel regret. Honestly, I was taught that they enjoyed causing harm through the subversion of wishes."

"You were also taught werewolves are evil," Vaughan reminded her, his voice filled with a teasing affection that made my heart ache. Not for him, since we'd never had that kind of relationship, but for the ease he had with his mate, an ease that I had only just started to experience for myself and might lose soon if we couldn't figure out a way to save Troy.

"I would love to know this guy's life story," Felix agreed enthusiastically. "Maybe if he survives the whole experience, we can invite him here and he can tell it to me himself."

"We're getting off topic," Vaughan interjected before I could. "So, Leo and the others will be able to join you to prepare for the attack. Do you need more backup than that? We have enough time to send another group up to you."

"I'm not going to say no to any additional manpower, but at this point, I'm less concerned about the external threat than the internal one. The former Beta was working against me and at least one of his accomplices, the one who shot Troy, is still at large. When the battle begins, I'm worried we'll be attacked from within our own side."

"Using the full force of your Alpha authority, you could root out dissenters," Vaughan suggested. "Under direct questioning from you, they wouldn't be able to lie if you really unleashed your power."

"That's only on a one-to-one basis, though," Felix protested. "She doesn't have the time or the energy necessary to interrogate the whole pack."

"Could that power be amplified somehow?" Calista wondered. "If the whole pack was gathered, would there be a way to have it affect everyone at once?"

"Like a megaphone, but for Alpha authority," Felix agreed enthusiastically. "That would be awesome."

"But does something like that exist?" I asked. I'd certainly never heard of it.

"Not that I know of," Calista admitted. "But we can do some research and get back to you."

Their willingness to help was appreciated, but it didn't move me any closer to solving the problem, and we hadn't even touched on the bigger issue yet. "What about the silver bullet? How could we get it out of Troy before it kills him?"

The silence on the other end of the line almost deafened me.

No one seemed to have any ideas until, after several long, quiet beats, a new voice spoke up.

"Maybe I could help? I don't really know what a bullet is, but if it's made of silver, that's a metal, right?"

"Of course!" Felix's exclamation was followed by a loud bang, as if he'd pounded his fist on the table to emphasize his point. "Amanda,

Evalina has the ability to manipulate metal. She can open any lock, and she made me the most incredible piece of jewellery. She's still learning the limits of her power, but there's a good chance she could remove the bullet without the need to cut your soldier open at all."

That sounded positive, but I needed more than a 'good chance' at this point. "How can we know for sure?"

"We'll have to do a test run," Felix said as if it were obvious. "Vaughan, shoot me in the foot with a silver bullet."

"Goddess help me," Vaughan muttered. "I am not shooting you."

"I'll do it," Calista offered. "I know how to cause a minimal amount of harm."

"Perfect," Felix replied. "He keeps a gun in the top left drawer of his desk."

Vaughan's growl filled the air. "You are both insane. No one is shooting anyone!"

Their conversation descended into argument, everyone talking over each other so much that I couldn't make out any of the individual sentences. Furniture rustled in the background, as if it were being pushed around, or perhaps someone was being pushed *into* it.

Finally, a bang rang out, much louder than the earlier one, and conversation ceased entirely.

"What the hell just happened?" I breathed.

"Calista shot him." Vaughan's voice was thick with disbelief. "I'm officially running an insane asylum here."

"Calm down and let her work," Felix said, his voice tight with pain but still strong. "Go ahead, Evalina."

Silence swallowed even the breaths on the other end of the call, and I held mine too, hoping for a miracle.

Ten seconds passed. Twenty. With each tick, I imagined the bullet poisoning Troy's heart, his life draining from him. How long could he survive once it lodged itself back in place?

I clutched the phone so tightly my fingers ached. Then came a sharp intake of breath and a muffled sound; Felix's voice, perhaps, but strained.

My heart stuttered. Did it work? Or was the silver wreaking havoc on him too?

The joyous sound of *laughter* ringing down the line answered my questions.

"Just like that," Felix exclaimed proudly. "It's out, Amanda, and she didn't even have to touch me. The wound's already healing."

Hope immediately leapt back to life inside me. "Really?"

"I saw it with my own eyes," Vaughan admitted grudgingly. "Looks like we might have solved one of your problems, at least."

Even if that was the only thing I got out of the call, it had been more than worth it. "Evalina, can you be here when the wish is undone?"

"I'll bring her up myself," Felix promised. "We'll leave in the morning, once my foot is fully healed."

"Unbelievable," Vaughan muttered, but he didn't contradict his Beta. In fact, he went even further. "I'll send another fifty men along with them, and in the meantime, Calista and I will look into a way to test your pack's loyalty."

My chest tightened with a gratitude so profound, I struggled to put it into words. "Thank you. This is above and beyond the requirements of our alliance, and I truly appreciate it."

"We're not just allies," Vaughan said, his voice turning gruff again. "With Sav as your Beta, we're family."

"And family looks after each other," Evalina added in her soft, lyrical tone.

Family. Not in the way Vaughan and I might have been, in another timeline, but the circle of people I could depend on was rapidly expanding.

More than that, I might have just found a way to save my mate's life.

Things were definitely looking up. All we needed now was for nothing else to go wrong in the meantime.

Chapter Forty-One

~**Troy**~

Savannah, Kalo and I cut a quiet path through the forest, heading towards the border where the Crimsontooth men would meet us. Although we debated taking a larger force for protection, ultimately discretion seemed more important. The fewer people who knew about our reinforcements, the better.

The sun had almost completely dipped below the mountain by the time we reached the rendezvous spot. More than a full day had passed since Kalo installed the barrier around our border, and during that time, no one had gone in or out. Now, that was about to change.

The sounds of the gathered warriors reached us before we saw them. Even doing their best to keep quiet, seventy-five men were hard to keep entirely silent. Feet shuffled in the dirt, people whispered to each other, and the odd cough punctuated the late-afternoon air.

At last, we broke free of the trees onto the beach where the men would cross over, and there they were: a large group of fit, trained werewolves, ready to join our cause. Ready to protect my Alpha, and my mate, and my heart filled with gratitude at the sight of them.

"Hey, Leo." Savannah raised a hand in greeting as one of the men at the front of the group stepped forward. I hadn't met him before, but from context, I could guess he was the pack Gamma, the leader of the delegation. He had the height of a ranked wolf but not nearly as much bulk as the other man who followed him out of the group, the one Savannah greeted as Darius.

Savannah quickly made the introductions all around.

"Guys, this is Troy from our border patrol team. The Alpha has given him full clearance on this mission. Troy, this is Leo, the Crimsontooth Gamma, and Darius, the Delta in charge of security.

We all exchanged nods of greeting, unable to shake hands with the barrier still in place between us.

"And this..." Savannah gestured with a flourish to the other man with us, the one who stuck out like a sore thumb among the group of rugged wolves, "is Kalo. He'll be the one getting you in."

The genie stepped forward and Darius' eyes narrowed in instant distrust. He and I were going to get along well, I could tell.

Leo, meanwhile, looked like he'd seen a ghost. His face went pale and he blinked so rapidly, I thought he might be about to pass out.

"Are you alright?" I asked him since nobody else seemed to notice his distress.

A muscle twitched in his jaw before he cleared his throat, seeming to regain his composure. "I'm fine. Just eager to get going. How do we do this?"

"I'll walk through the barrier to create an opening," Kalo explained. "It will form around my body only, so you will need to pass quite close to me in order to get through. One at a time. Some of you may need to duck."

His eyes scanned Leo's tall frame from head to toe, and the Gamma squirmed beneath his inspection. "Darius, you go first," he instructed. "If you can fit, the rest of us will."

The large Delta gamely stepped forward until he ran into the invisible barrier, the air refusing to yield to his bulk. On our side, Kalo walked to the same spot, roughly ten inches of space between them, and stepped through as if there were nothing in his way. He paused directly in the barrier's path, creating a bubble through it, exactly as he predicted.

Necks craned in the back of the large Crimsontooth pack to watch as Darius tried to push through the barrier. Hands in front of him, like a mime pressing against an invisible box, he inched closer to Kalo until, at last, his hand pushed through the air, almost causing him to lose his balance.

If the whole thing weren't so deadly serious, it would have been ridiculous.

Again as Kalo predicted, the spot where the barrier opened up didn't leave a lot of space for the werewolf to squeeze through, especially one the size of Darius. After making a couple of awkward attempts, his head blocking him one time and his ass the next, Darius let out a growl.

"Fuck it, this is stupid."

Before any of us could ask what he meant, he reached down to tug his shirt over his head. Once off, he tossed it through the hole in the barrier. His shoes followed, then his pants and underwear, leaving him naked and ready to shift.

Once wolf-sized, he fit through with much less trouble.

"Why didn't I think of shifting?" Savannah muttered under her breath, and I shot her a sympathetic smile.

"Didn't occur to me either but hey, look on the bright side. You get your own 75-man striptease."

She snorted in amusement. "Don't let my mate know, he'll never forgive them."

I wouldn't like the idea of Amanda standing there watching six dozen fit men get naked either, so I promised to keep it to myself.

In the interest of efficiency, Leo set up a production line where the men would strip and hand off their clothes to someone else, who passed it through the barrier to someone who had already come through. By the time the men shifted and crossed the barrier, their clothes were waiting for them. We were making good time and had managed to get almost three quarters of the men through when my wolf stirred restlessly in my head.

Do you feel that? he asked. *Something seems...off.*

Now that he mentioned it, the area around us seemed unusually still. The birds had gone silent, the usual rustling of small creatures in the underbrush absent.

I scanned the forest we'd come from, looking for any sign of trouble, when the crack of a branch snapped my attention upward.

"Sniper! Take cover!"

The men immediately scrambled, their training kicking in like instinct. Leo immediately leapt forward and grabbed Kalo, shoving the genie behind him while they made for the relative safety of the forest. Meanwhile, I went for Savannah, pulling her behind a large log on the beach. With her lying stomach-down on the sand, I covered her body with mine. They shouldn't have much of an angle at us, but I winced anyway when shots rang out.

Amanda would kill me if I got shot *again.*

"Did you see who it was?" Savannah breathed from beneath me.

"No. I just saw an arm and a gun. A hunting rifle, not one of the pack's defensive weapons."

"What does it matter what *kind* of gun he has?"

A few reasons, actually. It meant the weapon was likely to be a private one, which would be easier to trace if we could recover a bullet or two. It also meant the person shooting at us probably wasn't one of the pack's warriors, and the fewer of those we had to worry about turning against us, the better.

Out loud, though, I stuck to one main reason it mattered: "He'll run out of ammunition soon."

In fact, I'd barely gotten the words out of my mouth when the shooting stopped, and I immediately sprang to my feet.

"Darius?"

The Crimsontooth Delta appeared from behind one of the trees at the edge of the woods, ready for action.

"Follow me."

I ran full speed towards the tree where I'd spotted the sniper in the first place. Realizing he'd been compromised, the man dropped to the ground and shifted, clothes tearing off him as he bolted. I did the same, Darius close behind me as we took our wolf forms and sprinted off in pursuit.

Being from different packs, we couldn't mind-link, but our training had been similar enough that when I motioned with my snout to the left, he broke off that way while I took the right. Whoever the wolf was, chances were he would be smaller than both Darius and me, since few wolves were bigger. We could catch up with our longer strides and come at him from both sides, making escape all but impossible.

Hunter's paws pounded on the forest floor, leaving a cloud of dirt and fallen leaves in our wake. The wolf we were chasing panted hard, obviously running as fast as he could, but we were gaining ground. It didn't take long until I came up level on his right, Darius in step with me on the left. As soon as we both pulled ahead, my wolf let out a sharp bark and we both pounced. All three wolves tumbled together over the rocks and roots, coming to a sliding halt less than half a mile from the pack house.

Got you, you traitor, Hunter snarled.

I mind-linked Savannah. *We got him. Is everyone okay there?*

He got one of the men in the leg, we'll get him to the hospital, she replied. *Leo and Kalo are bringing the remaining men through. Can you send Darius back?*

Will do.

Clamping down on the neck of the captured wolf, I linked him directly. *Shift!*

Having no choice, he obeyed, the wolf transforming into a naked man I didn't recognize. I linked Devon for back-up and a change of clothes as I shifted too, quickly securing the man with his arms behind his back.

"Head back the way we came to help Savannah with the rest," I instructed Darius. "I've got him from here. Thanks for your help."

His wolf gave me a nod before turning and bounding back towards the lake.

I tightened my grip on the captured man's wrists, barely resisting the urge to shake him. If this was the bastard who nearly killed me that morning, who *wanted* to kill my mate, I wanted answers. "Are you working for Chad? How many of you are there?"

Despite his predicament, being restrained and subdued with blood dripping from a cut on his lip, he sneered at me. "There's more of us than there are of you. You should join us while you still have a chance. No one wants that bitch as Alpha."

I didn't remember making the conscious decision to punch him in the face, but the next thing I knew, my knuckles ached and he lay unconscious on the ground.

Once we got him to the cells, that would make one less man who wanted to hurt my mate out there, but we still didn't know how many others there might be, and we were running out of time to find out.

CHAPTER FORTY-TWO

~Amanda~

Savannah and Troy both tried to mind-link me at the same time.

Hang on a second, I told my Beta before responding to Troy. *What happened?*

His report simmered with barely-repressed anger. *More shots fired. Someone followed us and tried to do some damage. Everyone's okay, but you need to stay put. Don't leave that room. I'll come and give you a full debrief as soon as I get this bastard locked up.*

Did he even realize he was giving his Alpha orders? Based on his level of agitation, probably not, and as much as I wanted to snap at him for being overprotective, a part of me, the part that wasn't an Alpha first, thrilled at the way he instinctively shielded me.

You weren't hit?

No, he assured me. *I'm fine. I'll be there soon.*

Closing the link with him, I returned to Savannah. *How did it go?*

Her sunny tone completely contrasted with Troy's pessimism. *They're all through the barrier. It went perfectly, if we don't count the bullet in Andrew's leg.*

I rubbed at my temples with my fingers. She and I obviously had different definitions of 'perfectly'. *Andrew's one of the Crimsontooth warriors? Is he okay?*

He will be. Paramedics are on their way and it's not very deep.

Unlike Troy's wound, she meant.

I'll get the men settled in the temporary lodging Jasper set up and then I'll bring Leo and Darius to meet with you.

Bring Kalo too, I instructed. *Thanks, Savannah.*

Almost as if they planned it in advance, Savannah arrived just as my security guard was opening the door to let Troy and Jasper in. Suddenly, my quiet room was filled with people, the genie and the two Crimson-tooth commanders entering with my Beta. Without enough chairs for everyone, we all stood instead, forming a loose circle.

"Report, Savannah," I ordered to get us started.

"Kalo was able to open a gap in the barrier, as he proposed. The men had to shift to get through it, but they got through. Unfortunately, we had a sniper hiding in one of the trees, but luckily, Troy spotted him before he started shooting or it could have been a lot worse."

She gave my mate a grateful nod and he responded with a stiff one of his own, obviously unaccustomed to being singled out for praise. I could tell it pleased him, though, especially when his eyes briefly darted over to me afterwards, as if he wanted to double check that I'd heard her commendation.

As if I needed any more proof that he was heroic and selfless in the face of danger.

"Troy brought the man to the cells and I'll question him," Jasper added. "But my biggest concern is how he knew where to go."

Savannah's brow furrowed. "I assumed he just followed us."

"And climbed a tree without any of you seeing or hearing him?" Jasper shook his head. "Not likely. He must have been waiting there for you, which means he knew where you'd be. Who did you discuss your plans with?"

"Troy and I were the only ones who discussed the details," she stated. "And Leo, over the phone."

"Could someone have tapped the phone line?" I wondered.

"Not likely with the satellite phone," Jasper replied before turning back to his mate. "Where did you discuss it?"

"In my office."

The same thought occurred to all of us at the same time but Jasper was the one to state it out loud. "From now on, we assume both the

Alpha's *and* Beta's offices are compromised. Discussions in the pack house should only take place in this room."

"Or by mind-link," Troy suggested. "That would be even safer."

"This is getting ridiculous," I had to point out. "I'm practically a prisoner in this room, and now no one can speak out loud? Are there really *that* many traitors among us?"

I had fought beside these wolves, shared meals with them, trusted them with my life. Now, every familiar face was a question mark.

Disconcertingly, no one immediately answered.

I turned to my mate, hoping for some reassurance. "Troy?"

His shoulders straightened, as if bracing himself for the words he was about to say. "The man who shot at us claimed there were more people on his side than on mine. I believe that's an exaggeration, but I also think he wouldn't make such a bold claim if they didn't have a significant base."

"The former Beta is refusing to talk," Jasper added. "Or rather, he's talking non-stop but telling us nothing useful. He truly believes your time is limited, so all he has to do is wait us out. And if he won't give us names, I'm not sure how we can track them all down before the barrier comes down."

"There might be a way." Briefly, I recounted the idea Vaughan, Calista and Felix had suggested, of calling a packwide assembly and finding a way to use my Alpha authority to weed out dissenters there.

Troy immediately shook his head. "You'd have to go out in front of the whole pack. You'd be an open target for anyone who wanted to get to you."

Jasper wasn't so quick to say no, but he still had some reservations. "It's an interesting idea but I'm not sure how to amplify your power. Maybe one of the pack engineers could help."

"Except we don't know who can be trusted," Savannah reminded him. "Right now, anyone who isn't in this room is a potential suspect."

"I actually might have an idea."

The words came from Leo who, until that point, had been silent, and everyone in the room shifted to look at him.

"Ranked wolves have authority in their bloodlines too, though not as strong as the Alpha's. If we could form a perimeter around the assembly area, some kind of conduit running through various ranked members like an electric current, it might help to harness the energy inside the circle. I'm not sure what material could be used for the conduit, but Calista or perhaps Felix might have an idea."

"Felix will be coming here tomorrow," I announced to them all, trying to do the math in my head. That would leave me with Savannah, Felix, Leo and Darius as ranked wolves that I could trust.

And Troy, perhaps, Cinder reminded me.

Yes, perhaps him too. Hopefully the doctor would have his DNA results by then.

Would that be enough? I had no idea.

"In that case, Felix and I can work on it when he gets here," Leo offered. "We still have some time."

"But in the meantime, we should get started on the plans for when the barrier drops," Darius interjected.

"We'll do that in my office, with my team," Troy told him. "It'll be more secure there than in the pack house, and we'll have more room too. And there's food. I'm sure you're all hungry."

It was past dinner time according to the clock on the wall, so I did a quick inventory of what needed to be done before issuing my orders. "Alright. Savannah and Jasper, you're done for the day. Go home, have something to eat and get some rest."

"But..." they both protested, nearly in unison, but I shook my head.

"I need you on top of your game tomorrow. Take the night off." Not giving them a chance to argue further, I turned to the other men. "Leo and Darius, I'll leave you with Troy. Kalo, your input would be appreciated there as well if you don't mind."

"As long as there's food, I'll go," he replied easily.

"We'll all meet back here in the morning. Ten o'clock."

When their heads all bowed in acceptance, I added one more order through mind-link.

When you're finished, Troy, come back here to see me. It doesn't matter how late it is.

His eyes locked onto mine as he lifted his head. *Yes, Alpha.*

Everyone began to move towards the door, but Leo lingered at the rear, stepping closer to me as the others moved further away. "Do you have a minute to speak in private, Alpha?"

"Of course." Of all the men in the Crimsontooth pack, Leo had been the kindest to me during my short stay there, when we both thought I would be mated to his Alpha. He'd gone out of his way to give me all the information I needed to step into my role as Luna, and although it didn't work out that way, I would never forget the time and consideration he gave me.

A few minutes in return now would be the least I could do.

He called out to Darius, who had reached the door. "I'll meet you over there. Go ahead without me."

Darius nodded in agreement, and the door closed behind him, leaving me and the Crimsontooth Gamma alone.

"It's good to see you, Leo." I gestured to the chairs by my temporary desk since we were down to only the two of us. "Have a seat."

He sat across from me, as requested, but he didn't relax into his chair. If anything, he looked even more tense sitting than he had been standing.

"What can I do for you?" I prompted when he didn't say anything.

His jaw worked, throat bobbing with a tight swallow before he forced out the question. "What do you know about the genie?"

Where to start? "Well, your Luna knows far more about genies than I do. Most of what I know is what she's told me. Apparently, they're bound to an object, and when someone handles that object..."

"No." He interrupted me softly, lips twisting in a grimace. "Not genies in general. What do you know about *this* genie? About Kalo?"

Instantly, my senses were on alert. "Why? Do you think he'll betray us?"

I couldn't see how Leo would have come to that conclusion, and everything Kalo had done so far seemed to suggest he'd been honest about his motives, but too many lives were hanging in the balance for me to dismiss anything without hearing him out.

Leo let out a pained sigh. "No, nothing like that. This is a... personal question."

"Personal?" I was completely lost. Was he asking me what Kalo was like, as a person? Why would he be worried about that right now?

Leo ran a nervous hand through his short hair, scratching at the back of his neck on the way down. "This is going to sound crazy, but I think he might be my mate."

Oh.

Oh.

That hadn't crossed my mind for several reasons, one of which being that I had no idea Leo was gay, but the bigger one being that it seemed utterly impossible for any wolf to be mated to an immortal being that had been human thousands of years ago. How did that even work?

"You think? Your wolf doesn't know?" Cinder had been pretty damn clear when we met Troy.

Leo huffed a humourless laugh. "No, he's pretty certain. But without a wolf, Kalo obviously doesn't know. Sav said he's dangerous and very powerful. This is very unorthodox, and..."

"And you like rules," I finished for him. Perhaps more than anyone I'd ever met, Leo liked order and predictability. Kalo represented the complete opposite. "Well, here's what I know: he used to be human. He became a genie, and since then, he's had no free will of his own. He goes where he's called, performs the magic he's asked to do, and there seems to be some kind of curse attached to his magic. He's asked me to help get rid of his power, which might make him human again, or it might kill him. He isn't sure."

Leo absorbed all of that with growing alarm. "There must be a way to control the outcome."

"Sometimes, there isn't," I told him as gently as I could. "But I'm sure there's much more to his story than what I know. You should talk to him. Get to know him for yourself."

Leo swallowed again, his face pale. "I wouldn't know what to say to someone like him."

"Don't think of him as a genie. Talk to him like a person."

It only occurred to me after the words came out that maybe he didn't mean Kalo's species when he said 'someone like him'. Maybe he just meant someone as magnetic and unusual as Kalo, so I offered a suggestion.

"Tell him that I've asked you to get more information on his history, that I thought it might be useful for us to know about it before I make the final wish. That should get the conversation started, at least."

He nodded, slowly at first, then a little more confidently. "I could do that."

"Good." I gave him the most encouraging smile I could. "Congratulations, Leo. I know it's a shock, but the goddess usually knows what she's doing. If he's your mate, there's a good reason for it."

"Thank you, Alpha." He bowed low before taking his leave, and once again, I found myself alone.

Other than Cinder, who piped up in my head. *At least our mate isn't five thousand years old. Look on the bright side.*

The statement was so ridiculous, yet true, that I had to laugh.

Chapter Forty-Three

~Troy~

The planning meeting ran late, but we were making such good progress, nobody wanted to stop. The Crimsontooth men brought a fresh perspective to our situation, sharing tactics and strategies they'd developed that would be a departure from what our attackers might expect. Darius was firm and decisive while Leo sat back, absorbing everything before interjecting with a single sentence that shifted everything.

Even Kalo got swept up in it, sharing military strategies he'd encountered over the centuries, and though surprising our opponents with a fleet of elephants wasn't an option, his stories kept us all engaged, entertained, and surprisingly, offered a few useful insights.

By the time we finally broke for the night, exhaustion clung to my bones, mixed with a restless energy that wouldn't settle until I was close to one person in particular.

I glanced down at my watch and winced. Nearly midnight. Amanda should be resting and I hated the idea of disturbing her, but she'd said to come back to the pack house when I finished, no matter the hour. Besides, it might be one of my last nights on earth. Even if she never fully accepted me, I couldn't spend it anywhere other than by her side.

Outside her temporary room, the night guard had changed shifts. The new man stood straighter when I approached, giving a quick nod of respect, and I took a moment to check in. No suspicious activity since the shooting, he assured me, and no one had gone in or out of Amanda's room since Leo left hours ago.

"She ate and told me two hours ago that she was going to sleep," the guard added. "She said not to admit anyone besides Beta Savannah or... you."

Though he didn't voice it, his curiosity was evident. Savannah's access made sense, but me? A captain of the border patrol?

Rather than answering the unspoken question, I simply clapped him on the shoulder before slipping into the darkened room.

My eyes adjusted quickly in the dim light, my werewolf abilities kicking in, and I could make out Amanda's sleeping form beneath the covers of the same bed where I'd recovered from my injury earlier that day. She looked so peaceful, and for a long moment, I simply stood there, watching the soft rise and fall of her breath.

Eventually, I crept over to the ensuite bathroom, slipping out of all my clothes except my underwear and getting ready for bed. Unlike the night before in the cramped bunker, this bed was more than big enough for the two of us, so I could climb in without disturbing her. Though she said we would talk that night, I had no intention of waking her. We could wait until the morning, when she'd had a chance to rest.

However, when I returned to the bedroom, a lamp on the bedside table had been switched on, its gentle light creating a warm glow that illuminated the woman sitting up in her pajamas, hair tousled from sleep, smiling at me.My breath caught in an involuntary stutter. Even after all these years, she was the most beautiful sight I'd ever seen.

Though she didn't seem upset, I still had to apologize. "I'm sorry, I didn't mean to wake you."

"You didn't. Cinder did," she said with a soft laugh. "She felt you nearby and wouldn't leave me alone."

She pulled back the covers next to her and I wasted no time in settling into the empty space and leaning back against the headboard beside her. "Cinder is your wolf? That's a pretty name."

"She thinks so." Amanda's eyes twinkled in the lamplight, full of amusement and warmth. "What's your wolf's name?"

The excited howl inside my head made me wince.

"Hunter. He's losing his mind right now because we're talking about him."

This was a conversation we should have had a long time ago, things we should have known about each other as mates, but better late than never.

That went for everything about our relationship, including the way her body curled into mine as she relaxed, the warmth of her skin branding me. My pulse thrummed beneath her fingertips as she traced an absentminded pattern against my stomach, each touch sending heat swirling through my veins.

My arm circled her, pulling her even closer, and beneath the covers, my cock began to swell.

"How did the meeting go?" she murmured.

"If I go into detail, we'll be up all night," I warned her. "But it went well. We have some training to do with the men tomorrow but I'm feeling good about it. We'll be ready."

"That's good." She inhaled deeply, breathing in my scent, and my cock jerked, blood pumping fast. "Did Leo seem okay?"

"Um, yes?" The answer came out as a question because I had no idea why she was asking. "Shouldn't he have?"

"Of course," she lied, unconvincingly. "I was just curious."

As I thought back to Leo in the meeting, I couldn't remember anything that seemed off, but I *did* remember his strange behaviour earlier. "Although, now that you mention it, he had kind of a weird reaction when we brought the men into the territory. I have no idea what caused it. He said he was fine but he clearly wasn't. Do we need to be worried about him?"

"Not at all." Those words had the ring of truth. "He's a good man."

Hunter growled in my mind. *Why are you talking about other men? Get back to her wolf.*

I didn't want to talk about her wolf any more than I wanted to talk about Leo, but I *did* have something I desperately wanted to discuss.

Before I could get the words out, though, she spoke again. "I wonder why some people's mate bonds are simple and straightforward while other ones are so complicated."

How she made the leap from talking about Leo to wondering about complex mate bonds, I had no clue, but since that was exactly what I wanted to talk about, I didn't complain.

"I don't think there's a reason. Luck, maybe? It's like asking why some people are smarter than others, or prettier." My hand curled up to brush her hair behind her ear, my thumb softly stroking her cheek.

"I don't know if those are exactly the same thing," she protested. "People can study to be smarter, and makeup can make them prettier."

"And people can reject their mate bond," I pointed out, treading carefully onto that subject. "They can make it go away if it's too much trouble. But if you work at it, if you have to fight to make it work, I think you appreciate it more than if it came easily. Maybe it even makes it stronger in the end."

She pressed her face against my skin, as if she could climb inside it and find peace there. I knew the feeling. "I wish we could start over. Go back to that night and do it all differently."

How many nights had I spent lying in pain, wishing for the same thing? A week ago, I would have agreed with her whole-heartedly, but over the past few days, my perspective had shifted. "I don't."

Instantly, her head lifted off my shoulder and she turned to face me, confusion written all over her beautiful face. "What?"

"I don't wish that," I repeated, holding her gaze in the soft lamplight. "It would have been easier, certainly. And we would have been happy, I don't doubt that for a second. But I would never have fully appreciated a moment like this, holding my mate as we talked about our day, would never have seen it for the miracle it is, if I hadn't spent so long dreaming about it, convinced it would never happen."

She blinked as she processed that, her eyes still full of uncertainty as they searched mine.

"Besides," I added, "I think we've learned that wishing to fix something isn't always the best solution."

A reluctant smile crept across her lips as she conceded that point.

"If you accept me now, Amanda, I'll know that it's not just because of the mate bond. We've both had seven years to see what life apart would be like. And every day of those seven years, I chose you. I chose to wait for you, and to hope even when hoping seemed pointless. And that's far more powerful to me than any wish could ever be."

Her smile grew more understanding, more radiant, and her head bobbed in a gentle nod. "I wish I could say the same, but I think I held onto our bond more out of stubbornness than hope."

"There you go wishing again," I teased her, leaning down to place a soft kiss on her forehead. I would never take *that* opportunity for granted either. "Your stubbornness is part of what I love about you. Without your stubbornness, I would have died today. You just refused to let it happen."

At the reminder, her smile dimmed, just a little. "I was so scared that I'd lost you, Troy. Lost you before I even really had you."

"You have me," I promised. "You've had me since the first time I saw you, and even if I don't survive the bullet a second time..."

"Don't say that," she tried to cut me off, but I placed a gentle finger against her lips so she'd let me finish.

"Even if I don't survive, I will always be yours. That's never been in any doubt."

Our gazes held, her lips soft and full against my finger, the air thick with promise.

And then she said the most beautiful words I'd ever heard in my life.

"I'm yours too. I want to be yours. I accept you as my mate."

Chapter Forty-Four

~Amanda~

I expected a grin, or a cheer, or maybe even tears of happiness when I told Troy the decision I'd made, the decision that had grown over the last 48 hours from a possibility to the only logical choice.

But none of that happened.

Instead, he stared back at me blankly, blinking once, then twice, his thick eyelashes pressing together as if in slow motion.

Finally, he cleared his throat. "Sorry, can you say that again? I think I blacked out."

Joy bubbled into my laughter, needing somewhere to go. "I said that I accept you. We've wasted so much time, and I don't want to miss out on a second more. I can't wish away the past, but I can change the future, starting right now."

"You accept me." He repeated the words slowly, as if he couldn't quite believe it. "As your mate."

"Yes." I gave him an impatient nudge. "I think the normal response at a time like this would be to kiss me."

"Say it again," he whispered.

I rolled my eyes, but my grin grew even wider as I obliged. "I accept you."

"Thank the goddess."

At last, his head lowered towards mine and our mouths met. Cinder howled in delight as the sparks took hold, travelling through my body until every extremity tingled with both anticipation and fulfillment. My fingers dug into his bare chest, my hips instinctively seeking out his body, and the rest of the world ceased to exist.

It didn't take long for the kiss to turn hungry, Troy's hands moving from my face down my body, tracing its contours over the soft silk of my pajamas. I went even further, sliding my hand down his chest to press against his growing length. His breath hitched but the kiss didn't stop; if anything, his tongue only plunged in deeper.

Sex with him had been good the night before. Better than good, to be honest. *Amazing*. But now that we'd accepted the bond, each touch felt almost... sacred. Like we were sealing the agreement with our bodies, leading up to the marking that would make it official.

His fingers gripped the fabric of my pajamas, tugging it upwards, and we broke the kiss for a moment just to get rid of the unnecessary barrier between us. As soon as it disappeared, tossed over Troy's shoulder onto the floor, we came together again, skin to skin, heat flaring between us.

Troy rolled us over, his big hands cradling me as he shifted me onto my back. Once my head hit the pillow, his lips left mine again long enough for him to scramble out of his underwear, and when he knelt on the bed before me, gloriously naked, muscles tight and cock erect, I almost whimpered in need.

He might have given me an orgasm on the desk earlier that day, but *hours* had passed since then. I needed *more*.

My eyes dropped to the spot on his chest where the bullet had gone in, now completely healed. If I hadn't seen it myself, there would be nothing to give away how close we had been to never getting to this point.

"Goddess, look at you," he growled, and my eyes snapped back up to his face to find him staring down at me with the same intensity with which I'd been devouring him. "No man or wolf has ever been as lucky as I am."

"I don't know about that. I'm feeling pretty damn lucky myself." My voice was so thick with need, it had dropped several notes. "Now, get down here and get inside me."

He didn't need to be asked twice.

Brown eyes glinting with desire, he settled between my legs. Fisting his shaft, he brought his head to my entrance, a growl of approval rumbling in his chest when he felt just how wet I already was. Honestly, I'd been aching for him since he walked out of the bathroom in nothing but his underwear. How could I not?

Almost torturously slowly, he pushed into me, letting me feel each and every inch until he couldn't go any further.

"You feel so fucking perfect," he rasped. "It feels..."

I finished the sentence for him. "Right."

"Yeah."

His eyes met mine, full of all the longing of the last seven years and the promise of decades more to come as he began to move.

With my previous partners, I always preferred to be on top. Maybe it had to do with my Alpha blood, the instinct to command rather than submit, or maybe I just liked having the ability to walk away if I decided to. It gave me more control. Didn't require as much vulnerability.

But as Troy rocked inside me, thrusting deeply but gently, his fingers rubbing against my clit, I didn't mind letting him set the pace. I didn't feel out of control. I felt worshipped and treasured, and most of all, I felt *safe*.

Safe enough to let go.

With his steady rhythm, my orgasm built slowly. My hands gripped his strong shoulders and ran through his hair, but he did all the real work, leaving me to focus entirely on the sensations brought on by his actions. My need coiled tighter and tighter, until, almost without warning, one extra little flick of his finger sent me over the edge, not in a rush, but in a slow, gentle wave.

"Good?" he grunted above me, as if he really needed to ask.

"So good," I assured him through panted breaths. "But you don't have to hold back. Claim me, Troy. Make me yours completely."

His eyes turned nearly black above me, his wolf pressing close to the surface, as he shifted positions, hauling my ankles up over his shoulders.

I barely had time to gasp in surprise before he bent down over me, pressing my legs against me, folding me in half as he began to *really* fuck me.

I bit down the scream that threatened to come out, not wanting to attract the attention of the guard outside the door, and clawed at the bedsheets, mindlessly reaching for something to hold onto as pleasure flooded my body. His strength was brutal, his need raw and hungry, and each time his cock drove into me, I wanted him even more.

I was completely at his mercy, and I didn't mind at all.

Every movement felt like a vow. Every breath, a memory rewritten. Not erasing the past but building something on top of it that would be even stronger because of the foundation underneath.

While the first orgasm had been a slow build, the second one hit me like a steam train, rising to a sharp, sudden peak and dropping just as fast. If he even noticed it, I couldn't tell. His pace didn't let up, sweat forming across his brow as he claimed me over, and over, and over again.

When my body surrendered a third time, a long, drawn-out orgasm that clenched hard around his thick cock, Troy's movements finally stuttered, his thrusts turning erratic until, breathing out my name like a prayer, he came.

Now! Cinder urged in my head. *Claim him now!*

Troy released my legs, letting them fall open around him as he collapsed onto me. I kissed him hard, our chests heaving from the exertion, before trailing my lips down to the marking spot on his neck. It smelled so good, his sea salt scent making my mouth water.

Troy stilled, something shifting in his energy. Assuming it must be anticipation, his wolf probably urging him on just as mine was, I licked his throat, dragging my tongue along the spot in preparation for my mark.

Instantly, he pulled out of my arms and scrambled back from me. "N-no. You can't."

"What?" The words were so nonsensical to me, I thought he had to be joking. "Stop messing around. My wolf is going to have a breakdown."

"I'm not." He swallowed hard, face contracting in pain. "We can't mark each other, Amanda. I just can't do it."

Chapter Forty-Five

~**Troy**~

The look Amanda gave me when I turned down her mark instantly took me back to the hallway outside her father's office, all those years ago.

Confusion. Disappointment. *Betrayal.*

That look had haunted me since that day.

"What are you talking about?" Her voice cracked like dry wood as she sat up. "You're mine. You said…"

"I *am* yours," I promised quickly. "This is *not* a rejection, not in any way. For as long as I live, I will never reject you."

"Then why don't you want…"

She trailed off as she put the pieces together. There wasn't much my mate missed.

"As long as you live," she repeated. "Is that it?"

She'd hit the nail on the head, and I crept a little closer to her, on my knees, reaching for her hand. "If we're fully bonded, the pain you suffer if I die would be excruciating. I won't put you through it, not when I don't have to."

I didn't fear death, but having to die knowing I'd be leaving her in agony? That was another story entirely.

Amanda slid her hand into mine, but her eyes remained narrowed. "There are four problems with that argument."

I was willing to hear her out, even though I didn't expect anything she said to change my mind. "That's a pretty specific number. Hit me with them."

She didn't hesitate. "First, I'll be in pain no matter what. The bond breaking hurts whether it's been accepted or not."

"It's not the same and you know it." Resisting the bond had been slow and steady torture. Rejection would have been temporarily debilitating. But the death of a bonded mate? That was a pain unmatched among werewolves. Worse than torture. Some never recovered.

Just the idea of Amanda enduring that because of *me* made me want to tear the whole world down.

She must have had no comeback for that, as she moved onto the next point. "Second, you're not going to die. I've been busy today talking to people and making plans. There are things we can do. I'm not just going to let it happen."

I didn't know she'd been working on it, and that knowledge sparked gratitude and affection in my chest. But unless she'd found a 100% foolproof solution, it was still too much of a risk to take. "I appreciate that, but just because you don't want it to happen doesn't mean it won't. We have to anticipate the worst-case scenario."

Undeterred, she moved on. "Third: the bond will actually strengthen you. Once we've accepted it fully and marked each other, you can draw upon my strength too. It might make the difference between life and death."

That was the first point she made that actually made me pause. It was true that mated werewolves had better resilience, and were able to draw power from their mate, especially when that mate had Alpha blood like mine did. Having her mark and her strength behind me could make the difference if it came down to a close call.

I'd spent so long trying to protect her that I hadn't stopped to think *she* might be the one who saved *me*.

As I wavered, debating the issue in my head, Amanda pressed on. "And last, it's *my* life. *My* pain. You don't get to make decisions that will affect us both without consulting me. That's what got us into this mess in the first place."

She was absolutely right, and I bowed my head in acknowledgement. "I'm not trying to take control away from you. I just don't want you to suffer. You see my point, don't you?"

Her bold brown eyes were waiting for me when I lifted my head again.

"You were willing to die to protect me, Troy. Do you think that only goes one way? Don't you think I'd do the same for you? Do you really think that little of me?"

Those words would have brought me to my knees if I weren't already there. The idea that this incredible woman, the angel I admired all those years and the mate I yearned for, would *choose* to put herself in danger for me?

Inconceivable.

Unacceptable.

And so fucking amazing, my heart nearly burst with pride.

She leaned even closer, still naked and so utterly mesmerizing, I couldn't have looked away if the world was ending. "I would have taken my chances with you seven years ago if you gave me the choice. I said I accept you now, and I do, but only on the condition that we're a team from here on in. Any decisions we make, we make together. Can you accept *that*?"

I still believed that I made the right choice back then, to walk away to protect her, but Amanda was right this time. We *were* stronger together, and I respected her enough to admit when I was wrong.

"I do. You're right, and I'm sorry. If you're certain that's what you want, then of course I want your mark. I've wanted it for seven fucking years."

Hunter prowled just beneath my skin, every nerve singing in anticipation. This was actually going to happen. Except now, I'd ruined the moment, and I quickly racked my brain for a way to make it special again.

One thing I knew about my mate was that she never backed down from a challenge, so I decided to offer her one. "But I want to mark you first."

She stared at me for a moment, reading my sincerity, before her mouth curled up at one corner. A mischievous glint sparked in her eye. "You think you're faster than me, Captain?"

My muscles tensed, readying myself. "I don't need speed. I've got strength."

Her eyebrows raised, her smile both amused and full of challenge. "You do remember I'm the Alpha, right?"

Before I could answer, she pounced. Her weight wasn't much, but she *was* strong, and the angle knocked me off balance, pushing me backwards over the side of the bed. I hit the floor with a hard thud and she landed on top of me, knocking the wind out of me.

She lunged for my neck but I countered, rolling her under me. She kept the momentum going, using her legs to push me off. I hit the table hard, the lamp crashing to the floor.

"Alpha?" The guard outside knocked on the door. "Is everything alright?"

"Yes," she called back, and in the moment it took her to answer, I got myself back in the game. From a crouch, I leapt towards her, lifting her off the ground with me as I sprang up. We landed in a heap back on the bed, the frame creaking beneath the sudden assault. The headboard slammed into the wall.

Another knock at the door. "Are you sure you don't need help?"

"I'm fine!" she yelled back, more forcefully, her eyes narrowing on me as she wrapped her legs around my waist and pulled me down. Her nose grazed against my throat, sending sparks shooting through my body.

The urge to give in was strong, but I was having too much fun, and I could tell she was too. Summoning my strength, I pulled us backwards, off the bed once more and onto my feet, with her still wrapped around me. My arms went under her thighs, hauling her higher on my body so she could no longer reach my neck, but hers was now directly in my line of vision.

I had her and she knew it, her body going slack as I licked up her throat.

I didn't actually care about winning, though. I only wanted her.

"Together?" I offered.

Amanda sucked in a breath, clinging to me even tighter than before. "Together."

Bending my head to the side, I offered my neck to her while she did the same to me. We kissed and licked each other, need building inside me to a frenzy before Hunter howled and instinct took over. Her teeth pierced my skin half a second before mine sunk into her, connecting us not only in this moment, but forever afterwards.

Mine.

As the bond locked into place, her soul brushed against mine, wild and warm and achingly familiar.

At long last, I was whole.

Chapter Forty-Six

~Amanda~

I awoke to the sound of someone clearing their throat.

Repeatedly.

Loudly.

For a moment, it didn't register through the fog of sleep, but eventually, I groaned, forced my eyes open, and immediately regretted it. When did the room get so bright?

Savannah stood beside the bed, arms crossed and wearing a smirk that screamed trouble.

"Am I interrupting? You *did* say ten o'clock."

It took a second, maybe two, for my brain to reboot, until a warm weight shifted beside me and it all came rushing back.

Troy. The mark. Our bond.Kalo and the warriors and... The ten o'clock meeting. *In this room.*

"What the..." Troy mumbled before freezing. His arm tightened around me, and he blinked toward Savannah with a groggy scowl. "What the hell are you doing in here?"

She didn't flinch as she raised an eyebrow at him. "You should be glad it's only me. The rest of them are all standing outside, waiting to come in. It's five after ten."

"Shit." I scrambled upright, dragging the covers with me.

The room tilted and my head spun. It felt like I was hungover, even though I hadn't touched a drop.

"I never sleep in," I muttered, rubbing at my temple.

"Well, it's hardly a mystery." Savannah's smirk widened. "The marks on your necks say it all."

She was more right than she realized. Marking drained a wolf like nothing else. Soul-binding wasn't exactly light work, and since we'd completed it in the middle of the night, our bodies were still playing catch-up.

My mind was catching up too, and as I straightened, I narrowed my eyes at Savannah. Her blunt honesty was one of the reasons I chose her as Beta, but there were limits.

"If you figured it out, why are you still standing there? Protocol says you bow to your Alpha's mate."

Caught out, her arms dropped, and after a beat, she bowed her head to both me and Troy. "Sorry, Alpha. And... Luna? Congratulations."

The smirk had disappeared when she lifted her head again, replaced by a genuine smile.

"I want the full story later," she added. "But for now, we really do need to have that meeting."

I glanced at Troy and couldn't help but smile at the faint horror on his face at the word *Luna.* Not that we'd settled on what his title would be, but it wouldn't be that one.

"Can you stall them for five minutes while we get ready?"

She nodded and stepped out, leaving us to a frantic dash between the bathroom and bedroom. In under five minutes, we'd made ourselves presentable, if not entirely subtle. The scent change alone would've given us away, not to mention the fresh marks on our necks.

Just before I opened the door, I gave Troy a long embrace.

"Thank you for saying that," he murmured into my hair before pressing a kiss to my forehead.

I didn't need to ask what he meant. After everything he'd told me about his past, the way he'd been constantly dismissed and underestimated, most especially by my father, I knew he wasn't used to anyone standing up for him. But now that I knew the kind of man he really was, I would always be his champion, publicly and proudly.

Taking one last breath to collect myself from the whiplash of going from tangled in the sheets to hosting a meeting, I let the waiting wolves in.

Savannah hadn't spilled the news, judging by the stunned looks on Leo and Darius's faces when they walked in. Jasper, on the other hand, wore a knowing grin and bowed immediately. Savannah must have told him via mind-link and I couldn't blame her. Some things, a wolf *had* to share with her mate.

"Congratulations, Alpha," Jasper said. "And you too, Captain."

'Captain' suited Troy better than 'Luna,' but even that wasn't quite enough.

"It's Commander now," I announced. "As of today, Troy is in charge of pack security."

His voice echoed in my head through the bond, deeper and stronger than ever. *Are you sure? That position usually goes to...*

... someone who's proven themselves worthy of it, I finished for him.

I knew what he'd been about to say: traditionally, that role went to a Delta, someone who came from a ranked-blood family, but I didn't care.

As Alpha, I got to make the rules.

Kalo, the only person who couldn't smell the change or recognize the marks, looked between us with curiosity. "What are the congratulations for?"

Leo was the one who answered him, though he never once glanced in the genie's direction. "They're mates. Fated ones, unless I'm mistaken. That certainly casts a few things in a new light."

He didn't elaborate, but I could guess what he meant: my arranged match with his Alpha, maybe, or the way he'd seen Troy and I interact. Or maybe he was thinking about his own mate who stood five feet away from him, completely unaware.

"Ah." Kalo's golden eyes lingered on us a moment longer. "That explains it."

Again, his words might have multiple meanings, but we had no time to unpack them now.

I turned to Troy. "Commander, let's hear the update."

Half an hour later, everyone was caught up and the day's plans were in place. Troy, Leo, and Darius would work from the barracks, refining our defense strategy. Jasper would resume questioning the captives with Kalo accompanying him, and Savannah and I would focus on rooting out traitors before the barrier fell.

The men dispersed, Jasper kissing Savannah on his way out. Troy hesitated a step behind him, looking as if he wanted to do the same but unsure if he should.

I reached for his hand. "You can kiss me whenever you want," I whispered, pulling him close. "You outrank everyone now, except me. No one tells you what to do."

His smile was soft and reverent. "That's going to take some getting used to."

He stole one more kiss before slipping out the door after the others.

As soon as it closed, Savannah whirled on me, eyes wide. "What the hell happened? Two days ago, you were begging him to reject you!"

"Things change," I said with a shrug. "Remind me: how long did it take for you to go from thinking Jasper was a dangerous rogue to falling for him?"

She flopped down into the seat by my desk with a groan. "Fair point."

As I took my own seat behind the desk, she leaned closer, dropping her voice even though we were alone.

"You're really happy about this? It's definitely what you want?"

"I am and it is." I let my own smile take over, the one I'd been hiding throughout the meeting in an attempt to remain professional. "He's not the man I thought he was. He's so much more."

Savannah's expression softened as she took in my genuine delight. "Then I'm happy for you. But seriously... after seven years of tension, was the sex, like, *epic*?"

I almost choked on my laugh, which set her off, and soon, we were giggling and chatting the way I never thought I'd feel comfortable doing with another woman. Not as Alpha, not the way I saw other women in my pack laughing with their friends.

My Beta really might be that kind of friend for me, and now I had my mate too. Life felt on the brink of something truly wonderful, as long as we could get through the next day unscathed.

Eventually, my stomach growled, and I instructed the guard at the door to have lunch brought to us. When he knocked at the door a short time later, I called for him to come in, but instead of food, the doctor who I'd spoken to the day before stepped inside.

"Is this a good time, Alpha?"

"Yes, of course." I hadn't told Savannah about the DNA testing I'd authorized for Troy yet, but I trusted her to keep it discreet. "Did you get the results?"

"I did." The doctor walked over and passed me a file across the desk. "It's pretty much as I expected, but also, a bit of a surprise."

Savannah leaned closer as I flipped through the pages. Medical jargon blurred in front of my eyes, too much data and not enough context.

"What does it say?" I asked, handing the file back.

The doctor pulled out a page with three DNA charts and laid it on the desk. "I ran Troy's DNA against the genetic database, as I said. This one is his father."

I squinted down at it, as if the chart might suddenly turn into a picture. "You're certain?"

"Without a doubt. And this one shares enough of Troy's DNA to be a half-sibling on his paternal side."

My heart thudded at that unexpected news. This would be a lot for Troy to hear.

"Whose DNA is it? Who's Troy related to?"

"That was the surprising part," the doctor said. "His father is Alpha Craig of the Battle River pack."

Alpha? Cinder yipped in my head. *Did he say Alpha?*

The doctor carried on as if he were delivering the weather rather than monumental news. "Which makes the Alpha's son and heir, Alexander, Troy's half-brother."

"Wait." Savannah's eyes darted between me and the doctor incredulously. "Troy is the son of an Alpha?"

"The bastard son," the doctor corrected her, and before I could stop it, a growl rumbled in my throat.

The doctor leaned back in alarm, his eyes going wide.

"I'm sorry, Alpha, I didn't mean any disrespect. It's simply a fact. Troy's mother was not the Alpha's mate, and he is not a member of the Alpha's pack, which probably explains why, although he has the size, strength and healing ability of a highly-ranked wolf, he doesn't possess any Alpha authority here in the Ravenstone."

Perhaps, but it didn't change the fact that it *was* there in his blood. I relished the thought of throwing that in my father's face when I told him about our mating.

"Troy and I are mates," I announced to the doctor, gesturing to the mark on my neck. "We'll be formally announcing it tomorrow, but I'm curious: as my mate, will his Alpha blood become more prominent?"

"Congratulations, Alpha," the doctor said, dropping his head in acknowledgement. "And yes, I believe so. It's all there in his DNA. It might not have been nurtured while he was younger through the pack link, but through your bond, it might still reach its full potential. And this can only help him in the situation we discussed yesterday."

That was my hope too. I didn't care about Troy's lineage for myself; it made no difference to me if he were the son of an Alpha or the son of a rogue. But it could improve his chances of survival, and I'd take every advantage we could get.

Now, I just had to figure out how to tell him.

Chapter Forty-Seven

~**Troy**~

If someone had told me I might only have 24 hours left to live, I wouldn't have guessed I'd spend it in strategy meetings. But there I was, the new commander of pack security, drafting battle plans for *hours*.

Whether I died or not, the pack and Amanda had to be protected, so instead of worshipping my mate the way every cell in my body demanded, I sat around a table with Leo and Darius, running scenarios until we couldn't think of a single damn improvement. Every plan tested. Every possibility weighed.

Once we'd finalized our approach, we summoned our top warriors, the ones whose loyalty we'd never had reason to doubt.

Devon looked wiped when he walked in, probably pulling double shifts since I'd gone AWOL, but as soon as his eyes landed on the mark at my neck, he perked up.

You found your mate? His voice sounded in my head, tinged with excitement. *Congratulations!*

The grin on his face morphed into confusion a second later.

Wait... no one's been in or out of the territory. Who the hell did you find? Not someone who just got their wolf, right?

I had to fight hard not to laugh at the look of horror crossing his face.

Definitely not a teenager, I shot back. *I'll tell you everything later, I promise.*

We reviewed the plan with the warriors three full times, making sure they understood every detail. By the time we sent them out to run practice drills with their teams, the sun was already dragging the last of its light over the horizon.

"Should we head back to the pack house?" Darius asked just as Amanda's voice filled my head, closer and clearer than ever since we'd solidified our bond.

Felix and his mate are here. Savannah, Jasper and Kalo have just let them through the border. We'll reconvene back in my room as soon as you can get here.

I relayed the update to the others, already halfway to the door. *We're on our way.*

The Crimsontooth Beta had spent some time in our pack just a couple of weeks earlier, accompanying Savannah during her original visit, so I recognized him on sight. His mate, however, I nearly missed. Tucked against his side, she was almost two feet shorter than him, delicate and sharp-eyed. His protective arm wrapped tight around her as she peered out at the rest of us.

"This is Evalina," Felix introduced her, voice full of pride. "She's here to save the day."

She nudged him in the hip, the tips of her pointed ears tinting pink. "Don't exaggerate!"

"If you can repeat what you did yesterday, it's no exaggeration," Amanda replied, offering the fairy a warm smile. "We're grateful for your help, both me and my mate."

She reached for my hand like she couldn't stand for us to be apart, and I crossed the room to take my place at her side. All the stress of the day seemed to melt away with that simple touch.

Kalo stared openly at Evalina, golden eyes wide with wonder. "I've never seen anything like you before."

A low growl rolled through the room.

At first, I thought it must have come from Felix, but realized a second later it actually came from... Leo?

Everyone stilled, their eyes drawn to the Crimsontooth Gamma who looked almost as startled as the rest of us.

He cleared his throat with an awkward cough. "We should get started. We can socialize later."

"Let's start with Jasper," Amanda suggested. "How did things go with questioning Chad and the other prisoners?"

"They're still not giving up any names," Jasper relayed. "But we did notice something interesting. Whenever Kalo was close, they took my questions a little more seriously. At times, it almost seemed like they were on the verge of telling me something significant, but they pulled themselves back just in time."

That *was* interesting, and I felt the shift in Amanda's frame that suggested she thought so too.

"Does that happen a lot for you?" I asked the genie.

He shrugged in his casually elegant way. "People often confide in me, but I'm not doing anything to make it happen."

"You're not doing anything *intentionally*," Amanda amended. "But I wonder..."

She glanced over her shoulder to where the necklace that had summoned Kalo still lay.

"The necklace compelled me to touch it and speak a wish out loud to summon you. I assume it works that way for everyone, which means the necklace has some sort of magic attached to it. Perhaps you have the same sort of suggestive magic."

"What are you thinking?" Savannah asked.

Amanda wet her lips, and my gaze followed the movement, heat sparking in my blood. After hours apart, I ached for her. How we'd gone for years resisting each other seemed almost impossible. Now, even minutes felt unbearable.

"We're trying to think of a way to amplify my Alpha authority," she reminded us all. "What if Kalo *is* an amplifier? What if his suggestive power could make the whole pack respond to me more than they normally would?"

"Try it out," Felix offered, full of enthusiasm. "Order your pack members to do something right now."

All attention in the room moved to Savannah and Jasper, the only Ravenstone pack members present besides me, and Savannah sighed heavily. "Fine. Just don't make me do anything too embarrassing."

One corner of Amanda's mouth pulled upwards, a spark of mischief in her eyes, and my damn heart melted. I loved her playful side and wanted to get to know it much, much better.

Drawing a deep breath to centre her power, she addressed the two wolves. "Take a knee if you've ever had a risqué dream about anyone in this room besides your mate."

Even standing beside her, I felt the pull of her command like a tide. But since I'd only ever dreamed about her, I stayed upright. Jasper did too, thankfully; any other answer would've required a serious talk since Amanda would have been the only candidate.

Savannah, however, dropped to one knee, face scrunched in reluctant compliance.

Then Leo did too.

And Darius.

What the hell?

Amanda's command shouldn't have worked on anyone outside her pack, but if Kalo really was amplifying her Alpha pull, maybe it extended further. That boded well.

Felix burst into laughter at the sight of his Gamma and Delta kneeling. "I'm absolutely telling Vaughan you dreamed about his little sister."

"I didn't..." Leo started to say before snapping his mouth shut again. "Never mind."

That was weird. If he hadn't dreamed about Savannah, who *had* he dreamed about?

Amanda gave everyone a sheepish shrug. "Alright, I think that's enough. Please stand up."

Jasper offered Savannah his hand to help her up, looking less than pleased with the whole situation.

"It was a long time ago, and nothing actually happened," she muttered under her breath. "Someone change the subject."

I was happy to comply. "That was impressive, but can we scale it to affect the whole pack?"

Amanda's lips pursed thoughtfully. "Maybe we could form a perimeter around the group, like four corners of a square, with Kalo at the centre to help concentrate it. Alphas and Betas projecting and reflecting authority."

"Four?" My eyes darted around the room, double checking my math. "We only have one Alpha and two Betas, though."

Amanda and Savannah exchanged a glance and Savannah cleared her throat. "Why don't we move this meeting back to our house? We could all use a drink and our Alpha could use some time with her new mate."

The suggestion seemed to come out of nowhere but Amanda nodded in agreement. "Reach out to me by mind-link if anything major happens, but otherwise, we'll all reconvene here in the morning."

Everyone said their goodbyes and shuffled out of the room until only Amanda and I remained. Instinct urged me to take her in my arms, but the stiff set of her shoulders added to the strange tension created by everyone else's sudden departure.

"What's going on?"

She crossed to the bed and sat on the edge. "Come sit with me."

I followed, but reading the weight in her voice, I left some space between us. She obviously only wanted to talk.

"I spoke with the pack doctor again today," she began. "He ran a genetic test on you yesterday, trying to understand how you healed so fast. He suspected you might have ranked blood somewhere in your lineage."

I truly tried to follow her train of thought but it seemed completely unrelated to anything else going on and irrelevant in the grand scheme of things. I didn't care about my lineage and I didn't think she did either. "What are you talking about?"

Amanda reached for my hand, warmth sparking as our skin met. Her thumb traced circles over my palm, soothing and grounding, and in her eyes, I could see her affection, her determination, and a hint of vulnerability that made her all the more impressive to me.

"Troy," she said softly. "I know who your father is."

Chapter Forty-Eight

~Amanda~

As I expected, Troy blanched the moment I said I knew his father's identity. His whole body recoiled, and if I hadn't been holding his hand so tightly, he might have pulled away entirely.

"My father?" he echoed, swallowing as if the words tasted foreign in his mouth. "He's from the Battle River pack. I already know that."

He'd told me that in the bunker, when we'd let our walls down for the first time. I recited the rest of what he'd confided that night, wanting him to know I'd been paying attention.

"You said you went there looking for answers about your mother, but they turned you away."

He gave a slow nod, guarded and cautious, like he could sense a storm coming and was bracing for the first crack of thunder.

I hated that I had to be the one to tell him, that I had this truth before he did. Like I was keeping it from him even when I wasn't.

We both knew the price that came from keeping secrets, though, so I took a steadying breath and gave him the news as gently as I could. "It makes sense that they didn't want you asking too many questions. According to your DNA results, your father is the Battle River Alpha."

A long blink followed that announcement, his eyes going slightly unfocused as he processed the words. "The... Alpha?"

"Yes." I gave his hand a small squeeze, doing my best to anchor him. "After the doctor told me, I looked through the records we have on their pack. Eight months before you were born, Alpha Craig's mate gave birth to a son of her own."

I could almost see the pieces clicking into place behind his eyes.

"He was mated? And his mate was pregnant when he slept with my mother?"

His face contorted, jaw clenched as disgust hit hard and fast. He pulled his hand free and stood, pacing the room with a palm pressed to his mouth like he might be sick.

"It might explain why your Alpha authority never fully manifested," I offered gently, trying to give him something to hold onto. "You weren't born of mates or raised in his pack, but the blood is still there. Enough to heal you and enough to help me tomorrow."

That context didn't seem important at the moment but I mentioned it anyway as a reminder of why I'd ordered the test in the first place.

He didn't seem angry with me about that, at least. He also didn't respond directly to my comment, still pacing in tight circles in a room that was too small for a man of his size to truly work his frustration out.

"My aunt always said it was a one-night stand. That my mother got drunk in the city, went to bed with a stranger, and regretted it."

"I imagine she *did* regret it once she found out he had a mate," I said softly.

He didn't even pause. "She would have seen his mark. I can't pretend she didn't know. But she still kept trying to get him to acknowledge me. Now it makes sense why he never did."

I stayed quiet, letting him talk out loud as he processed it.

"It would've been a scandal," he muttered. "If his mate didn't already know..."He trailed off, reaching out and bracing his hands on the wall as he reached the end of the room again. For a second, I thought he might punch straight through the drywall, but he just stood there, breathing like he'd run miles, every muscle wound as tight as a drawn bowstring. When he finally turned back to face me, there was such raw, stricken horror on his face, it nearly broke me.

"He killed her, didn't he? She must have threatened to go public and he decided to shut her up for good."

My throat tightened, but I forced myself not to feed his suspicion even though the thought had crossed my mind too. "We don't know that, but now that you're in a position of power here, they can't dismiss you so easily. We'll get answers. When all this is over, I'll speak to Alpha Craig. Or his son. Or both."

At the word 'son', Troy stiffened. "How many others are there?"

"His son is the only one the doctor mentioned, and I couldn't find any other children listed in our records either. His name is Alexander, and as I said, he's about eight months older than you."

Having never had a sibling of my own, I could empathize with the shock Troy must have been feeling to suddenly learn he had an older half-brother he never knew about. His nostrils flared as he took a heavy breath, grappling with that fact.

"He's probably just like his father," he muttered.

That was the shock talking, so I stood from the bed and went to him, wrapping my arms around him and laying my head against his chest. "You don't know that. Am *I* just like my father?"

"No," he admitted. His arms circled my back, and his breath came out shaky against my hair. "But I can't imagine he'll be happy to find out about me."

"Maybe not at first, but you're not a threat to him. He's the older between you and you have your own pack anyway. You have your own path, and you're not trying to take anything from him. If he has any sense, he'll see that."

We stood there for a long moment, holding each other as the storm inside him gradually quieted. My fingers traced small circles over his back, grounding us both.

When I looked up, my heart swelled at the sight of my mate, wounded but still strong, protective but willing to take my protection. Stubborn and loyal and so very *mine.*

"Tell me what you need," I said softly. "Tell me what will make you feel better."

His thumb stroked gently down my cheek, reverent and hungry at once. "I need *you*. I want to lose myself in you until we can't move or even think. Just you and me, and nothing else. In case this is the end. In case it's only the beginning."

A rush of heat moved through me, fuelled by the fire in his eyes. I wanted it too, that escape and that connection, now more than ever before.

His mouth hovered just above mine, his breath warm and uneven, and my whole body leaned into him like it knew exactly where it belonged. The heat between us wasn't new, but in that moment, it carried something heavier: a need not just to be wanted, but to be known, inside and out.

Rising onto my toes, I brushed my lips against his and whispered, "Then take me. If it's the last night of the world, let's make it count."

Chapter Forty-Nine

~**Troy**~

Before I even fully woke the next morning, I felt Amanda, warm and quiet beside me, her breath a steady rhythm against my chest. We'd worn each other out the night before, just as I wanted, and if my life did end that day, I could go with no regrets about how I'd spent my final night.

I let my fingers trace the edge of the sheet near her hip, almost touching her but not quite as the revelations of the previous night repeated in my head.

My father, an Alpha.

Blood I never asked for, that seemed hotter than ever as it ran beneath my skin.

It changed nothing, and yet, nothing felt quite the same either.

Amanda stirred, stretching beside me like she already knew I was awake.

"You okay?" she asked, voice soft and heavy with sleep.

That was a loaded question, but I nodded anyway. "We've got work to do."

Although I still hated the idea of putting Amanda in front of the whole pack when someone had tried to kill her only two days earlier, I'd been unable to come up with an alternative that would give us the same results. So, once we were dressed and invited the rest of our small task force into the room for one final debrief, Amanda sent out a pack-wide mind-link.

All-pack meeting at the assembly field in half an hour. Attendance is mandatory. An attack is planned against our pack for later today. Stay calm and report to the field for your orders.

"That ought to get everyone's attention," Jasper said grimly. He carried a bag filled with silver handcuffs, as many as the pack could spare, so he, Leo and Darius could detain anyone who failed Amanda's loyalty test. We had no idea how many defectors to expect.

"We'll go and keep an eye on things as people gather," Savannah offered. "Alpha, you should wait until the last minute and take an unexpected route."

She didn't say why but we all understood the danger another would-be assassin posed. I'd already had the same thought. "I'll bring her when it's time. Everyone else can head out."

We barely waited five minutes after the others left before we also left the pack house. Rather than heading towards the assembly site, we went the opposite direction, holding hands as we took a roundabout route through the forest. Neither of us spoke, our attention focused on watching for danger, but it felt good to be outside with her and doing something as ordinary as going for a walk. Maybe when all this was over, we'd be able to do it regularly.

By the time we arrived at the field, members of the Ravenstone pack stood in large clusters, murmuring amongst themselves. Uncertainty hung thick in the air. At the centre, Kalo stood out. Even though Leo had insisted he dress in borrowed clothes to try to blend in more, his white hair and golden eyes still gave him away. Of all of us, he was the only one who didn't look on edge. Perhaps he'd been in so many life-or-death situations before, it no longer phased him.

Felix was already there too, arms crossed over his chest, scanning the crowd like he expected trouble and was almost looking forward to it. His little mate stood beside him, attracting her fair share of attention too, especially among the younger wolves who seemed to realize they had something special in their midst.

On the opposite side of the crowd, Savannah stood in place with Jasper, the two of them whispering to each other as they surveyed the gathered crowd.

I would have liked to stay at my mate's side, but I couldn't, not when she needed me to form the fourth corner of the square. Instead, I pressed a fierce kiss to her temple.

"You've got this. You're stronger than anyone I know."

Clear and determined eyes met mine as I stepped back, and I bowed my head to my Alpha before striding away from her, eating up the distance as quickly as possible until I reached the back of the crowd. Directly in a line with Kalo in the centre and the podium from which Amanda would speak, I took my assigned position.

When she stepped forward onto the platform, posture unyielding and head held high, my breath caught. She looked just as much like an angel as she had that day I first saw her, magnificent in her beauty. I could barely breathe just looking at her.

Her eyes met mine for a heart-stopping second before she began to address the pack.

"Thank you all for coming. As I mentioned, the pack is under threat and we have a plan to deal with it. However, there's another threat we also have to deal with, which is the main reason I called you here today. A threat from within, from those among us who would betray us and perhaps already have."

A ripple of shock moved through the group, furtive glances flying back and forth as everyone tried to guess who she might be talking about.

"You know who you are," she continued, her voice growing even more resonant as Cinder pushed close to the surface, her wolf's authority mingling with Amanda's own Alpha power. In my chest, a humming started. "Now, you're going to reveal yourselves to me."

Ahead of me, Kalo stood centred in the middle of the group, facing Amanda. Closing his eyes, he began to rotate in a slow circle, and when he turned in my direction, I almost staggered back. The power that emanated from Amanda suddenly tripled in force, pressing down on me like gravity thickening in the air. Rather than letting it go through me, though, I focused back on the crowd in front of me, doing my best to reflect it back onto them, hitting them from all sides.

And as that power flowed through me, for the first time, I *felt* it: Alpha blood, burning clean and true in my veins. Not because of the man who gave it to me, but because of the woman who stood at the head of the pack and made me *hers*.

My fingers tingled, my breath slowing to match the steady beat of power thrumming in the air. Felix straightened to my right, and to the left, Savannah leaned forward, pushing back against the invisible force.

Fuck, that's strong, the Beta's voice panted in my head. Felix nodded as if she'd spoken to him too.

The square held, its power contained within, and when Amanda spoke again, I didn't just *hear* her words. They echoed in my very bones.

"All traitors step forward. *Now.*"

The silence that followed was so total it felt like sound itself had frozen.

And then... someone moved.

A woman near the front edge of the crowd, wearing the uniform of the border patrol. Someone from *my* team, I realized, my stomach sinking. Lily, one of the team leaders I'd fought beside as recently as a few days ago.

Her face twisted in pain, hands shaking like she was trying to fight the movement, she stumbled forward.

Behind her, more followed. A young man from the supply team. A nurse from the hospital, a close friend of the Beta's wife. A couple more, and a few more after that. One by one, they moved to the front of the crowd and dropped to their knees in front of Amanda, chests heaving, sweat on their brows.

Ten people, all told, in addition to those already being held in the pack's prison. Though any and all betrayal stung, it also wasn't the full-scale revolt we'd been threatened with. I breathed a sigh of relief, and across the distance separating us, I thought Amanda did too.

Meanwhile, the crowd erupted in anger, accusations and disbelief hurled at the self-declared traitors kneeling at the front. From the side, Jasper, Leo and Darius stepped forward, cuffing the traitors.

As the last person was secured, Amanda's expression softened and she turned back to the crowd. The swell of power over the clearing faded, the air becoming lighter, and I inhaled a deep breath of it, my body still buzzing with what it had just achieved.

"Thank you to the rest of you for your faithfulness and support. We've faced fear together in the past and we'll do it again, but I want to offer you something else today too. I want to share *hope.* I want to share with you that, after all these years, I've claimed my fated mate."

Another rush of whispers swelled through the crowd, these ones filled with curiosity and interest rather than suspicion and fear.

"He grew up in this pack and has spent the last ten years working to protect us all. Now, he will take on the role of Commander of the pack's security, both internal and external. I'm delighted to introduce you all to…"

Her eyes met mine across the distance between us, and even with all that space, I felt the spark of our bond simmering along with the remnants of the power she'd shared with me.

But before she could speak my name, her eyes rolled back and she crumpled where she stood, collapsing onto the platform like a puppet with its strings severed.

"Amanda!" Her name came out in a roar as I broke formation and ran, dodging stunned pack members as the field exploded into noise and chaos.

Chapter Fifty

~Amanda~

Darkness surrounded me. Not cold or terrifying, but more like the deep quiet of an underwater cave. Peaceful, in a way. Inside the blackness, my thoughts floated, sluggish and weightless as the dark beckoned me to go even deeper.

Before I could sink into it, though, a voice cut through the murk, rough and trembling with panic.

"Amanda? Open your eyes. Please. You're going to be okay. Please be okay."

Troy.

My mate's voice anchored me, jumpstarting me out of my lethargy. I clawed toward the sound, the connection between us a golden thread through the dark, and when I finally broke through to consciousness, I surfaced with a gasp.

Light and sound slammed into me all at once.

"Back up! Give her air!" Jasper barked.

Savannah's voice was softer and nearer. "Troy, let the medic…"

"No! No one touches her."

My eyes blinked open to find his face above me, drawn tight with worry, sweat beading at his temples. His hand cradled the side of my head, and another held mine like he might lose me if he let go.

"I'm okay," I rasped, though my tongue felt heavy and dry.

He shook his head, as if he knew better than I did how I felt. "You were out for almost three minutes. That's not okay."

Each second of uncertainty over a mate's health felt like an eternity. I knew that as much as anyone, and now he had just a small idea of how I'd felt the other day when I watched him die.

"I used too much energy," I admitted softly. "Pulled too much power through the pack. It hit me all at once, but I'll be fine."

Troy exhaled shakily, brushing his forehead against mine. "Thank the goddess. You scared the hell out of me."

Around us, the crowd buzzed in the distance, their voices growing dimmer as the chaos subsided. Savannah's voice carried as she ordered the pack members incapable of fighting to retreat to their safe zones. Jasper shouted instructions to the warriors and reserve fighters. I could feel the shift in energy as the pack fell back into order, rallying behind us.

So much for my big announcement. The happy news would have to wait for another time.

Assuming we survived.

"We need to move," I said, already pushing myself up with his help. "The attack's coming. We still have to prepare..."

"You need to rest," Troy contradicted even as he helped me sit. "You just dropped like... like..."

He couldn't even force the words out, but I knew what he meant. *Like he had when the bullet hit him.*

"You're not getting rid of me that easily. But maybe after this, we stop nearly dying on each other, alright?"

He blew out a long breath that broke into a weak chuckle. "I'll try."

I reached up to cup his cheek, admiring the handsome face I got to call mine for just a second while I had the chance. "Help me stand. That's all I need."

My feet almost left the ground as his solid strength lifted me upright, and I found myself face-to-face with Kalo. The genie looked almost as relieved to see me unharmed as my mate did.

"You need to undo the wishes," he reminded me. "Before the barrier falls."

Because someone had the chance to kill me in the attack, he meant. The implication wasn't lost on me. If I died before I could make the wish, he would remain trapped until he found another person willing to make the wish. Given how long he'd waited to find even one, I couldn't blame him for not wanting to take his chances on locating another.

We were all counting on this working.

"I'll do it as soon as everyone's in place," I promised. "The defensive teams are getting in position now. Troy will go to the hospital and…"

"No," my mate interrupted before I could finish. "I'm going to the frontlines with you."

What on earth was he talking about? "When I undo the wishes, the bullet returns. You need to be in the hospital so the doctors can help you."

"Evalina will help me," he insisted, determination flaring in his eyes. "Between her magic and the power of our bond, my odds of survival are just as good in the forest as in an operating room. As Alpha, you need to be with the warriors, and I'm not leaving your side."

Damn it. As much as I wanted to argue, part of me understood. After all the years he'd spent watching me from a distance, protecting me from the shadows, of course he wasn't going to step away now when he had the chance to stand at my side. I wouldn't either.

"Evalina," I called, scanning the perimeter. The petite fairy was already moving toward us, Felix trailing after her like a silent shadow. "Do you need anything special to work your magic? Electricity or refrigeration or… I don't know. Anything?"

She shook her head. "We don't have such things in my world. The magic works on its own."

Gold light shimmered at her fingertips, casting a soft glow, and Troy raised his eyebrows at me, a silent 'see?' coming through loud and clear.

"You, however, need food and water," Felix interjected, eyes fixed on me. "You look drained."

"There's no time…"

"I'll mind-link someone to bring it to you," Savannah interrupted as she and Jasper returned. "You'll need to stay sharp if you're going to survive the next few hours."

"We've locked the traitors up," Jasper added. "They didn't resist. Whatever you and Kalo did, it shook them to their core. The warriors will be in position within twenty minutes, so we shouldn't wait much longer.

I nodded, adrenaline rising to replace the weariness still tugging at my limbs. "Then let's move out. We'll find a place near the front to undo the wishes, where Evalina can work her magic and I can still lead the troops."

It all came down to this; three days of planning and preparation, and within the next hour, we'd know if we'd done enough.

Troy stepped into place beside me, taking my hand in his. "Together?"

In an instant, I was back in the moment we marked each other, agreeing to move forward as equals. Just as it did then, the warmth of his presence chased away the last shadows of my exhaustion, bringing a sense of resolve and certainty, even though nothing about the next few hours was guaranteed.

"Together," I agreed.

Chapter Fifty-One

~**Troy**~

The forest had never felt so quiet.

Not even the birds dared to sing as we stood just inside the tree line, the enemy's forces visible beyond the edge of Kalo's barrier. Shadows moved between trees across the clearing. They'd noted our approach and were watching and waiting to see what we would do. A massive wolf, bolder than the rest, made no attempt to hide as he paced, almost taunting us to make a move.

Everyone was on edge.

I could hear every heartbeat around me, but Amanda's stood out among them, fast but steady. Strong. My mate stood at the centre of the circle we'd formed, her body lit by faint tendrils of sunlight breaking through the canopy. Wearing the black sweatshirt and sweatpants that served as our pack's pre-shift uniform, her hair pulled back into a ponytail, she still looked like an angel, but an avenging one, ready for war.

In front of her stood Kalo, hands behind his back, golden eyes focused and unreadable. Leo hadn't moved from his place at Kalo's side since we'd arrived. His body was turned slightly toward the genie, as if he were guarding Kalo from some invisible threat.

Evalina hovered a few feet away, her small hands twitching in nervous preparation as she stared at me with wide, watchful eyes. She didn't say a word, but her posture told me she was ready to move the second I needed her.

Savannah and Jasper stood behind Amanda, side-by-side like sentinels, also ready to shift. Darius was to one side of them, and on the other, Felix waited near Evalina, arms crossed, his gaze sharp and focused.

And me? I stood right beside Amanda, fingers clenched tight around her small hand. I'd already taken my shirt off since Evalina would need access to my chest, and sweat beaded across my brow despite the cool breeze that whispered through the trees.

We had one shot at this. One shot to undo the wishes, save my life, defeat the invaders and prove to everyone that Amanda was the one and only rightful Alpha of the Ravenstone pack.

"Are you ready?" Amanda asked softly, turning to me.

In the brown eyes that locked on mine, I saw the woman who would have defied her father for me if I asked her to. The woman who always put her pack first, even when it meant moving away to take another Alpha as her mate. The woman who saved my life, and the one who made it worth living. She was everything to me, and if I had to risk everything for the chance to live a life with her, I'd do it every single time.

"For you? Always."

Her hand brushed my chest, resting for a second over my heart where the bullet would soon return. I watched her throat work as she swallowed.

"I'll stay as long as I can," she said, voice barely a whisper. "Don't take too long, okay?"

My stomach coiled but I nodded firmly. "We've got this, Alpha."

Clearing his throat, Kalo stepped forward. "There are only a few minutes left. We should proceed."

Amanda swallowed once more. "Let's go, then."

From inside his coat, he drew the necklace that Amanda had used to summon him. How he got it, I had no idea. The last time I saw it, it sat on Amanda's desk in the room where we'd been sleeping.

The object dangled from his hand as he eyed it with a mix of reverence and loathing. It was a sign of his immortality but it also served as a prison for him. After this, he'd be free of it, but would he still be alive?

No one knew.

We had that much in common.

Amanda reached for it, taking the piece of jewellery from him. No one else noticed how her hand trembled, but I saw it.

"You're sure about this?" she asked the genie, giving him one last chance to change his mind.

His golden gaze met hers without hesitation. "I've never been more sure of anything."

Inhaling deeply, Amanda turned back to the group. "When I speak the wish, the barrier will fall. Get ready."

Felix nodded and leaned over to whisper something to Evalina. Jasper and Savannah tensed, her eyes glazing over as she passed the order on to the troops waiting nearby.

Amanda raised the necklace, the pendant catching the light as she held it aloft. Her voice rang out clearly across the quiet space.

"I wish that every wish this genie has ever granted is now undone."

The instant the words left her mouth, the air snapped.

A pulse of energy rolled outward from Kalo, knocking dust and leaves into the air. The barrier shimmered violently, becoming visible as it moved. Cracks appeared in it, fracturing into pieces like shattered glass before it vanished with a low hum that made my bones vibrate.

Across the clearing, the enemy forces stirred and, with a shout, our men attacked, shifting in the charge so that yells turned to growls. Around us, Felix, Savannah, Jasper and Darius all shifted and joined the attacking force.

Kalo, meanwhile, began to… flicker? I didn't know how else to describe it. I could almost see through him and then he solidified again, his body appearing to fade in and out as the wish's full effects took hold.

"No!" Leo growled beside him, grabbing hold of him to try to keep him there. It didn't seem to help; his hand gripped empty air where Kalo's shoulder had been a second earlier. Eyes wild, he glanced around, looking for help, but none of us knew what to do.

Besides, I had other things on my mind.

Evalina rushed to me just as the full force of the bullet hit.

Pain exploded in my chest, the sharp sting of the silver radiating outwards and beginning to sap my strength almost immediately. My legs buckled and I dropped to my knees with a strangled grunt, clutching at my chest as if I could claw the bullet out myself.

"I'm here." Amanda's hands were on me, the sparks of our bond helping to keep some of the worst of the pain at bay as Evalina knelt beside us.

"It's back," I hissed, each breath scraping raw against my ribs. "I feel it. Here."

My chest burned like fire. I couldn't breathe properly, my lungs spasming against the invading pressure.

"Lie down," Amanda instructed, helping to bring me to the ground even as her eyes darted towards the sounds of fighting in the distance, calculating how long she could stay before she needed to go and lead the charge.

With forced effort, I pulled my hand away from my chest, my fingers clenching in the dirt instead as my nails bit into the soil.

Evalina placed her palms over my chest and I could *feel* her magic begin. Warm and steady, like a blanket that wrapped around the searing pain and held it in place. My vision swam, spots dancing across the edges.

Amanda's fingers threaded through my hair, her beautiful face hovering above me. "Just a little longer. I've got you. Stay with me."

"I'm not going anywhere," I ground out even as blackness began to close in. A tugging feeling joined the searing pain in my chest, as if something was pulling on the bullet, bidding it to move. My gaze moved to Evalina but she didn't look at me. She stared down at my chest instead, her face scrunched in concentration, her cheeks turning red from effort.

A howl sounded in the clearing, making the trees around us shake. The howl of an Alpha, without a doubt.

Amanda's head snapped up and I forced one more word out. "Go."

Her head shook immediately. "Not yet. You need me."

When I opened my mouth again, no breath came, so I spoke to her in my head instead. *Your pack needs you. Go.*

A new round of pain sliced through me as the bullet began to move. I could feel its slow progress. The magic was clearly doing something, but would it be in time?

Amanda pushed back as the sounds of the fighting swelled, but a moment later, she reappeared, pressing her lips to mine in a fierce kiss that temporarily erased every other thought from my head. Her breath pushed down into my lungs where mine had ceased, and at the same time, with a slick, sickening, slurping sound, the bullet came free.

"I've got it!" Evalina exclaimed, both triumphant and exhausted as she held the bloody bullet up for us to see.

Amanda didn't wait to hear more. In a blur of fur, she was gone, and my eyes closed as the darkness took me.

CHAPTER FIFTY-TWO

~**Amanda**~

Only a few minutes into the fight and already, the forest reeked of blood.

My paws pounded across the ground as I tore through enemy lines, each muscle coiled with fury and purpose. The trees blurred in streaks of green and gold, the scent of strange wolves mingling with blood and churned-up earth. Cinder was fully in control of our body, our thoughts one and the same. *Protect the pack. Protect our mate.*

Ahead of me, chaos raged.

Snarls, howls, and bone-crunching impacts echoed through the woods, a soundtrack to the violence ripping Ravenstone apart. Bodies collided. Blood sprayed. And above it all, I felt the threads of the pack link, each one a thread connecting me to my people, strain and tighten.

Suddenly, one snapped.

A strangled sound left my throat as I stumbled mid-sprint. Somewhere to the west, one of our warriors fell. I didn't know who, not yet, but the loss reverberated through me like the strike of a hammer. As a new Alpha, I'd never felt the death of one of my own before, and I didn't know it would feel like *that*.

Another snapped. And another.

Pain lanced through my head as if I'd been physically struck. I staggered, momentarily blinded by the grief, until Cinder shoved us forward again. *Later,* she growled. *Mourn later. Now, we fight.*

A flash of fur came into view on my right as Felix, the Crimsontooth Beta, recognizable from his scent, tore into one of the attackers.

To the left, Savannah's sleek wolf was locked in a vicious clash with a grey beast, their bodies rolling through the mud in a blur of fang and fury.

Although I wanted to help, I had to trust my team to look after themselves. I had one target, one I could see up ahead, watching me come.

The Alpha on the other side.

He stood apart from his pack just beyond the clearing, larger than any of the others, his coat dark as coal, his eyes dark and cruel, even in his wolf form. His aura rolled off him in heavy waves, a dominance that rivalled my father's, but it didn't shake me.

I was an Alpha too.

Cinder snarled, and we lunged.

He met my charge with a thunderous growl, his claws slashing forward. We collided in a tangle of snapping jaws and raking limbs, teeth catching fur, skin, and bone. His fangs scraped my shoulder, but I twisted beneath him, forcing him off-balance and slamming him into the ground.

Before he could recover, I pounced, sinking my teeth into the soft flesh at his side. His howl contained no fear, only rage as he kicked out with powerful hind legs, knocking me back just enough to flip onto his paws again.

Panting, we circled each other, blood already staining the dirt between us.

The skin around his teeth pulled back in a snarl, revealing sharp, unforgiving teeth, and I returned the gesture, refusing to back down. This was *my* land. *My* pack. Who the fuck did he think he was to have any right to it?

A flicker of movement behind him, another wolf, tried to catch my attention but I didn't spare him a glance. My warriors would deal with the rest. My entire focus had to stay on the Alpha.

In the blink of an eye, he lunged again. I dodged left, ducked underneath him, and tore at his leg.

He stumbled, losing his balance, and hit the ground.

Now! Cinder urged.

I leapt, jaws open, aiming for his throat...

... when something slammed into me from the side, mid-air.

Teeth clamped down on my flank with searing force. I crashed to the ground, stunned and breathless, pain flaring white-hot through my ribcage. Blood instantly soaked into the earth beneath me.

My limbs scrambled for purchase, but the second wolf was already on top of me, heavier and broader than I expected. His teeth tore into my shoulder, and I screamed, both in my wolf form and through the bond.

I felt Troy's pain even before I heard his voice through the link, weak but urgent. *Amanda!*

I couldn't answer.

I couldn't breathe.

The enemy Alpha rose to his feet again, his form blurring through the dust in my eyes. Above me, the second wolf's breath bore down against my neck. He could have taken a decisive blow, but he didn't. He offered me up to his Alpha instead.

And that was his mistake.

Gathering all my strength, I rolled over on my back, towards the second wolf, and dug my claws into his belly above me. He yelped in surprise, or pain, or both, but I didn't hesitate as I rolled back, using his own weight for leverage, and released him straight into the Alpha wolf as he lunged towards me to finish me off. The two collided with a heavy thud, bones smashing together as I retracted my claws and rolled out of the way.

Alpha! Savannah's voice reached me just as her wolf appeared. *I've got the second one.*

Sure enough, she leapt at the wolf who'd brought me down, leaving me one-on-one with the other Alpha as he gave his head a hard shake, trying to reorient himself.

I wouldn't give him that chance.

Cinder pounced onto his back, smashing his head down into the dirt, her teeth finding the soft, unprotected flesh of his neck and growling deep and low with an unmistakable order in the language of wolves.

Surrender or die.

He snarled back, bucking in a wild attempt to throw her off, but when she bit down harder in one final warning, he got the message.

The clatter of battle around us dimmed as he sent out a mind-link to his pack, telling them to back down.

I did the same.

I've got the Alpha. Hold your positions.

When everything had gone quiet, the wolf beneath me shifted back to his human form, the ultimate surrender in any battle.

He shoved me off, defiant even in his loss, and pulled himself up to face me.

Blood streaked his human skin. His breaths came ragged, chest rising and falling heavily, but I could only stare at his face.

His eyes. His jawline.

The shape of his mouth.

I knew them all, or at least, a younger version of them. I'd kissed them just a few minutes earlier.

His face looked just like my mate's.

Chapter Fifty-Three

~Troy~

A scream tore me from unconsciousness; my mate's cry, dragging me out of the dark with violent force. My body protested, my chest still aching from where the bullet had been, the silver still working its way out of my bloodstream. I needed rest, needed time to heal, but none of that mattered when I heard her.

She was in pain. She needed help, and I wasn't there.

I forced myself to sit up and nearly blacked out again immediately.

A soft, small hand pressed against my shoulder.

"Stay down," Evalina murmured. "You're safe. Felix said you should stay here."

Her face came into focus, the pointed ears poking out beneath her braided hair. Behind her, I could see Leo kneeling over an unmoving Kalo. The genie seemed solid again, no more fading in and out, but I couldn't tell if he was dead or alive. Leo's face was pale, his body tense, with every ounce of his attention focused on Kalo as if nothing else existed around them. He didn't even glance my way.

The still-healing wound in my chest pulled tight as I pushed to my feet, ignoring Evalina's protests. No way in hell was I lying there a second longer, not when Amanda needed me.

"Thank you for your help," I managed to bite out before I took my wolf form.

Never had shifting been so ragged or painful. Bones cracked, muscles strained, and every heartbeat felt like it might tear me apart, but eventually, four legs supported me rather than two. My fur might be slick with sweat and blood, lungs rasping for breath, but Hunter let out a howl anyway as we took off in search of our mate.

Dozens of scents assaulted me as I went but hers cut through it all, pulling me forward. My Alpha.

My Amanda.

I followed her scent until the sounds of battle quieted and the trees opened into a clearing. There, I stumbled to a stop, ribs screaming in protest, and stared.

Amanda's wolf stood tall, bloodied but unbroken, and my chest clenched painfully with relief. Thank the goddess she was okay.

In front of her stood a man: naked, bloodied, and defiant. Still broad-shouldered and solid in his late forties, his eyes glittered with contempt.

Recognition hit me all at once, slamming into me with all the subtlety of a steamroller.

For the first time in my life, my own features stared back at me, the ones I've never shared with anyone in my mother's family. Not an exact match, but close enough that the truth couldn't be denied.

This man had to be my father. Nothing else could explain it.

'Father' wasn't the right word though. This was the man who never wanted me. The man who let my mother die alone. The man who made me a bastard.

Before I could speak or even fully process what I was seeing, another wolf limped forward and shifted, collapsing onto two legs at the older man's side. This one was younger, leaner, his face less hardened, but the resemblance was unmistakable. The eyes, the brow, the proud, angular chin.

Again, he wasn't an exact copy of the older man, or of myself, but there were enough similarities to make it devastatingly clear who he must be.

My brother.

"We're willing to negotiate," the younger one panted, voice wary as he glanced between Amanda and the older man. "I'll speak for our pack."

Hunter snarled, deep and violent. *Negotiate? After what they did?*

I stepped forward out of the shadows, shifting mid-stride despite the agony tearing through my body. Muscles screamed and bones cracked as I emerged naked, panting, and full of raw fury.

"There's no negotiation here. You'll follow the Alpha's orders or you'll die."

Both men turned. My father's gaze met mine and a flicker of realization darkened his eyes. Cold calculation lingered there, followed by something else.

Regret? Disgust?

Maybe both. A heartbeat of heavy silence passed before he snarled, "I thought you'd be dead by now."

The words were designed to hurt, so I didn't give him the satisfaction of flinching. "Disappointed?"

The younger man, my brother, stared openly, confusion written across his face. "Who is he?" he demanded, turning to his father.

Alpha Craig didn't answer. His eyes remained locked on me, disdain radiating off him like heat.

Amanda shifted beside me, brushing my arm with her own in silent support as her voice rang out sharp and cold. "This is my Commander, and my mate. He speaks for me."

I never looked away from my father. "You'll pull every single one of your wolves off Ravenstone land immediately or I'll take the life she spared you."

The younger man bristled, but he deferred to his Alpha. The older man's jaw clenched so tightly, I thought his teeth might crack.

Finally, after a long beat, Craig nodded stiffly. "Alexander, send the order."

Alexander hesitated only a second before bowing his head and sending the retreat through their pack link. One by one, enemy wolves slipped away into the trees.

Amanda's voice cut through the silence like a blade. "You two will accompany me to the Ravenstone pack house. We'll settle this with reparations for your unprovoked attack."

Craig's lips twisted into a sneer. "As you wish... Alpha."

I almost cracked a smile at the way he unknowingly echoed Kalo's words. Ironic, since Kalo's magic had been instrumental in buying us the time we needed to stave off this attack.

Hopefully the genie would be alright now that the rest had been handled.

Medical staff, attend to the wounded, Amanda directed through a pack-wide link. *Report any unauthorized wolves to your unit leaders. Stand down, everyone. Well done.*

To a smaller group, she sent out one more message. *Jasper and Savannah, take our guests here to the pack house. I need to see the doctor, but I'll be there in a minute.*

I immediately spun to face her, my eyes roaming her body. "Where are you hurt?"

It didn't take me long to spot the jagged teeth marks along her side and a growl rumbled deep in my chest.

"I'm going to fucking kill him."

"I think you should try to get some answers first." She gave me a smile that only partly masked her pain. "Come on, let's both get checked out by the doctors, and then we can deal with your father, together."

Together. That word would never sound anything less than magical to me.

Reluctantly, I stood back while Jasper and his men led Alpha Craig and Alexander deeper into our territory while I stayed by my mate's side until the doctor arrived.

My father had a lot to fucking answer for.

Chapter Fifty-Four

~**Amanda**~

Troy sat in the chair opposite my desk, bare-chested under a loose hoodie he hadn't bothered to zip, his skin pale but unbroken. I didn't need the doctor's praise to know how lucky he was, but hearing the words didn't hurt.

"I've never seen anything like it," the doctor said, shaking his head as he checked the last of the readings. "The wound should have killed him a second time. Instead, it closed as if it had never been there. Your bond, the fairy's magic, and his genetics... somehow, it all worked together." He turned to me with something almost like awe. "Whatever force is protecting him, Alpha, don't let it go."

He was preaching to the choir. I wouldn't let Troy go again for anything in this world.

The office door clicked shut behind him, leaving me and Troy alone for a brief moment of stillness. I leaned against the edge of my desk, watching Troy as he flexed his fingers slowly, testing his strength. "You good?" I asked softly.

He glanced up, those pale brown eyes meeting mine with a small, almost crooked smile. "Getting there. We survived, Alpha."

I exhaled slowly. There'd be time later to process the trauma of the battle. For now, there was still unfinished business.

Jasper, bring them in, I mind-linked, my tone sharp again. *All of them.*

A few minutes later, the door opened and Jasper entered with Beta Chad, shackled and sullen. Sweat gathered on his flushed brow. Alpha Craig and Alexander followed, uncuffed but closely watched by Savannah and Darius. Alexander's expression held wary curiosity while Alpha Craig feigned boredom.

I knew enough about putting on a show to cover up your true feelings to recognize when someone else was doing it.

I motioned them further into the room. Troy stood as soon as Alpha Craig approached, and the temperature in the room seemed to drop ten degrees.

"Sit," I ordered. They all obeyed: Chad glaring, Craig lounging arrogantly in the chair across from me, and Alexander looking increasingly uncomfortable next to his father, fingers twitching against his thigh while his gaze returned to Troy again and again.

My mate remained standing, towering over the other men as he came to stand next to my desk.

I let a long pause linger in the air, forcing them to feel the weight of the moment. Their fate rested in my hands, and they needed to understand that.

"Clearly, you two," I nodded toward Craig and Chad, "were working together to take my pack. What I want to know is who was foolish enough to start it and who was the idiot who went along with it."

Silence followed, a silence during which Chad gave Craig a hard side-eye until Craig's lips curled in faint amusement. "*If* I was working with your Beta, and I'm not saying I was, it would seem he did a piss-poor job of holding up his end."

"And if I was working with you, I'd say you exaggerated your pack's strength," Chad snapped back.

Craig growled, his mask slipping with the insult. "You told me they wouldn't fight. That morale was crumbling. Instead, we got a rallying she-wolf and a magical force field."

"It's not my fault someone blocked the assassin's shot. And even then, the genie was supposed to..."

"The genie," Craig snarled. "You put so much fucking faith in this genie and all he did was keep us out while they regrouped!"

They're admitting to everything, Savannah marvelled in my head.

Indeed they were. I just had to dangle a little bit of rope and they scrambled to hang themselves with it.

"Enough." My voice cracked through the room like a whip and both men flinched. "Chad, you and the others who supported you are banished from the Ravenstone, effective immediately. Including your eldest son, who I assume slunk off with the other Battle River men. You'll leave today."

"You can't..." he tried to bluster.

"Oh, yes, I can. I am the Alpha of this pack, *your* Alpha, which you seem to have forgotten. Your years of loyal service to my father are the only reason you're leaving with your life. Step foot on my land again, and I'll tear your throat out myself."

I nodded at Jasper who called two of his men in and passed on my instructions. Stone-faced, they accompanied Chad from the room, leaving me with the two Battle River wolves.

When the door closed, I shifted my gaze to Craig.

"As for you, your pack lost. You invaded us and you failed. Under the ancient surrender terms, you owe us damage costs and blood prices for the fallen."

The doctor had confirmed to me that four men were dead. Three more were in critical condition, but they were hopeful they could be saved. Guilt twisted at my gut at the idea that anyone had died because of me, but Troy, sensing my despair, assured me that every warrior was ready to die for his pack and would be proud of the part they'd played. It simply came with the territory of being a warrior in the first place.

It didn't make it any easier.

Craig's expression twisted in disdain at my declaration. "Send me the bill, then. Are we done here?"

A growl rumbled from my left, and I knew without looking that it came from Troy. "Don't speak to her that way, you bastard."

Craig simply scoffed. "I don't think I'm the bastard here."

Troy lunged before I could react, but Alexander was quicker, stepping in front of his father and Alpha.

"What the hell is going on?" His eyes swung from Troy to Craig and back again. Seeing them so close together, the resemblance was impossible to miss.

"Oh, I know." Savannah raised her hand, her tone both bright and sarcastic. "Troy is Alpha Craig's son. It's kind of obvious, isn't it?"

I shot her a warning look as Alexander blinked in surprise. "That's not possible."

"Oh, it's possible," Troy said, ice in his voice. "Your father slept with my mother while *your* mother was carrying you. Real class act."

All the colour drained from Alexander's face as he turned to his father. This time, there was no deference in his expression, only disbelief and something like grief. "Is that true?"

Craig's jaw flexed, hard and sharp. His voice, when it came out, was cold as stone. "You were the only son that mattered."

The silence that followed was suffocating, sucking all the air from the room. Alexander slowly sat back down, visibly struggling with the truth that had just been revealed, while Troy stepped away, as if he couldn't trust himself not to attack Craig again with nothing between them. He prowled the edge of the room instead.

I stood slowly, folding my arms across my chest. "Alexander, you're free to go. Return to your forces and take them home. I'll be in touch about the reparations."

He didn't react for so long, I wasn't sure he even heard me.

"What about him?" he finally asked, gesturing to his father.

"Alpha Craig still has some questions to answer for us."

That was too much for the Alpha, who leaned forward, slamming his fist on my desk. "I don't answer to you. You can't keep me here without violating werewolf law."

He tried to stand, but Jasper immediately shoved him back down, giving me a nod to continue.

"For the battle, no. Murder, however, is another matter."

"What murder?" Alexander asked, sounding like he didn't really want to know.

Troy answered for me, each word clear and strong.

"The murder of my mother."

Chapter Fifty-Five

~Troy~

My wolf could smell blood.

It might have been Amanda's, or it might have been my father's own blood from their earlier battle. Either way, the scent lingered on his skin, in his hair and beneath his nails.

Or maybe it was blood from long ago, the blood of my mother that still stained his hands.

All I knew was that Hunter wanted blood in return, and so did I. Only the self-control I'd learned over years of staying away from Amanda kept me from tearing him limb from limb immediately.

I might still do it eventually, but first, I wanted answers.

Amanda gave me the floor. Her office was silent except for the creak of the leather chair under my father's weight and the slow tick of the clock. Despite having been dismissed, Alexander didn't move. My mate stood behind her desk, arms crossed, silent and powerful.

Backup, if I needed it.

I wouldn't.

"What happened to my mother?" My voice scraped against the inside of my throat like broken glass, rough and raw, as I finally got to ask the question that had haunted me my whole life.

Craig didn't blink. "She was a mistake. We only ever spent one night together. I was on a trip and my mate's pregnancy had been... difficult. We both drank too much. It didn't mean anything."

My jaw clenched, but I didn't interrupt. I had suspected as much, and his version of events matched up with what little my aunt could tell me. He didn't seem to be lying.

"I didn't even know her name, not until she tracked me down weeks later and said she was pregnant. Meanwhile, my mate had just given birth. I told her to deal with it."

"Charming," Savannah muttered, and Jasper shot her a look, half-affectionate and half-warning. She mimed zipping her lips shut as Craig continued.

"That should have been the end of it, but she came back a couple of years later. Told me she went ahead and had the baby and wanted me to acknowledge it."

It. Hunter growled in my head at the throwaway insult, and I could see Amanda's fists clench.

"I offered her money," he declared, as if that should have been enough.

"But she didn't want money," I guessed, already knowing the answer deep in my heart.

"No. She wanted you to have a father. My name and a position within the pack. I told her it was impossible but she wouldn't listen to reason. Tried to tell me that my honour mattered more than my reputation."

"So you killed her." The words barely made it past my teeth.

Craig arched a brow. "I didn't. My men did."

Even though I'd long suspected she was dead, hearing it confirmed landed like a ball of hot lead in my stomach. The floor seemed to tilt beneath me and I stumbled back a step. I couldn't hear anything but the rush of blood in my ears.

Amanda moved towards me but I shook my head at her. I needed to do this on my own.

"If they killed her on your orders, it's still down to you."

My father's face was all sneer. "She tried to sneak onto Battle River territory after I told her never to come back. The border team caught her at the perimeter. They treated her like any rogue would be treated under our laws. That's not murder. That's enforcement."

I could feel my wolf pacing, claws digging in. "You'll pay for it."

"I *already* paid for it. I told your Alpha, who was her Alpha at the time, that one of his pack members crossed my border and was killed. I paid the reparations. That was years ago and it's settled. You can't touch me."

Amanda's silence finally snapped.

"So, you covered up the real reason she was there, twisted it into something palatable for my father, and paid him off."

Craig offered her a cold smile. "And he accepted it, which means it's done. Legally and politically. You want to dig that up again, you're going to end up looking worse than I will."

His gaze slid towards me, sharp as a knife.

"Not to mention you'd be declaring your mate's lineage, or lack of it, to the whole world. You want to shout from the rooftops that you're sleeping with a bastard?"

The air in the room vibrated as Amanda let out a deep growl, her wolf barely beneath the surface.

"Troy isn't responsible for the circumstances of his birth. You are, and I'm pretty sure that makes you the bastard here."

Craig scowled at the insult but held his tongue. Next to him, Alexander stared at his father as if he'd never seen him before.

Slowly, Amanda exhaled, her arms dropping to her sides as she looked over at me. "As much as I hate it, if what he says is true, if my father accepted payment and treated it as a territorial violation, then under the laws we're bound to, we can't hold him accountable."

My voice came out hoarse as I stared at her in disbelief. "So that's it?"

"I'm sorry," she said, and I had no doubt that she meant it. "I can't make him answer for it legally."

Craig pushed to his feet with a satisfied grunt. "Well then, if we're finished here..."

It was my turn to growl, the force of it causing every head to turn my way.

"We are *not* finished. Maybe she can't hold you accountable, but I can. I challenge you, Alpha Craig of Battle River."

The room dropped into a heavy silence, charged with electricity, like the forest before a storm. Savannah and Jasper exchanged wide-eyed looks while Alexander stared at the ground in a daze. My wolf pressed against my skin, claws scraping inside my bones, desperate to play his part.

Craig blinked once, then again, like he was trying to decide if he misheard. "You what?"

"You heard me. You say the law protects you, but it's not the only law we live by. I challenge you for leadership of the Battle River pack."

Amanda stepped forward, concern written across her face. "Troy, you just healed..."

I held out a hand to stop her. "I know what I'm doing. I'm not letting him walk away from this."

When no one else spoke, Craig forced a laugh. "You think the pack will follow you? You don't even know them. Even if you pulled some kind of magic trick with your genie and force field and Goddess knows what else, Alexander is my heir. You'd have to take him too."

For the first time since learning I was his brother, Alexander's eyes met mine. He looked exactly as I'd expect a man whose whole world had just shattered to look: stunned and a little lost. But as our gazes held, his lips pressed into a grim line and he nodded once.

It wasn't much to go on. It could have meant a thousand different things. But in that moment, facing each other man-to-man, I took it as a nod of understanding. A confirmation he wouldn't stand in my way.

I looked back at my father. "No magic. No tricks. And let me worry about the pack. When I beat you, I'll make sure they know what kind of Alpha you really are."

Craig's eyes narrowed. "You'll regret this."

Hunter howled in my head, a war cry that I echoed in my own way.

"Not nearly as much as you will."

Chapter Fifty-Six

~Amanda~

This was madness.

Troy had barely survived a silver bullet less than an hour earlier. His wound was healed, by fairy magic, Alpha blood, and sheer will, but that didn't mean he was ready to take on an Alpha with decades of battle experience.

And yet, there he stood, squaring his shoulders like stone and preparing to fight his own father.

Maybe I should have tried to stop him. I could have reminded him that we had just been given a second chance, the opportunity to have a real life together, and risking it would be reckless.

But I kept my mouth shut. I could see in his eyes just how much it meant to him to get justice for his mother, to get some closure, and to reclaim his past in a way he could live with.

Since I couldn't stand in the way of that, I'd have to stand beside him instead.

"Savannah, Jasper," I said, using all my training to keep my voice steady. "Gather anyone who's available and willing to stand witness at the training field. Make sure the perimeter remains heavily guarded though. If anyone from Battle River so much as sneezes over the border, I want to know."

Savannah nodded, her eyes glazing over immediately as she relayed my orders by mind-link. Jasper was already moving toward the door.

"Troy, Alpha Craig, make your way over there but don't start until I arrive. If we're going to do this, we're going to do it properly."

Still glaring at each other, they strode out of the room without a backward glance.

I turned to Alexander, who still sat awkwardly in the chair next to the one his father had just vacated. "If you want to recall a small group of witnesses from your pack, I'll allow it. You can decide how much of the reason for this challenge to share for now."

He looked at me for a long moment, a pain and loneliness in his eyes that I recognized all too well. Just a few weeks ago, I'd been like him, realizing the man I admired and looked up to all my life wasn't exactly who I thought he was. Was anything more disheartening than realizing that not only is your father flawed, he's not even a good person?

Alexander blinked, seeming to snap out of his daze. "Should I take one of your men as a chaperone?"

"I'll go with him," Savannah offered. "I'll take Felix too. He can be a neutral observer to all of this, not on either side."

I nodded before glancing around again, noticing we still had a couple of people unaccounted for. "Has anyone seen Leo? Or Kalo?"

Savannah shook her head. "Not since the battle ended."

Unease flickered through me, but I pushed it down. It would have to wait until later. For now, the challenge demanded my full attention.

Only when everyone else had left the office did I notice I was shaking.

"Please," I whispered into the stillness of the room, not to any genie or even to the goddess, but simply to the universe itself. "If he survives this, I promise I'll never wish for anything ever again."

No answer came.

Drawing in a deep breath, I straightened my spine and headed out to the training field.

Troy stood with his back to me as I approached, stretching and loosening muscles that had only just healed. He was shirtless again, boots already off, barefoot on the grass of the training field. Pack members had started to gather in a wide circle around the centre, murmuring to one another as they watched us. The sun cast long shadows over the grass as it lowered over the mountains, night almost upon us.

"Are you sure you want to do this?" I asked softly.

He turned to me, a mixture of apology and determination in his eyes. "I have to."

"I know." I stepped closer, reaching up to touch his face. "Just promise me you'll win. For your mother, and for me."

Troy took my hand and pressed a kiss to my palm. "I will. I just need to finish it."

Although my chest ached with fear, although it went against every instinct I had to protect each member of my pack, I nodded and stepped back, leaving him to face the fight alone.

Across the field, Alexander returned with a small group of his own men. Craig removed his shirt slowly, almost theatrically, and shifted first. As I'd already seen up close, his wolf was huge: towering and broad-shouldered, with dark, glossy fur and golden eyes that gleamed with contempt. The sight of him alone silenced the crowd.

Troy shifted next, and my breath caught as Hunter burst forth in a blaze of movement, his frame leaner than his father's but no less powerful. His eyes scanned the crowd once before settling on Craig, and they began to circle each other.

"You all know the rules," I called out, my voice sounding surprisingly steady given the way my hands continued to tremble. "No one can interfere. The fight is to the death unless the challengers themselves negotiate a surrender. You may begin."

The echo of my voice faded into the evening air, an air that crackled with tension as the two wolves faced off.

Craig made the first move. He lunged forward, attempting to overwhelm his son with sheer force, but Hunter was quicker. He darted to the side and snapped at Craig's flank, drawing blood, but Craig spun and caught Hunter with a shoulder, sending him sprawling.

I flinched with each blow as if I could feel it myself.

"Come on," I whispered. "Come on, get up."

Hunter did, shaking off the hit and charging, aiming low. He caught Craig's front leg, his teeth digging deep, and Craig staggered back with a snarl. Hunter went for him again, and again he pushed Craig back. It felt like he was gaining the upper hand, and hope surged in my chest.

That hope turned out to be premature. Craig twisted violently and slammed Hunter into the dirt, pouncing on him before he could escape. His jaws clamped around Hunter's neck, and my heart stuttered.

"No," I breathed, my voice cracking. Someone gripped my hand tightly, and I realized that, at some point, Savannah had come to stand beside me. I'd been so focused on the fight that I hadn't even noticed.

Hunter thrashed, kicking and twisting, but he couldn't get leverage. Craig pressed harder, teeth tightening around the vulnerable spot between neck and shoulder. Blood stained the ground beneath them.

"Troy," I choked out. "Please..."

"Let him hear you," Savannah urged, squeezing my hand even tighter. "He'll fight for you."

I wasn't supposed to interfere. Those were the rules.

But this was my mate, the man I'd waited seven long years for, so just this once, I couldn't care less about the fucking rules.

"I love you."

Every head in the circle turned towards me as I shouted the words loudly enough that Troy could hear. I could have mind-linked him instead, but I wanted everyone to hear it. I wanted them to know what I knew.

"You're the best man I've ever met, and I'm so proud you're my mate. Show him who you really are."

Hunter's body went rigid. His ears twitched, his hind legs braced against the ground, and with a roar that split the air, he twisted violently and launched Craig off of him.

The crowd gasped as Craig skidded across the ground, unprepared for the impact.

And Hunter pounced.

He didn't give his father time to recover. He descended like a storm, claws and fangs flashing in a flurry of precise, punishing strikes. Craig fought back, but he was off-balance and slower than before, rattled by the unexpected reversal.

With one last snap, Hunter caught his opponent by the scruff and slammed him to the ground, pinning him fully.

"Is he actually going to kill…"

Savannah didn't even finish her question before Hunter leaned down and dug his teeth into Craig's throat. With a violent tug, he ripped the skin loose. Blood sprayed out as the wolf on the ground let out a yelp of pain that quickly turned into a pitiful gurgle.

The wolf's body twitched and shuddered before going still.

The last rays of sunlight disappeared beyond the mountaintops, and Alpha Craig was dead.

Chapter Fifty-Seven

~Troy~

The field fell silent.

I stood naked under the darkening sky after shifting back to my human form, my breath fogging in the cool evening air. The sharp scent of blood clung to my skin, mingling with damp grass and the faint acrid tang of sweat. Somewhere behind me, my father's body lay motionless, but I didn't turn. I wouldn't give him another second of my time, not even in death.

Instead, I stared ahead, muscles still twitching with the aftershock of the fight, heart thudding low and steady in my chest. For just a moment, I thought I felt a gentle weight at my shoulder, the ghost of a hand, a whisper of warmth.

Mom?

No sooner had the thought crossed my mind than the weight disappeared, leaving behind a sense of peace I hadn't known before.

A Ravenstone warrior stepped forward, pressing a folded bundle of clothes into my hands and I quickly got dressed, the fabric rough against my skin. Every nerve still felt raw and on edge, just like the silence surrounding me.

As I finished pulling the clothes on, two figures approached from opposite ends of the circle. Amanda's steps were quick and sure, her eyes locked on mine. Alexander walked slower, his shoulders squared but not combative.

I reached for Amanda's hand, the soft spark of our bond grounding me instantly, before turning to face my half-brother.

"I did what had to be done. It wasn't about you."

Those were the first words either of us had said directly to the other since he learned the truth. Before, Alpha Craig had been the focal point; with him gone, we were on our own.

He gave a small nod, jaw clenched tight. "If someone killed my mother, I'd have done the same. But some of the others might question the outcome."

His gaze flicked to Amanda, making his meaning clear. From a distance, Amanda's shout could've looked like interference, but it hadn't been the deciding factor. Not really.

"When he had me pinned, the Alpha mind-linked me," I told them both. "I didn't even know that was possible outside a pack or mate bond, but I guess blood has its own link."

"What did he say?" Amanda asked.

My teeth gritted at the memory. "He told me that the day she died, he'd *invited* my mother to the territory. Told her to use an unofficial crossing to come and meet him so they could discuss me. Then he sent his guards to watch the area, knowing they'd kill her for trespassing. He set her up so she wouldn't be a problem for him anymore."

Amanda stiffened beside me, her fingers tightening around mine. "He really did murder her."

I nodded once before focusing back on my brother. "That's what gave me the edge. Not Amanda's shout, even though it meant everything. It was his arrogance and the lack of remorse, right to the end."

Alexander cleared his throat. "I believe you. He could be cruel when it suited him. I tried not to see it, and I never thought he'd go so far, but... it's hard to defend any of this."

His answer was so mature, so graceful in defeat, that it erased any doubts I might have had about what I intended to do next.

Behind him, the wolves from Battle River stood in a loose half-circle, whispering amongst themselves and watching us carefully.

"Well, I'll leave the job of convincing the pack about the validity of the challenge to their next Alpha."

Alexander's brow furrowed. "What do you mean? *You're* the next Alpha."

I shook my head, looking him dead in the eyes. "I never wanted to lead the Battle River pack. The challenge was the only way I could force him into a fight, but my place is here. I already have an Alpha to serve. This is my home. *She's* my home."

Even without looking at her, I could feel Amanda's smile.

"In my one and only act as Alpha of the Battle River pack, I give the pack to you. You're the one trained for it, and you're one of them. They'll accept you. It makes sense."

You're putting the pack's needs first, Amanda's voice whispered in my head. *That's exactly what a true Alpha does.*

I happened to agree with her, but I had one more thing to add. "There is one condition, though."

Alexander stared at me as if he wasn't sure whether or not to believe any of this. "What's the condition?"

"That our two packs are now at peace. You can make the reparations as we discussed, this challenge will be recognized, and we can all move on."

He blinked a few times, looking for a catch, but in the end, he couldn't find one. "You're serious?"

"I am." Holding out my right hand, I let my wolf claws extend from my left hand and scratched a thin line across my palm. "I transfer any claim I have over the Battle River pack to you, Alexander."

I extended my hand to him, but before taking it, Alexander bowed his head to me in an open sign of respect. His men murmured behind him as he stepped forward to shake my hand.

A surge of electricity passed between us, not like the sparks of the mate bond but something equally deep and primal. For a second, Alexander's eyes seemed to glow before settling back to their normal colour.

He turned around to face the others, and they all immediately bowed in acknowledgement and acceptance of his authority.

Amanda's hand found mine again, and I looked down to see her eyes shining as she gazed up at me, her smile full of pride and love.

"You didn't have to give it away," she said quietly. "You could've been an Alpha in your own right."

I reached out and tucked a strand of hair behind her ear, letting my thumb brush her cheek. "I don't need the title. I already have everything I want right here."

We said our goodbyes to the Battle River men, with Amanda extending an invitation to Alexander to come back for a visit soon so we could get to know each other properly, and hand-in-hand, we headed back towards the pack house.

Most of the pack had already retreated to their homes as night fully set in, but Savannah intercepted us near the steps. Her braid was falling apart and her clothes were torn, but she grinned at us like she didn't have a care in the world. Jasper stood a few feet behind her, arms folded, looking equally tired but content.

"Go to bed," Savannah ordered, waving us toward the door. "Whatever nightmares the world throws at us next, they can wait until the morning. For now, rest. You both earned it."

Amanda raised a brow at her. "Are you giving me orders now?"

"Just a very aggressive suggestion," Savannah quipped. "The kind a Beta and friend gets to make when you've been through hell."

My mate surprised me by letting go of my hand and wrapping her arms around Savannah. I couldn't recall ever seeing her hug anyone before. The Beta looked equally surprised, but she quickly returned the hug.

"Thank you both for all your help," Amanda said as she stepped back, giving Jasper a smile too. "We'll see you in the morning."

We climbed the stairs in silence, the day's exhaustion finally settling in. Rather than returning to the room where she had been staying, though, Amanda led me to her own bedroom. To the room that would now be *ours*, and she turned and leaned against the door as it closed behind us.

"We actually survived," she said, voice hushed like she was afraid to break the spell. "*You* survived."

I stepped closer, pressing my forehead to hers. "We both did. And now we have time..."

"...to make up for all the time we lost," she finished for me.

Her hands slid into my hair, and I leaned in to kiss her, slowly, deeply, and reverently. There was no urgency this time, no desperation like before. Just the quiet certainty that we had found each other at last and this time, we wouldn't let go.

I undressed her carefully, worshipping every inch of her as if memorizing her all over again. And when she pulled me into bed beside her, we moved together without any rush or need to prove anything. We had all the time in the world.

Time to laugh.

Time to heal.

Time to love.

Afterwards, with our legs tangled and her head resting on my chest, I whispered the words I should've said years ago.

"I love you. I'm yours. Always. No matter what."

And just before sleep claimed me, I heard her murmur back, "And I'm yours. Forever."

Chapter Fifty-Eight

~Amanda~

The morning sun spilled golden light through the pack house windows as Troy and I descended the staircase, hand-in-hand. My muscles still ached from the battle and the effort of channeling my Alpha authority the day before, and my thoughts were still tangled in everything we'd survived, but for the first time in a long time, I didn't feel like I was carrying the weight of it all alone.

In fact, I was pretty sure I'd never have to do it alone again.

Muted voices and the faint scent of woodsmoke met us in the foyer. The Crimsontooth warriors had gathered near the front doors, most of them spilling onto the deck outside. Felix gave instructions with his usual cheerfulness, Evalina at his side. Darius leaned casually against the wall, speaking with Savannah and Jasper.

And off to the left, behind them, stood Leo and...

Kalo.

I stopped short at the sight of him. In the rush of everything that happened after the battle, I'd forgotten to ask for an update on the genie. Seeing him alive and whole should've brought nothing but relief, but something about him had changed.

Not just the clothes, which were now modern. Not just his eyes, either: still golden, but lacking that otherworldly glow.

No, something *else* was different, and I couldn't quite put my finger on it until I noticed, just above the collar of his shirt, a mark.

A werewolf's mark.

Leo's mark.

My eyebrows shot up, and when Kalo turned and caught me looking, he tilted his head slightly, letting me see the mark more clearly, as if he knew exactly what had caught my attention.

Doing my best to pick my jaw up off the floor, I stepped closer. "I'm glad to see you're still in one piece. I owe you more than I can say. You protected my people and you gave us time when we had none. Thank you."

His head dipped in acknowledgement. "Thank you for keeping your word. You gave me my freedom... or something close to it, anyway."

His golden eyes flicked to Leo beside him, and the Gamma's shoulders tensed. In his stiff posture, I couldn't see any of the happiness a newly-mated wolf normally radiated, and my gaze darted between the two of them, trying to work out the situation between them without asking directly.

"Are you leaving us, Kalo?"

He nodded. "I need to figure out what comes next for me. That means going with the Crimsontooth men, at least for now. But I'm glad things worked out for you, Amanda. I'm glad you got what you wished for."

This time, his eyes found Troy, who had gone to talk to Felix, and his meaning couldn't have been clearer. He wasn't talking about the wishes I made with him; he meant the one my heart made, seven years earlier, on that night in the moonlight when Troy and I first met.

With a wistful smile, the former genie bowed his head once before stepping outside to join the others.

Leo watched him go, a mixture of longing and regret on his face. Since no one else was nearby, I didn't bother dancing around the issue any longer. "What happened?"

His jaw tightened, as if the prospect of speaking about it pained him, but he spoke the words anyway. "After your last wish, Kalo started fading. I don't mean metaphorically; he literally *faded*, like his body was being pulled out of this world one thread at a time. I could *feel* it. He was dying."

I had a sinking feeling where this was going. "So, you marked him to anchor him here?"

He nodded. "I didn't ask his permission. I didn't have time. It was either mark him or lose him forever."

Although I could understand the desperation he must have felt, perhaps better than anyone else, I still winced. "Leo…"

"I know," he said, almost too quickly. "I know it was wrong. Rule number one of being a werewolf: never mark your mate without consent. And I never would have done it under any other circumstances, but it was the only way to keep him alive."

"And now he's angry?" I guessed.

"He's quiet," Leo corrected grimly. "Which is almost worse. He looks at me like I betrayed him, like I took away his freedom all over again, but I was only trying to save him."

I knew a little about what it meant to take someone's choice away. What it had felt like when Troy walked away all those years ago, thinking he was protecting me by choosing *for* me. I knew how easy it was to confuse protection with callousness, and how the feeling of betrayal could linger.

But I also knew the power of the bond, and that wounds *could* heal when you were honest and brave.

"Give him time," I suggested gently. "It's a lot to adjust to, but time has a way of untangling even the messiest knots. If it's meant to be, he'll come around."

Leo looked down, and I could have sworn it was because he didn't want me to see the tears in his eyes. "I hope you're right. Take care, Alpha Amanda."

Keeping his head bowed, he turned and followed the others out the door, staying close enough to Kalo to keep an eye on him but not *too* close.

My heart ached for them both, and with a deep sigh, I made my way over to where Troy stood with Felix, Evalina, Jasper, and Savannah. They all turned to me with warm smiles, and a strange feeling of belonging warmed my chest, chasing away the melancholy that had just been there.

These were *my* people, a strange sort of hybrid family bound together by chance and by choice, and I couldn't be happier that they were all in my life.

"I want to thank you both," I said to Felix and Evalina. "You went above and beyond to help us here. Tell Vaughan that if he ever needs help from Ravenstone, all he has to do is ask."

Felix wore his usual grin. "We might just take you up on that. The last few months have been anything but ordinary."

"No kidding," Savannah said. "Spirits, the fairy realm, genetic experiments, and a genie? And every one of us finds our mate in the middle of it."

"Fate has a strange sense of humour," Jasper added.

Evalina beamed up at Felix. "It's not a joke, though, so I think it must be by design."

Felix squeezed her against his side, still smiling, but I could see concern lurking in his eyes. "One thing's certain: the world around us is shifting. All this supernatural activity and the way the mate bonds have aligned... it has to mean something. I don't know what, but I have a feeling we're going to find out soon, whether we want to or not."

That sobering thought silenced us all for a beat, until Troy slipped his arm around my waist.

"Normal or not, I wouldn't change a thing about the way things have turned out."

On that, we could all agree.

Outside, the Crimsontooth men began to disperse, disappearing into the trees as they marched back to the border to begin their trip home. I could see Kalo's white hair bobbing among the crowd and Leo following a few steps behind him. Kalo never looked back at his mate.

When we could no longer see them, Troy leaned down to kiss my forehead. "So, Alpha, what do you want to do today?"

I took a breath, letting the peace of the morning settle deep in my bones. "Honestly? I'd like to go right back to bed and make up for even more of that lost time."

He chuckled in a way that made it clear he agreed. "I'd love that too, but unfortunately, we've got a pack to run."

We had a pack to run.

Goddess, how I loved the sound of that.

~The End~

THE STORY CONTINUES...

If you enjoyed the book, please take a moment to leave a review.
Thank you!

The fifth book of the *Rocky Mountain Wolves* series, Death Knows Our Name, follows Leo and Kalo on their return to the Crimsontooth Pack. Coming in the summer of 2026!

Keep In Touch

For more about my other books and to keep up-to-date with new releases, find all the links here:
https://linktr.ee/melodytyden